PASSION UNTAMED

By Pamela Palmer

Passion Untamed
Obsession Untamed
Desire Untamed

PAMELA PALMER

PASSION UNTAMED

A FERAL WARRIORS NOVEL

AVON

An Imprint of HarperCollins*Publishers*

AVON BOOKS
An Imprint of HarperCollins*Publishers*
10 East 53rd Street
New York, New York 10022-5299

For Peggy, Holly, Vonnie, Michelle,
Cheryl, Debbie, Andrea,
Cici, Laura, and Bettina
for books, champagne, and precious friendship.

Acknowledgments

Thanks to all the wonderful, talented people who helped me bring this book to life, in particular, May Chen, Helen Breitwieser, Laurin Wittig, Anne Shaw Moran, and Kyle Poulsen. I couldn't have done it without you.

To Denise McInerney for a million things.

And to my family for their support and patience when deadlines took priority. You're always first in my heart.

Virginia, 1738

The newly marked Feral Warrior, Black Panther, prowled the wide, flat stone overlooking the raging Potowmack River. Snow swirled around him, driven by a harsh wind as he waited for the ritual that would, goddess willing, transform him into a shape-shifter, one of the most powerful creatures on Earth.

Months ago, the animal spirit of one of the deceased Ferals had marked him as his own. A bare week later, as he'd set out to find Feral House, the Mage witch Ancreta had tricked him, capturing him. For long months he'd endured her torture as she viciously tried to pry loose the animal spirit inside him, burning a rage into his soul that never eased.

Now the time had come to know if she'd succeeded.

Around him, the six Feral Warriors paced barechested, a thick gold armband snaking around each man's arm as they raised the mystic circle. In their midst stood the Radiant, the lone woman accompanying them—the one through whom they pulled their power from the Earth. The mystic circle would enclose the great rock and hide all within it from the prying eyes of the Indians that still occasionally hunted these woods.

The day was dreary, the cold biting against the bare skin of his upper body, a body broken too many times beneath Ancreta's torture.

Hatred curled in his belly. Fury lived in his blood. For seven months he'd been her captive, the third of three newly marked Ferals the witch had captured over the past two years.

Only two had survived, Vincent and him. Ten days ago, Vincent had escaped. Nine days ago, he'd risked capture and death to return. Black Panther tilted his head, letting the wind brush his long black hair from his face. Vincent had returned for *him*. And finally, this very day, they would complete the ritual, *the Renascence*, to be reborn as Feral Warriors in truth.

Vincent stood beside him. The leather strip that bound his blond hair at his nape had loosened, and his hair whipped around his face, hiding and revealing eyes lit with a humor that never died, even when Ancreta had done her worst. The two newly marked, soon-to-be shifters stood as one, their wary, fascinated gazes taking in the Feral Warriors, the pride of the Therian race. To a man, the warriors were as tall as they were—all well over six and a half feet, with strong, powerful bodies. Black Panther remembered and relived the awe he'd felt the morning he'd woken to find the claw-mark scars across his eye and known he'd been chosen to join them.

As he watched, the warriors took their places around the circle, raising their voices in chant. The magic might keep out prying eyes, but it did nothing to dissuade the weather. The biting wind raked across his skin, the snow swirling around his ankles.

The woman pulled her billowing cloak tight around her, a petulant look on her face. "Why we cannot wait a mere day or two to perform the ritual, I do not understand. 'Tis snowing!"

The Chief of the Ferals, Lyon, met her discontent with calm command. "The warriors have been through much, Oudine. They need your radiance, and I need their strength added to our numbers. We've been six for too long."

The woman huffed. "You said yourself they may be too damaged by the witch to shift. They may be useless."

"Silence, Oudine." Lyon's voice was no less harsh for its quietness.

Black Panther's hands fisted at his sides. *Useless.* The word ripped through him like a cold steel blade, chilling his blood with sharp crystals of frost. Had Ancreta destroyed everything he'd lived for?

From the moment he awakened to find the feral marks across his eye, he'd waited for this moment. No, in truth, from the moment he was born. His grandmother, the Tauxenent tribe's seer, the woman who had given him the name *Black Panther*, had predicted at his birth more than 140 years ago that he would someday walk the Earth as both panther and man.

All these years he'd believed. All these years he'd waited.

Yesterday, arriving at Feral House at last, he'd learned that the Feral Warrior killed by the Mage shortly before he himself was marked had in fact been the black panther. The prophecy would, at last, come true. But only if Ancreta had not destroyed his ability to reach that animal as she'd sought to do. A Feral Warrior who could not shift would not live long.

"We shall shift as we were meant to," Vincent said quietly, curling his arm over Black Panther's shoulder. "Never doubt it."

Black Panther met his friend's level gaze, feeling a deep and abiding bond, deeper than any he'd felt for another. It was Vincent who'd kept him sane and strong through the months of shared torture. It was Vincent who'd shared his grief when the third of their number, Frederick, had finally died. And it was Vincent who'd found his way out, yet returned, risking everything for his friend.

He owed the man his life.

He nodded to his companion. "We shall shift." Tempered excitement lifted his pulse as he prayed to the goddess of the Therians that his hope wasn't in vain.

"It is time," said one of the Ferals, a man with cold pale eyes, the one called Kougar.

Lyon turned to the woman, the Radiant. "Prepare yourself, Oudine."

With a disgusted huff, the woman sat in the middle of the wide rock, her woolen skirts and cape billowing in the harsh wind.

As the men formed a broad, loose circle around her, Lyon motioned to the two newest members. "Join us."

Vincent at his side, Black Panther stepped forward, into the circle, with a mix of tense anticipation and pride. As he watched, Kougar slashed a knife across his own chest, slapped his palm against the bright red ribbon, and curled his fingers into a fist around the blood. Then he handed the knife to the warrior at his side. One by one, each man did the same until all held a fist damp with his own blood. The last of the six handed the knife to Vincent.

His friend took the blade with a rueful frown, then cut himself as the others had. "Bollocks," he muttered. "Have they been taking lessons from Ancreta?"

"Silence," Kougar said evenly.

When Vincent handed him the blade, Black Panther cut his own chest with the bloodied knife, the pain radiating through his body in an arc of fire, but dulling rapidly as his body healed the insult to his flesh. He slapped his palm to the warm stickiness and fisted his hand. As the others shoved their fists into the air, he did the same.

Lyon nodded. "It is time, Oudine."

Sitting at their feet, the Radiant pushed back the sleeves of her gown and raised her arms above her head.

The chief turned and met his gaze, then Vincent's. "New Ferals, you cannot drink the radiance directly until after your first shift. If you touch her, you will die."

The six moved to stand between the newcomers and the Radiant. Lyon opened his fist and pressed his bloody palm atop Black Panther's fist. A second pressed his palm atop Lyon's and a third atop his. The other three gathered around Vincent in the same manner.

Kougar began to chant, and the others joined in. "Spirits rise and join. Empower the beasts beneath this sky. Goddess, reveal your warriors!"

Thunder rumbled. Black Panther tensed as the rock beneath his feet quaked and trembled. Power raced through his body in an arc of excruciating pain. He clamped down against the unwarriorlike urge to yell his misery to the heavens and hung on.

His vision clouded with small, sparkling lights as something started to shift deep inside. Pain erupted within his body as if he were being stabbed by a thousand knives. Only by sheer dint of the strongest will did he remain upright and not fall to his knees in agony. In the distance, he heard the sound of Ancreta's laughter. He fought the pain, embracing the power that rushed through him, transforming him.

And suddenly his vision shifted. No longer was he standing at the height of men, but far lower, on four legs. His sight sharpened. Sounds bombarded his ears. Scents overwhelmed him—the snow, the forest woods, the river, and the men and woman surrounding him. Each carried a different scent, each heart beat at a different pace, and he was suddenly, strikingly, aware of them all.

Joy coalesced within him, rare and pure, despite the pain that continued to stab at his body. He threw his cat's head back and roared in triumph. He was, finally, *incredibly*, a black panther in truth. Ancreta had not won after all.

"Shift back to a man, Black Panther." Lyon's low voice landed softly on his ears.

He stilled. How was he supposed to shift back?

As if hearing his question, Lyon spoke again. "Will yourself a man, warrior, and it will be so."

He did. He wished himself to be a man once more and in a second burst of colorful lights and mind-ripping pain, he returned to his human form. Panting from the dulling pain, filled with an odd mix of rage and elation, he turned to Vincent.

A strange flatness lay in his friend's eyes.

"Henceforth," Kougar intoned at Lyon's side, "you will be known among us as Paenther."

Vincent studied him, his eyes hard as his gaze dipped. "You accomplished the feat, B.P. You bear the armband."

Paenther looked down at the thick gold snaking around his upper arm. At one end, a panther's head glowed with emerald eyes. His gaze snapped to Vincent, to his friend's arms, devoid of gold. And with piercing, painful clarity, he understood.

"You did not shift." The realization came out on a hard burst of disbelief.

Vincent shook his head, his expression as grim as Paenther had ever seen it. Even during all those miserable months, Vincent had been the one who believed they'd eventually get out of there. That they would eventually become Feral Warriors. Now it seemed even that was to be stolen from him.

Paenther frowned, his head moving in denial. "You shifted before. You should not have been able to, but you did."

"Perhaps 'tis why I cannot now. Ancreta and her dark magic have fouled . . . *destroyed* . . . the one good thing in my life."

"We shall try one more time," Lyon said, drawing their joint gazes. The Chief of the Ferals' expression was grim.

Paenther stilled. "And if he fails to shift a second time?"

Lyon shook his head. "A Feral Warrior who cannot shift cannot receive radiance and will eventually die."

He knew it to be true. The third captive, Frederick, had been trapped in Ancreta's dungeon for nearly two years when his immortality began to wane. He'd bled to death from one of Ancreta's tortures as an immortal never would have.

"We are at war with the Mage," Lyon continued. "We cannot wait two years to replenish our ranks."

The rage boiling beneath Paenther's skin found an outlet as he whirled on the Chief of the Ferals. He lunged forward, stopping a mere yard before the powerful chief, baring his human teeth. "You shall *not d*estroy him."

Lyon growled low in his throat, a sound of warning. "Then he must shift."

Paenther whirled back to his friend with fierce determination. "Did you feel anything? Anything at all?"

Vincent shook his head. "I heard Ancreta's laughter."

"As did I. In the distance."

"No. I heard it as clear as if she stood at my side."

Paenther's lip curled. "She still has her claws in both of us. More so in you." He turned back to Lyon. "The witch must die. This day. Before we try again."

Lyon held his gaze, his own hard. "The Earth retaliates when we kill the Mage. The Elemental has already died this day. The witch is safely locked away in our prison. It is enough."

Paenther held firm. "She must die. Her power over us must die for Vincent to shift."

The Chief of the Ferals shook his head, unbending. "We shall try again, this moment."

Fury and denial stole Paenther's fraying control. Before Lyon could turn away, Paenther ripped the knife out of Kougar's hand and plunged it into Lyon's breast, pressing it against his heart.

In a lightning-fast move, Lyon grabbed him around the neck, his claws sprouting and sinking deep into Paenther's throat until the blood ran warm down his chest.

Animals growled all around him, the tension on the rock turning thick as tree sap in winter. If Paenther killed their chief, he'd never take another step. But none dared tackle him when doing so might cut out their leader's heart.

Lyon's fangs dropped, his eyes turning the glowing amber of a lion's. "You would kill me?" he growled, his voice calm, but deadly.

"Not unless you give me no choice. I will do whatever I must to save his life as he saved mine."

For long, breathless moments, the two bleeding men stared one another down. On some dark level of his mind, Paenther knew he was sacrificing his status as a Feral Warrior in order to preserve Vincent's. The devastation of that thought was nothing compared to his desperation to save his friend.

Finally, never taking his eyes from Paenther's, Lyon spoke, his voice clipped and tight. "Get the witch. She'll die this day. Before we try the ritual again." In those hard amber eyes, Paenther saw the truth. The Chief of the Ferals had made the choice to comply with his demand. If he had chosen to kill his attacker instead, Paenther's throat would be gone, and he would be the one with the blade in his chest.

Paenther withdrew the knife and offered the hilt to Lyon. He'd won the concession he'd wanted. Now he would suffer the consequences. He understood all too well the law of the pack, as he'd been raised by the law of the tribe. If you challenged the chief, you killed him. Or expected to die.

If Lyon chose to take his life for the attack, he would accept his death like the warrior he was.

Vincent stepped beside him, shoulder to shoulder, his tone hard as granite. "You'll only destroy him through me."

Lyon growled, a low, threatening rumble, his hand tightening around Paenther's neck, his claws digging deeper with a fiery pain. Abruptly, Lyon released him, his gaze traveling slowly between the two newest Ferals.

"I would punish you severely, both of you, if I did not believe the witch had already done so. You've emerged from that hell with a rare loyalty toward one another. Turn that loyalty toward the nine, and you'll make fine Feral Warriors. If you do not . . ." His eyes glittered with warning. " . . . if either of you ever threatens one of us again, I'll clear the way for your replacements without a second thought."

Paenther stared at the man, taking his measure, finding both strength and fairness, making him all the more proud to be a Feral Warrior.

"Return to your places within the circle," Lyon growled.

Paenther slammed his fist against his chest as he met Lyon's gaze. "My loyalty is yours."

Lyon nodded once. "Good."

By the time Ancreta was dragged onto the rock, Paenther's hair was dripping from melted snowflakes, his hands nearly numb.

The blond beauty cowered at his feet in fear.

"Face your fate!" Paenther snarled, a borrowed knife in his hand. He looked at Vincent. "The head or the heart?"

"The head."

Paenther nodded once, then shoved the struggling witch onto her back. He wanted her to see death come for her. As fear lanced her copper-ringed irises, he saw again the innocent young beauty he'd believed her to be as he'd come to her rescue all those months ago. A bit of chivalry he had rued every moment since.

He knelt beside her, lifting his blade to strike, Vincent mirroring his action on her other side.

"Die, witch," they said as one.

As Vincent's blade hacked off her head in a shower of blood, Paenther's blade carved out her heart. Raw, savage satisfaction poured through his body, doing much to heal his soul.

It was done.

The two men rose as one, blood-splattered but grimly satisfied.

"Are you ready to try again?" Lyon asked.

Vincent nodded, a glimmer of a smile lifting his mouth, though his eyes remained hard and wary. "Ready as a stallion in rut."

Once more, the circle formed, blood bloomed on the warriors' chests, fists rose into the air. This time Paenther didn't shift, but in a flash of sparkling light, Vincent did. Where he'd stood, a huge black-and-green snake now curled on the rock, his scales shimmering as he grew in both length and width. Nine feet long. Twelve feet. Fifteen feet.

In a second flash of light, Vincent reappeared, grinning like a loon, his hair gone, his bald head gleaming, a gold armband with the head of a snake curving around his arm.

Paenther felt a rush of joy five times what he'd felt when he'd shifted himself.

"Henceforth," Kougar intoned, "you will be known as Vhyper."

Vincent/Vhyper whooped, a grin splitting his face as the two men embraced, slapping one another on the back. They pulled apart, grasping one another's shoulders.

"Is it not an astonishing feeling to shift, my friend?" Vhyper asked. "The rapture. The utter feeling of well-being."

"It is a fine feeling, Vhyper," Paenther said. The others had told him to expect as much. But for him, the shift had brought only pain. A pain to match the rage Ancreta had burned into his soul. The witch might be dead, but he feared her legacy would torment him until the very end of his immortal existence.

His hatred of all things Mage would endure through eternity.

Chapter
One

Paenther floated, his mind in a sensual fog trapped somewhere between dream and reality. Remembering . . .

She held out her hand to him, an ethereal beauty with short, dark hair and soft eyes the color of a summer sky. Eyes that smoldered with passion as she led him behind the building, through the parking lot, and up the steep, heavily wooded hill behind the Market deep in the Blue Ridge Mountains of western Virginia.

He didn't even know her name.

Beyond the sight of prying eyes, he pulled her to a stop and kissed her, passion exploding as he pressed her against the nearest tree, desperate to be inside her. The deep rumble of a truck sounded in the distance. She kissed him back frantically, as if she feared they didn't have much time. The feel of her hand on his zipper made his blood pound. The touch of her fingers along the length of his bare flesh nearly stopped his heart.

Gentleness and care be damned, he needed her now. Shoving his hand beneath her dress, he found her bare and ready. His finger probed her depths, and she forced him deeper, whimpering with desire.

Yanking her dress up to her waist, he lifted her, positioning her sheath to his height. As she wrapped her bare thighs around his waist, he pushed inside her, filling her in a single, perfect thrust.

Heaven. Nothing in his life had ever felt more right. Within moments, her release broke over her with a cry, her inner muscles contracting hard around him, driving him over the edge.

"Look at me," she cried.

And he did, staring into eyes suddenly encircled by shiny copper rings.

The eyes of a Mage.

Paenther fought his way back to consciousness like a man hacking a path through a fog-shrouded jungle. Little by little, he parted the misty enchantment that encased his brain, impressions flying at him through his senses. Cold, rough stone dug into the bare flesh of his back as he lay with his arms pulled taut above his head. He flexed his muscles and tried to move, but harsh metal bit into his wrists as the sound of chains clanked against the rock.

Icy disbelief clawed through his mind. His pulse began to race.

He was chained. Naked.

Finally, *finally*, his vision tore free of the enchantment. His eyes snapped open, and he stared around him at the unlikely sight. He was alone.

In a cave.

High above him, dozens of daggerlike stalactites dripped from the roof. Floating around them were small flames encased in luminescent bubbles. A sight he hadn't seen since Ancreta's dungeon. A sight that filled him with cold dread.

Mage lightwicks.

He fought against his bonds in furious desperation as he struggled to remember what had happened.

The beauty. Innocence and wisdom shining from eyes the color of a summer sky. He'd buried himself inside her and found a passion and release more intense, more incredible, than any he'd ever known. Until, at that moment of raging perfection, she'd revealed herself to be Mage, and he'd felt the net of enchantment snare his mind.

The memory stopped his breath, cramping his guts. For the second time in his life, he'd been captured by a Mage witch.

Fury charged through his body, a yell of denial roaring through his head as he struggled to free himself.

This couldn't be happening. He had *not* fallen into another Mage trap! He'd barely survived the first one.

Goddess, he had to get out of here.

He studied his cage with a strafing gaze. It appeared to be a room, an uneven room roughly fifteen feet by fifteen feet, with a steel door that had been left open. Through the doorway, he glimpsed more stone, telling him he was probably in one of the extensive caverns that riddled the Blue Ridge. The air was damp and cool, but he barely felt the chill through the rage boiling his blood.

The rock slab beneath him appeared to be high off the ground yet attached to the wall like some kind of wide, natural shelf. The wall curved just enough to shield him from the mineral-laden water dripping from the stalactites into the puddles on the floor.

As he tipped his head back to look behind him, he caught the odd sight of a showerhead sticking out of the rock. Plumbing? Was this actually the Mage stronghold, then, and not simply a prison?

He turned to look in the other direction behind him, and froze. Hanging from wooden hangers, from a single peg on the wall, were three softly colored dresses in a shapeless, long-sleeved style he recognized all too well. *Hers.*

Fury ripped through his mind as he remembered, in painful clarity, lifting the hem of one of those soft, worn dresses and sliding his hand beneath to encounter only warm flesh and damp heat. A heat the witch had invited him to drive himself into. He had, and it was an act he'd regret for the rest of his life.

He wondered just how long that would be, now.

Ice congealed in his heart. His only reason for being in these mountains at all was to find Vhyper. Something had happened to his friend during a ritual a few weeks ago. He'd been cut by the Daemon blade, as they all had. But unlike the rest of them, Vhyper had changed. Some of the Ferals thought the evil in the blade had stolen his soul.

Paenther refused to believe it. He would save Vhyper just as Vhyper had saved *him* all those years ago. But he had to find him first. Getting trapped and chained in a witch's lair sure as hell wasn't the way to go about it.

His muscles corded as he fought the chains with every ounce of strength he possessed until his skin was damp with sweat and his wrists slick with blood. Yet he accomplished nothing. He was pinned fast, his arms trapped above his head, his legs spread and tethered.

Ah, goddess. If only you'd stopped me. No fate could be worse. He'd have sold his soul to have escaped this.

Heaven help me. His soul was probably the very thing the witch wanted. To finish what Ancreta had started all those years ago—tearing him loose from his animal once and for all.

"Go! Flee!" Skye clapped her hands at the small herd of deer gathering around her. Pouring her will into the air, she set them to flight with a swish of their white tails. "I'm death," she cried, as they scattered into the surrounding woods. "I'm nothing but death to you!"

But even as the beautiful creatures disappeared, Skye knew they'd return. They always returned, drawn to her as deeply as she was to them. Tears burned her eyes. Not for the first time, she bitterly wished she'd never been born with this affinity for the Earth's creatures. The gift that should have been a source of joy had turned her life into a living nightmare.

Skye collapsed back against the nearest tree trunk, her heart thudding with agitation, her stomach sick from the weight of hatred.

"Dear Mother," she prayed. "Take Birik and burn him in Hell!"

But the Mother never heard her. How many years had she been trapped in this darkness, chained to this mountain as surely as the warrior she'd captured was chained to the rock slab in her room, even if her chains were less visible?

Two days ago she'd been sent to capture him—a shape-shifter. One of the elite Feral Warriors. One of the most rare creatures in the world and, without a doubt, the most beautiful. He'd shown her such extraordinary gentleness, such fierce passion, and she'd repaid him with the ultimate betrayal.

But she'd had no choice. If only she could end this nightmare. If only she could escape Birik and this mountain!

The nudge at her hip had her sinking to her knees to embrace the doe who'd come right back to her. "Ever loyal, aren't you, Faithful?" The white-tailed deer with the notch out of her ear was her favorite. Her only true friend. One she would never take into the caverns. Ever.

The doe nuzzled her cheek, staring at her with those huge brown eyes, giving her the only loyalty she'd known in too many years. Unhappiness burned the backs of her eyes. Fear twisted inside her. Though Birik had assured her he had no intention of killing the Feral, she was terrified he'd lied.

She curved both arms around Faithful, burying her face in her soft brown neck, wishing for a miracle that would save them all. But she'd long ago ceased believing in miracles.

Slowly, the other deer returned to gather around her, as did several dozen other forest creatures. Drawn to her, every one, much to her joy . . . and sorrow.

With a last caress, she said good-bye to Faithful, sending her away as she chose another doe to accompany her back to the caverns, along with several smaller animals.

As much as she dreaded facing the Feral, dreading the anger she knew she'd see in those dark eyes that had looked at her with such gentleness, she had to get back to him.

And pray she could keep him alive.

Paenther caught the witch's scent, that delicate, damning smell of violets, moments before she stepped into the doorway, the ethereal beauty who'd shown him heaven between her thighs, then captured him in her net of bewitchment. At the sight of her, lust slammed into him all over again.

Even as hatred seared its way through his blood, his gaze drank in the vision. She was slender, with few curves revealing themselves beneath the soft, shapeless blue dress. But her short hair accentuated a long, graceful neck and features that were too fine, too delicate for a coldhearted witch.

Mage or not, she stole his breath.

She watched him, her eyes wary, as she gently stroked the rabbit in her arms. At her side, a doe pressed her head against the witch's hip while several excited squirrels chased one another around her ankles.

He'd thought she was human.

Closing his eyes against the sight of her, he prayed that grave error didn't turn out to be the last mistake he ever made.

At the soft sound of her movement, he opened his eyes and watched her cross the room, leading her small menagerie to a cage in the corner. The rabbit and squirrels ran inside, and she fastened the door, then tied the docile doe loosely with a rope attached to the wall. Empathy for the creatures jolted him. Creatures she'd captured as surely as she'd captured him.

The animals seemed to like her. Pets, no doubt. A growl rumbled low in his throat. He would never be her pet.

The hatred inside him was so raw, so pure, if his gaze could kill, she'd be dead. Goddess, he couldn't remember the last time he'd let his cock do his thinking for him. No woman had pierced his icy control in centuries. The fact that this one had should have rung a thousand warning bells that she wasn't what she seemed.

"*Witch*," he snarled. "What do you want from me?"

She rose from her animals with the grace of a dancer and turned to him. There was a fragility about her that tried to tug at his protective instincts. But like everything about her that pulled at him, he knew it was a lie. If he ever managed to free himself from these shackles, he'd carve the heart out of her chest just as he had Ancreta's.

"What I want doesn't matter." Even her soft voice, rich with a regret he didn't believe, held a musical lilt that stroked his senses. "I'm sorry to have brought you here."

"Then let me go."

"I can't." She came toward him, stopping at the foot of the stone platform where he was chained. To his consternation, she watched him, her gaze sliding over his flesh. His body rose, hardening, as if her hands and not her gaze caressed him.

The faint scent of her arousal stole across his senses, tripping a wild rage inside him. How many times had Ancreta forced him to rise for her, then impaled herself on his unwilling body before beginning the torture of trying to free him from his animal?

Placing her palms on the waist-high rock, the witch pulled herself up and knelt between his legs with a swish of soft cotton.

Paenther went feral, that place halfway between man and beast where his fangs erupted, his claws unsheathed, and his black eyes turned the glowing green of a jungle cat's.

"You touch me, you die."

The witch laced her fingers together in her lap tight enough to turn her knuckles white. The sympathy and remorse in her blue eyes almost seemed real. "I've been where you are. I wouldn't wish it on my worst enemy." She leaned forward, her voice strong and low, and laced with steel. "I know you don't believe me, but you aren't my enemy."

"You *are* mine," he bit out.

She sighed. "I know." Sitting back on her heels, she loosened the knot of her hands. "I'm sorry. I have to touch you, but I won't touch you *there*." Her gaze caressed his shaft. "Not unless you want me to."

"I'll kill you first."

With a single nod, she splayed her cool palms lightly across his bare thighs. With that simple touch, sensation rippled across his flesh, a heady, electric heat that sent the blood surging through his veins. He fought the desire that blasted him, clawing to hang on to the icy control that had molded his life, but his mind betrayed him as thoroughly as his body. All he could think of was the way her silken thighs had felt beneath his hands as he'd spread her in the woods, as he'd entered her.

The scent of violets washed over him. The sight of her mouth, ripe and unsmiling in that delicate face, reminded him of the taste of her kiss, like clear, sweet raindrops. Even knowing what she was, even knowing she'd lured him into her trap with a siren's song of lust, he couldn't stop wanting her.

Her palms slid along the tops of his thighs, across his flesh as if he were an animal to be petted. It was all he could do not to purr. Without his consciously willing it, his fangs and claws retracted.

"You hid your Mage eyes," he snarled instead.

Her mouth twisted in a wry, frustratingly engaging shadow of a smile. "You wouldn't have come with me otherwise."

Paenther tried to growl, but the feel of her hands was doing things to him in parts of his body that had nothing to do with sex. Almost as if she were soothing the rage burned into his soul by Ancreta all those years ago.

"You're beautiful," she murmured. "Your skin is warm as the sun. Your hair like black silk." Her words flowed over him, as irritatingly pleasing as her touch. "The animal inside you purrs."

Paenther froze. Dammit, he hadn't even tried . . . Closing his eyes against her, he called on the magic deep inside him and tried to shift, praying his panther's paws would be able to slide free of his shackles.

Nothing happened.

As he opened his eyes, the witch's copper blue gaze met his. "The manacles steal your power, warrior. You can't shift as long as you wear them."

"How long have you known I was a Feral?"

"I knew the first time I saw you. I felt the animal inside you. Just now, I felt you call to the power he gives you."

He scowled. "You couldn't possibly have felt that."

She watched him with those eyes as deep as the oceans, but said nothing.

Witch.

His body went rigid as a thought occurred to him. He hadn't been alone. What if Foxx had been captured, too? He forced himself to look into the siren's face, guarding himself against the tug of her beauty, steeling himself for her answer.

"How many of us did you catch?"

"Just you, warrior. Your companion got away."

He stared at her, wanting to feel relieved yet not trusting her at all. Still, maybe Foxx *had* escaped. He would call Lyon, and they'd initiate a rescue. He hated the thought of his unbridled lust putting his brothers in danger; but knowing the others would come, that he wasn't doomed to spend the rest of his life here, helped calm his storm-tossed mind.

His thoughts evaporated as the witch leaned over him, her dark, sleek head dipping toward his body as if she intended to take him in her mouth.

The growl that erupted from his throat was that of an animal, dark with warning, even as part of him longed for the feel of her wet tongue stroking his length. But her lips landed well to the right of his heavy erection, brushing a light, damp kiss on his hip bone.

Paenther sucked in a hard breath, sweat beading at his temples. Even that small brush of her lips sent heat rushing through his body. His arms shook as they strained against their bonds, his driving need shifting from retribution to pulling her on top of him and burying himself in her heat.

How could he want her so badly when he hated her so violently? She was a fire in his blood. A need raging out of control.

The heady musk of her arousal thickened in the air, and he knew he wasn't the only one feeling the desire. She lifted her gaze, heat a living thing in her eyes. The woman was a potent, dangerous blend of false innocence and a siren's temptation. His body burned to possess her again.

She bent down, her mouth trailing soft, damp kisses along his hip to his thigh, her lips inches from the base of his hard, throbbing shaft. He wanted her to touch him, to take him into her mouth with a need bordering on desperation. But he would never admit it. Never.

What is she doing to me?

A flash of dark light near the ceiling jerked his thoughts from the pleasure arcing through his body. He frowned at the dark, pulsing sphere that clearly wasn't a lightwick. His eyes narrowed with recognition. A power orb. Scanning the ceiling, he saw others nestled high against the ceiling, pulsing with light, throbbing to the beat of his pounding heart. As if they were somehow feeding off him.

Or feeding off the passion riding him.

"You're collecting power," he accused.

She looked up, her lids heavy, her lips damp. Sexy as hell. "That's the reason you're here."

He stared at her, unsure if her words relieved him or infuriated him more. His only purpose for being here was to fill those orbs with his lust? To be chained and petted by a beauty of a witch until he was out of his mind with wanting?

No way in hell. He knew the Mage too well to believe for a single moment the answer was that simple.

"What are you going to do with the energy once the orbs are filled?"

She raised up and sat back on her heels, shrugging delicately even as her chest rose and fell on rapid, shallow breaths. "I don't know. It's for Birik. All I know is that if we don't raise enough . . . he won't be pleased." Her gaze rose to the ceiling, as if studying the orbs and measuring the results of her play. "It's not enough."

As one soft hand moved back to his thigh, she reached up and covered her breast, squeezing the small mound through her dress. She gasped, her back arching as her head tilted back. His cock jerked with a hunger of its own.

The scent of desire swirled around him. Heat rushed through his blood, pooling in that one part of his anatomy until he was thick and throbbing and nearly out of his head with needing her.

He struggled to turn his mind elsewhere. "Who's

Birik?" Even his voice strained against the driving desire to feel her tight around him.

Slowly, she released her breast and lifted her hand off his thigh to rake both sets of fingers through her short hair. With a shuddering breath she said, "He's the archsorcerer in charge of this stronghold and ruler of all who reside here. He reports to the Elemental himself."

"And he wants the power from these orbs?"

"Yes."

Power from passion. He'd never heard of dark power raised in such a way, but he knew little about Mage orbs. Less still about the use to which they might try to put that energy.

What if they were making some kind of weapon to use against the Ferals? The thought made him ill. What if he'd somehow become the instrument of the destruction of his brothers?

Goddess, he couldn't live with this. He couldn't let this happen.

She looked up at the ceiling again and sighed. "It's enough."

With a last featherlight pat to his thigh, the beauty climbed off the stone and walked to the door with a natural, barefooted grace, leaving him hard and distended and throbbing.

Witch. Fury burned inside him. But as she disappeared out the portal, it took every ounce of control he possessed not to call her back.

Chapter
Two

Skye fled the cell that served as her bedroom and hurried through the passages that twisted and turned through the rock following eons of water erosion. The open areas and passages of the cavern remained in their natural state, though Birik's extensive quarters and most of the bedchambers, kitchens, and ritual rooms had been transformed into comfortable living areas complete with furniture, carpeting, wallpaper, and more.

Only Skye lived in an unadorned cell within the rock, though she spent as little time there as possible. Most of her days she stayed outside in the woods, or wandering among the unused parts of the cave, where she headed now.

Low in her body, unrelieved passion made her

throb and ache. Regret for her part in the capture of the beautiful shape-shifter ripped at her heart.

At last she reached the dagger fields, the raw, uncleared part of the caverns where the daggerlike stones, the stalagmites, rose from below as their counterparts hung from above. The air smelled of cool, damp limestone with the only trace of light-wick smoke from the single flame that floated behind her, lighting the darkness. Few Mage ever ventured this deep into the caves. It was here she came to think when she wasn't in the forest. Lowering herself to a small, dry patch of stone tucked into the curve of a low wall, she struggled to gather her wits, wits that had scattered to the winds with the first touch of the man's thighs beneath her palms.

Pulling her knees tight against her chest, she buried her face in her skirt and shook. Her body wanted, it *needed* what she'd found with him in the woods earlier. That temporary, explosive quenching of the fire that had burned inside her from the first moment she'd seen him in the Market two days ago.

Birik had warned her that shape-shifters would be coming. He'd sent her to watch for them, ordering her to choose one for her own. Nothing good would come of it for either her or the shifter, she'd known that. But she'd long ago quit fighting her fate and accepted that she could never thwart one of Birik's commands.

So she'd done as directed and begun to haunt the small human Market, waiting for her prey.

When he'd first stepped into the store, she'd felt the Earth come to a stop, as if the very air had caught its breath. Though she'd pretended to be engrossed in the magazine in her hand, she'd been excruciatingly aware of him with his huge, leather-clad body, his arresting face with the high, pronounced cheekbones and savage claw marks across his eye, and the feeling of fierce, tense control rolling off him in waves.

And when he'd turned that dark gaze on her, her knees had gone weak even as she'd been filled with a strange, shimmering joy. She'd felt herself smile even as her pulse had threatened to race away. It wasn't until after he'd left the store that she'd realized she'd felt his animal. And realized what he was. That he was one of the very creatures Birik had sent her to capture. But by then it was too late.

At the realization, her heart had pounded as confusion clouded her mind. Deep inside, she'd known he was hers. But taking him meant Birik would have him, too.

When he'd returned the next day, he'd walked straight to her, where she'd waited at the corner of the building.

She'd been so overwhelmed by his wild, masculine presence and her own confusion, she'd said nothing, merely backed around the corner, knowing he'd follow. And he had. He'd stared at her with such hunger in his eyes. The animal inside him had leaped in greeting, rubbing itself warmly against her mind.

Walking into his arms had been the most natural thing she'd ever done. The moment their mouths had touched, passion had exploded. All thought had flown from her head as she'd drunk of his clean, wild taste, diving her fingers into his silken black hair. Time had ceased to exist, Birik and his demands all but forgotten.

She'd felt this wild need rising inside her. And he'd known it. His hand had slid beneath her skirt, between her thighs. As one long finger burrowed deep inside her, she'd felt a pleasure she'd barely been able to credit. A pleasure so intense, she'd wondered if she could die from it. And she'd wanted him as she'd never wanted another.

But Paenther's redheaded friend had come looking for him, and she'd run.

That was yesterday. Today they'd finally mated, a joining she'd never believed possible. Without pain. Without cruelty. And she'd rewarded him for his tenderness by enthralling him, trapping him in a captivity from which he'd never escape. Now he hated her, *hated* her, with a vehemence that tore tiny strips from her soul.

Pressing her back against the rock, she raked trembling fingers through her hair, aching with regret and bitterness. He was hers, all right. Her prisoner. Her enemy.

If only she could have saved him. But if she'd sent him away, Birik would only have forced her to capture another. Birik always got his way. *Always.*

She'd had to choose a Feral.

And from the moment she saw him, she'd known *this* Feral was the only man she would ever want.

Paenther's gaze remained fixed on the door as he waited for the witch's return. Part of him, the part that hated, never wanted to see her again. But another part of him hungered for the sight of her. For another whiff of her violet scent. And he both dreaded and craved another touch of her hands. She'd woven her spell of enchantment over him but good, there was no doubt about it.

She had yet to do anything more than touch him, but he knew the Mage. The pain would come. He'd escape this captivity more damaged than he had the last.

If he escaped at all.

His gaze slid to the ceiling, to one of the lightwicks floating high above his head. The first time he ever saw a lightwick was the day he met Vhyper. After his ill-fated attempt to rescue a beauty who'd turned out to be Mage, he'd woken in a musty, dark cellar, chained on his back as he was now.

That time, though, he hadn't been alone.

Welcome to Hell, my friend, Vhyper had said. His face had taken on a fierce, fervent look. *We are going to get out of this together. Do not doubt it. Do not ever doubt it.*

And he hadn't.

Paenther fisted his hands as his gaze moved from the lightwicks to the stalactites and back again. Vhyper's words that day, repeated nearly every day of his captivity, had kept him focused through months of torture of the worst kind. They'd kept him sane.

Now he made a similar, silent promise to his friend. *I won't give up until I find you, Vhype. Until I save you as you saved me. Don't ever doubt it.*

But, dammit, he had to get free if he was ever going to be of any use to either one of them.

At the sound of footsteps outside the room, steps too heavy to be the witch's, Paenther turned his head to face the entrance.

And came face-to-face with Vhyper.

His friend walked casually through the door, looking the same as he always did, his sleek head gleaming beneath the lightwicks, a single earring in the shape of a snake dangling from the lobe of his right ear. He was dressed in his usual attire of open leather vest over a bare, broad chest, the golden Feral armband curled around his arm.

Paenther's heart lurched with triumphant relief, then plummeted to his stomach as he stared into Vhyper's eyes. Those dark blue eyes that had always glimmered with humor and warmth, even in the direst of circumstances, lay cold. Flat.

Soulless.

The eyes of a stranger.

Paenther felt the loss like a physical blow. *What have you done with my friend?* He could only pray that the man he knew, the man he'd trusted like no other, was still in there somewhere, trapped within the dark magic and not lost to him completely.

"Well, well, if it isn't my old friend, B.P. I must say, you're looking a little underdressed." Vhyper sauntered over to him, his mouth lifting into a smile that held no humor. "I knew you'd come to *rescue* me. Catching you was easy as child's play."

"Why are you here, Vhype?" Paenther asked evenly. His emotions were always under tight restraint, caught with the rage he battled every minute of every day.

Vhyper shrugged. "You know why."

"Do I? All I know is Zaphene turned you against us. What did she do to you, Vhyper?"

Vhyper tugged on his earring, his brows lowering. For a moment, Paenther thought he saw the old Vhyper walk through those eyes.

"Truthfully, I'm not sure it was the witch's doing. I think it happened the night we raised the spirit of the lion. I got bitten by that Daemon blade the same as the rest of you, but it changed me, B.P." His eyes narrowed in thought. "It rid me of my conscience. I'm not entirely sure it didn't steal my soul." Vhyper grinned suddenly, the coldness like frost over his eyes. "A hell of a way to live."

Paenther stared at him, railing at the fates. *Not Vhyper. You can't have Vhyper!* He owed the snake his sanity. His life. Grinding his teeth together, Paenther fought back the tide of anger. The Ferals would come. He needed to learn all he could.

"Are the Mage still trying to free Satanan and his Daemon horde?"

Vhyper tugged at his earring. "Of course."

"*Why?* How can you help them unleash that evil?"

Vhyper shrugged. "And what is evil, B.P.? Is it evil for the owl to kill the mouse?" He smiled coldly. "Depends on your point of view, doesn't it? On whether you're the owl . . . or the mouse."

"Satanan will destroy this world."

"Will he? Or will he simply feed from it? The Daemons were always at the top of the food chain."

"You're not a Daemon."

"True. But I'm not looking for power out of this." Again, his old friend's eyes narrowed, something approaching confusion entering their dark blue depths. "It's a compulsion, B.P., to free the evil."

"The evil's infected you, Vhype. It's controlling you. *Fight it.*"

As quickly as the confusion had entered the shape-shifter's eyes, it disappeared again. His grin turned malicious. "It's not controlling me, Paenther. Nothing controls me now. Not even my conscience." He shrugged as if he were admitting a weakness for porn. "I find I've developed a taste for the misery of others."

Paenther shook his head. This wasn't the man he knew. "Why am I here?" His gaze flicked up to the pulsing orbs above his head. "To raise power to fill those? Or something more?"

Vhyper's smile was cold. "Depends on how much you raise." He lifted his hand and turned. "Later, B.P."

"Vhyper, wait. What about Foxx?" He had to know if the witch had told him the truth. Not that he could trust anything Vhyper said, either.

The man glanced back. "He got away. The witch wasn't interested in him and by the time the other Mage realized there were Ferals on the mountain, he was already gone. But the mountain has a magic all its own. If he started up the mountain at all, he'd have been snared by the spell."

Dread curled in Paenther's gut. "What spell?"

"An incantation to confuse. As soon as it took hold of him, he would have forgotten why he was there, forgotten all about you until he'd driven a good long way away. By then, he wouldn't even remember where he'd last seen you."

Vhyper laughed. "Had you hoped for a proper Feral rescue? Not going to happen, B.P. Foxx won't be able to lead them back here. You'll never leave here alive."

As he stared at the man who used to be his friend, something real moved through Vhyper's eyes, a glimmer of warmth. A hint of pain. A glimpse of the friend he'd known for so many years.

It was there and gone in an instant, swallowed by the evil. But Paenther's pulse began to pound. He knew what he'd seen. The Vhyper he'd give his life for was still in there. Subjugated to the darkness, but not lost. Not completely.

"Vhyper, *fight it.*"

"There's nothing to fight, Paenther," he said coldly. "There's no one here who will help you. You have a role to play, just as we all do." Vhyper's eyes began to glitter. "It's going to be amazing, B.P. Things are going to happen you won't believe. And you won't want to miss. You'll have a front-row seat, old friend. I'll make sure of it."

Vhyper turned and walked out the door.

"Vhyper!" Paenther strained against his shackles, rattling his chains on the rock until his body was damp with sweat, and the coppery scent of his own blood coated his nostrils. Desperation, fierce and terrible, vibrated through his body as he fought to free himself with every ounce of strength he possessed.

Foxx was safe, but unless both Vhyper and the witch had lied to him, he wouldn't be leading the others back here. Paenther was as lost as Vhyper unless he could somehow find a way to reach his friend beneath the cold eyes of the evil that had ensnared him. Unless he could find a way to free them both.

He remembered thinking, after the witch Zaphene infiltrated Feral House, turning Vhyper, that things couldn't get much worse. He hadn't had a clue.

Now he was caught in trouble as deep as the blue of the eyes that had ensnared him. And he had a bad feeling this trouble had only begun.

Chapter Three

Skye rose from her private sanctuary in the dagger fields and brushed off her soft knit dress, her pulse finally back to normal—or as close to normal as it was likely to get with the Feral strapped to her bed. She had to get back to him. As much as she dreaded facing those hate-filled black eyes, she needed to make certain all her creatures were okay—the ones who walked on four feet and the very large, very masculine shape-shifter who at present walked on two.

Her stomach clenched. Midnight was not far away.

She retraced her path, dodging puddles and dripping stone, the rock cool beneath her bare feet. In the distance she heard the sounds of voices as the sorcerers prepared the evening rituals and the women of the cavern readied the evening meal. At one time, she would have helped them. But not anymore. She was no longer one of them.

She alone still possessed a soul.

Her stomach growled. It had been two days since she'd last eaten. But as she turned a corner in the rock and spied Birik talking to one of his sentinels, her appetite fled.

Birik was striking in his way, with his fawn-colored skin, long white hair, and cruel green eyes, his body as lean and quick as the thorn whip he'd used on her as a child. Curled around his neck and draped over one shoulder was a large black rat snake. Two gray-and-copper corn snakes slithered around his feet.

She didn't mind the snakes. She was drawn to all creatures. But the man was another matter. If she could do anything to avoid him, she would, but there was no other way back to her room from here. So she averted her gaze as she approached where he stood, seeking to avoid his notice as she always did. But as she tried to pass, stepping around his snakes, he grabbed her arm, his cruel fingers digging into her flesh and pulling her to a stop.

Fear shivered up her spine.

Birik released her only to lift those thin, brutish fingers to her cheek, making her swallow hard. The brush of his fingers was unnaturally gentle, doing nothing to quell the speeding of her pulse. His gentleness always scared her more than his casual cruelty. Skye held perfectly still, knowing better than to let him see her fear.

"You did well, enchantress." His eyes glittered with excitement. "The power was more than I'd hoped for, and you've yet to ride him."

She didn't ask how he knew she hadn't mated with the Feral since bringing him into the cavern. Birik always knew more than he should. "He's not ready to be mounted."

Birik laughed. "He's male, and clearly drawn to you. A few strokes of your hand or tongue, and I guarantee he'll be ready."

Skye swallowed again, nodding. There was no use arguing. Birik neither understood nor cared that the Feral's hatred of his captivity and his captor made him fight the attraction, or that she'd succeed far better if the man, like any creature in captivity, were given a few days to calm to her touch.

The Mage who'd been her master, teacher, and tormentor since she was eight grabbed her jaw, squeezing until she thought he might break the bones in her face, hurting her until the tears she struggled to hold back clouded her vision.

"Don't fail me, Skye. You won't like the consequences."

Apprehension fluttered in her stomach. She knew the consequences all too well. "I won't fail you."

The moment Birik released her, she hurried past him, descending the ancient stairs carved into the rock as she fled to the relative safety of the prison cell that had become her bedroom when she was eight. She'd fought Birik back then. Bitterly. He'd taken everything from her, all comfort, all warmth. And when that still hadn't forced her compliance, he'd hurt her, terribly, over and over and over again until he'd finally broken her will.

Giving up hadn't been easy. It had never been in her nature to acquiesce. But the pain had become more than she could stand. And she'd finally understood there was nothing more that she could do but accept her fate.

As she neared the door to her chamber, she thought of the beautiful man trapped inside. And what she had to do. Her fist pressed against the harsh ache of guilt lodged beneath her breastbone. She wasn't the only one who suffered because of Birik's control over her. If she wanted to keep the Feral alive, she had little choice but to make him suffer more.

She reached her room to find him as she'd left him, chained and furious. A man chained and naked as he was should look helpless. But dark, angry eyes speared her as danger rolled off him, filling the very air of the room. He was the most powerful, most unsettling, male she'd ever encountered. Just being in the same room with him sent her pulse pounding in a way that had only a little to do with fear.

A thrill of energy rolled across her skin, drawing her eyes to the orbs. Birik had drained them while she was gone, yet already they were beginning to glow again. Lust shimmered in the air. Hers, certainly.

Did he feel it, too? There was so much fury in his eyes, it was difficult to say. But then her gaze traveled the length of his hard, muscular body, coming to rest on the arousal standing straight up from his groin, long and thick and rigid.

Oh, he felt it, all right. And wasn't the least bit happy about it.

"Free me," the man growled between clenched teeth as he watched her with a predator's stillness.

Skye went to where the animals awaited, greeting them silently as they greeted her, running her hands down the neck of the doe and bending to let the sweet creature nuzzle her cheek as Faithful always did. Sharp grief pierced her heart at the thought of this deer's future.

"If I could free you, I would." She'd free them all, herself included. But freedom from Birik was impossible. She'd tried. Over and over she'd tried until Birik made certain she would never try again.

With a last stroke of the doe's soft coat, she crossed back and closed the steel door to the room, a door Birik had installed years ago to keep her in. She rarely bothered to close it anymore. It had never kept anyone out. But she closed it now, needing no audience for what she must do.

With a deep breath that did little to calm her, she moved slowly toward the cold slab of rock that had acted as her bed for so many years. The Feral's black eyes watched her every step of the way. As she drew near, she couldn't find the courage to meet the anger in his eyes and looked away, letting her gaze wander over his powerful male body instead. He was truly magnificent. Mage males tended toward slim physiques and few overt muscles. Not so the Ferals.

This one in particular was a sight to behold. His skin was a beautiful shade of bronze, his chest broad and muscular, adorned with a thick, intriguing tattoo—an intricate interweaving of curves and lines. Around one of the thickly muscled arms chained above his head curved a golden armband. At one end, the head of a panther stared out at her, its eyes twinkling with emeralds. She knew the armband could not be removed except by the wearer himself.

Birik had tried.

With a deep breath, she forced herself to meet that dark, angry gaze.

The moment she did, he growled at her. *"Free me."*

"I can't." Her breath caught, her pulse fluttering as she felt the pull of those eyes. She had the oddest sensation that if she wasn't careful, she'd find herself tumbling into those black depths, becoming the captive instead of the captor.

Lifting her hand, she reached for him, sliding her palm across his warm, granite chest, tracing his tattoo, feeling the ripple of hard muscle against her skin. Desire arced through her body.

His masculine scent rose up to meet her on a rush of dark, carnal pleasure.

The animal inside him, pacing angrily, turned its head toward her in greeting.

"Don't touch me," the man snarled.

"I have no choice." She stared into those furious eyes, forcing herself to hold his gaze. "Hear me, Feral. Your only chance at survival is to cooperate with me. If you fail to prove useful, Birik will destroy you. And I don't want that."

A muscle in his jaw leaped. "Then let me go."

"I can't." Her palm slid down to his abdomen to brush the edge of the thatch of hair springing up around his root. His muscles tightened, quivering beneath her touch. "Let me mount you, warrior."

"Never." But his erection twitched, jerking. His will denied what his body craved.

What both their bodies craved. She knew he remembered as well as she did what it had been like, that slide of flesh within flesh. The pleasure . . . *good Mother*, the pleasure. She hadn't realized it could be like that. Her body had been breached more times than she could count, yet sex had never brought her anything but discomfort or pain.

Until this man walked into her life. From the moment she first saw him, her body had throbbed almost continuously, pulsing and contracting with desire, dampening her thighs. Now that passion, that power arced through the room, thickening.

The sound of a vicious animal rumbled from the Feral's throat. "That hand gets any closer to my shaft and I'll rip your head from your shoulders."

Skye released a sigh. "I don't want to force you."

"Then don't," he snapped.

"You don't understand!" If only she had the time to back off and let him calm beneath her touch for a few days. But Birik had never been a patient man. And she sensed the anger ran deep in this Feral. A few days, or even weeks, might not be enough.

"I understand all I need to," he snarled.

But he didn't. Not at all. She had no choice but to raise the passion between them in whatever way she must. Skye dipped her head to his chest, kissing his warm skin. He smelled of night forests, wild and untamed. Darting her tongue out, she tasted him, as pleased by his taste as by his scent. Everything about him made her want him more.

Moving a step to the side, she pressed her mouth to his abdomen, then to his hip bone, scenting the faint musk of his erection.

She lifted her head and looked at him, her breathing uneven, her eyes growing heavy with desire. "Can I kiss you there?"

"*No.*"

She continued to his broad, rock-hard thigh, kissing, licking.

"*Witch.*" His growl was still one of furious warning, but beneath the anger, passion vibrated.

"I want you inside me, warrior," she said huskily. "Just as you want me. Your body longs to press deep within mine."

"I don't want you. I never want you."

"You wanted me before. In the woods."

"That was before I knew what you were."

She sighed. He'd thought she was human. Birik had given her the ability to hide the copper rings around her irises for just that purpose.

Something had happened when they'd kissed yesterday. A strange sexual energy had passed between them, bonding them in some indefinable way. All night her body had wept for release, a release only he could give her. She'd woken knowing he'd come back to her.

And he had.

Unfortunately, Birik's orders had been as clear and sharp as a piece of cut glass. When the Feral returned, she must capture him.

And she had.

Skye curled her fingers around his leg, caressing his inner thigh as she stood beside the stone where he was pinned, letting her fingers slide almost to his groin. "Let me touch you, warrior."

"No."

Stubborn man. He needed more time. If she forced him now, so violently against his will, his hatred would only grow stronger and more impossible to breach. She'd never calm him, never get him to accept his place here. And he must accept it.

She couldn't give up.

The alternative meant his destruction.

Fury clouded Paenther's mind, rage blurred his vision. His body burned to slake its need on the witch whose soft hands stroked his thigh, whose softer lips laid kisses on his hip, seducing. Tormenting.

He fought the attraction, struggled to feel nothing as he had so many times in the past. But, as in the past, his body had a will of its own.

How many times had Ancreta come to him as he'd lain chained in that cellar? How many times had she taken him into her mouth and sucked him hard? He could still feel the torment of those golden curls tumbling over his hips as he fought the arousal and lost. Every time, he'd lost.

She'd lift those miles of skirts to her waist and straddle him, cruel laughter in her eyes that he'd fought her, and she'd won yet again. He'd buck and try to throw her off, but she'd clamp that surprisingly strong hand around his shaft and squeeze him until he quit bucking, then guide him into her hole, taking him inside.

Hatred ran like blood through his memory. Gregor would invariably join them. As Ancreta rode him, as he fought to withhold his seed, Gregor would grab his head and begin chanting, digging his fingernails into the flesh of his skull until blood ran down his temples and through his hair. And as Paenther lost the battle, coming in a hot rush of pleasure and fury, his mind wrenched open, Gregor would delve into his mind and rip at the animal spirit that had only recently joined him, trying to remove him, to steal him, the pain beyond anything Paenther had ever endured before, or since.

And he hated.

Lost in the memory, he barely distinguished between the blond Ancreta of his nightmares and the dark-haired witch with the blue eyes whose hands even now slid over his body, one over his arm, the other trailing up his hip, the fingers tangling in the hair at the base of his shaft.

A growl rumbled in his throat, his mind a haze of fury and memory. As her soft hand closed around his shaft, he turned feral, his fangs and claws unsheathing. He attacked her in the only way left to him, striking at the arm that had ventured too close to his mouth.

His animal's fangs sank into her forearm, ripping off a thick hunk of her flesh. Warm blood drenched his mouth. Raw satisfaction burned through the haze of his anger as he watched her jerk away, her face ashen. He spit the flesh onto the floor. *Witch.* If he were loose, he'd kill her. He'd shift into his panther form and rip open her throat, then eat out her heart.

He snarled, waiting for her retribution, tensing for the pain she'd deal, and not caring. But the witch only stumbled backward, holding the wounded arm in front of her, the blood flowing steadily down the front of her dress. She backed up until she reached the far wall, then sank to the floor beside the doe, cradling her injury.

Paenther watched her, searching for pleasure in her pain, and found it frustratingly absent. His fangs and claws retracted. She wasn't Ancreta. This witch was too damned fragile-looking. And she wasn't acting like he'd expected her to. No scream. No tears.

Ancreta would have been beating him by now, with the closest weapon. Stabbing him. Cutting chunks out of his own flesh, her eyes brilliant with vengeance.

Was this witch more controlled than Ancreta? More clever, perhaps, planning her retribution more thoroughly?

As he watched her, the blood stopped running. The flesh grew and knit until, at last, other than the stain on her gown, she was back to normal.

Still, she sat there as the doe nuzzled her cheek, leaning into the animal's touch, her eyes closed, a deep unhappiness in the lines of her body. Finally, she looked up and met his gaze, nothing but sad emotions in her eyes.

With a sigh, she looked up at the ceiling. "They're not full," she said wearily. She met his gaze again with those deep, fathomless eyes. "We have to fill them. I know you hate it, but neither of us has a choice."

She rose and came over to him, climbing onto the stone and settling back on her heels between his parted legs as she had before. He waited for the cruelty of her touch, expecting it. Wanting it. Needing to know he'd broken through that calm facade of hers. But the hands that brushed his thighs were as soft and gentle as before.

She puzzled him. Was there no cruelty in her? A gentle witch? Now, *there* was an oxymoron if he'd ever heard one.

"How can you touch me softly after I attacked you?" he heard himself ask.

She didn't meet his gaze. "You've done nothing more than any wild creature would do when trapped."

He scowled at her and at the twinge of guilt he felt for hurting her, the evidence of which darkened her dress.

Dammit, I won't feel guilty. Her gentleness, her vulnerability, were just an act. A lie. Maybe even flat-out enchantment. He'd be a fool to trust her in any way. And he'd already been fool enough to last an immortal lifetime.

His successful strike and her silent acceptance of the pain had taken the edge off his fury but done nothing to dampen his desire. As she knelt between his legs, caressing his hips, thighs, and abdomen, touching his shaft with only her heated gaze, he felt the sexual energy roll over his flesh and pound in his blood.

His breathing turned labored as he struggled not to rock his hips, as he fought against the need to demand she take him into her body and bring him to release.

Finally, she lifted her hands and moved to his side, to sit with her back against the curve of the rock shelf. Her face was flushed, her own breathing labored, her chest rising with each harsh breath.

Slowly his body cooled, slowly she quieted, not quite touching him until she laid her palm against his rib cage.

"The animal inside you calms to my touch. I wish you could, too, warrior."

"Never." But the word was without heat.

A gentle witch. Was it possible?

She climbed down off the rock and went to her animals, freeing them. For long minutes, she stroked them, one after the other, whispering to them as they clamored for her attention. Finally, she walked toward the door with a tense unhappiness that pulled at him, her animals pressing around her as they had when she'd first walked in.

"Where are you going?" he asked.

She looked back at him, over her shoulder. "It's almost midnight," she said quietly.

He saw the glisten of tears in her eyes.

Chapter Four

Skye danced, as she did every midnight, her hands high above her head, her body swaying and twisting to the music of the Earth, clad only in the blood of the sacrifices.

The power of her gift rode her flesh as she danced, a harsh tingling that sank into her muscles and bones and tore at her heart. High above her, the orbs tucked in between the stalactites and flickering lightwicks sparkled and spit with energy.

In a loose circle around her, the sorcerers chanted.

"Faster," Birik snapped from the corner of the whitewashed room. His pale hair glowed silver in the cool light, his cold gaze pinned to the power orbs as one of his snakes, a rattler, curled across his shoulder. Beside him stood the doe tied fast to the rock.

Skye's gaze fell to the desperate animal, to her large, frightened eyes. And to the bloody dagger in Birik's hand. Grief threatened to swallow her, and she tore her gaze away and spun faster, her feet sure on the blood-slick stones. She felt as if it were her soul that was being slaughtered.

If only it were Birik's blood drenching her body! But the small flare of dark emotion died as quickly as it rose, snuffed out by the crushing weight of desolation.

It didn't matter. Nothing mattered. For years and years, the creatures of her heart had died at midnight, and there was nothing she could do to stop it. Nothing she could do to change her fate or theirs. The Mother, the goddess, had long ago forsaken them all.

Now she'd been forced to drag a man, a Feral, into this hell. Fear for him cut like broken glass.

She danced, struggling to forget, to block out the raw smell of the blood coating her hair and skin, fighting to crawl into her mind, away from the savagery, away from the cries of the doe struggling to reach her, begging her to save her.

Inside, she cried out her own frustration at the wrongness, at the horror of what she was forced to do. Because she couldn't save her. She couldn't save any of them. The only thing she might possibly be able to do was keep the man, the Feral, from ending like all her other creatures. She *must*. Her soul would die if she were forced to dance in his blood as well.

As the doe's cries ended abruptly, Skye threw back her head, her chest pierced with a pain she couldn't show, her mind echoing with an anguished, silent scream.

Moments later, she heard Birik approach from behind and closed her eyes as warm blood slid over her scalp and cascaded down her body, spreading fingers of warmth against the chill of the cavern air, carving holes in her heart.

Skye flung her hands into the air above her, pulling the power Birik demanded, desecrating her precious tie to the creatures of the Earth.

The blood ran down her cheeks like tears.

Paenther scented violets even before the witch stepped into the room. She returned without her animals, her hair wet as if she'd just showered, her eyes hollow. Without a word, without meeting his gaze, she crawled up beside him, between his body and the wall, and lay down, curling against his hip. He could feel her trembling.

As much as he hated her, he'd always had finely honed protective instincts toward women and children, and they rose now. Something had hurt her. He reminded himself he didn't care. But as he felt her slowly calm, her breathing evening out in sleep, the tension eased from his own body.

He wasn't sure when he'd drifted off, but he woke to the sound of water dripping from the stalactites into the puddles scattered across the room and the feel of the witch's silken head on his chest. She had one arm wrapped around his waist, the other hand tucked against her neck. That second arm was nearly within reach of his mouth. But he'd lost the desire to hurt her. Her gentle touch and her acceptance of his fury had taken the edge off his need for revenge.

He blinked, feeling . . . strange. Almost . . . relaxed.

With disbelief he realized what was wrong. Or what was right. The rage, the ever-present rage he struggled to contain day and night, the rage burned into his soul by Ancreta nearly three hundred years ago, had inexplicably left him.

How? Was this simply more magic?

Did he care?

Chained atop this cold stone, deep in the bowels of a second Mage captivity, he felt more at peace than he had in years. Eased. Whole in a way he hadn't felt in centuries.

Had she somehow, miraculously healed him? Or was her nearness affecting him in a way he'd never imagined anyone could?

The implications rocked him. He almost hoped it was just enchantment. Just a lie. Because if it wasn't, if this easing of the torment he'd lived with for centuries was somehow coming from her. . .

A witch.

Heaven help him. The last thing he wanted was to need her. More than he did already.

Paenther woke to the sound of footsteps moments before the steel door crashed in against the rock. The witch startled awake, rearing up, filling him with the scent of sleep-warmed violets and the acrid tang of fear.

In the doorway stood a man with the slim build of a Mage and hair a dozen shades paler than his skin. His face was long, his lips thin, and his copper-ringed eyes blazed with a cold fury.

Paenther's muscles tensed for a battle he wouldn't be able to fight, fury of his own raging through his body as he strained against his shackles until they bit into his flesh. The strange peace he'd felt when he woke during the night had vanished with the woman's fear.

"Birik," the witch breathed, her eyes wide, her voice tight with dread.

"I warned you," the Mage said coldly, and started toward them.

"But . . ."

The Mage latched onto her upper arm and yanked her off the rock. As the witch stumbled, he pulled her to the wall, grabbed her shoulders, and slammed her back until her skull collided with stone with a sharp crack.

Paenther's body went taut with outrage, but the bastard wasn't through. He grabbed her face, holding on until the witch's eyes widened with pain and the smells of burning flesh and blood assailed his sensitive nose.

Finally, the Mage released her. As the fragile woman sunk to the ground, he leveled several hard kicks to her ribs and one to the side of her head, then strode out of the room without a backward glance.

Paenther stared at the woman lying on the damp, rocky floor like a broken doll, blood running down her cheek from where the bastard must have cracked her skull. For long moments, the only sound in the room was the drip, drip, drip from the rock daggers and the faint, thready beat of her heart.

"Witch?" he called softly. But she gave no indication she heard him.

Minute by minute, her heartbeat strengthened as her immortal body healed the ravages of the assault until, finally, she stirred. Slowly, painfully, she curled into a ball as if to protect herself from further attack. But like the attack itself, she took the pain without a groan, without a cry. Her suffering was somehow all the more difficult to bear for its terrible silence.

His gut contracted as he remembered tearing at her arm. And how she'd suffered that time, too, without a sound.

He wasn't sure what to make of her. She'd hidden what she was, enthralled him, and captured him. She was everything he hated. Yet now he was forced to wonder if she'd had any choice in the matter.

Had he misjudged her? Was there really such a thing as a gentle witch? One thing was certain, this one was nothing like Ancreta.

His muscles bunched as she pushed herself onto her elbows, as if he could somehow lend her strength. She struggled to sit up, then collapsed back against the wall with a grimace that told him what the move had cost her. He looked at her smudged and bloodied face and wanted to beat the hell out of the man who'd done this to her. Birik.

"Why did he beat you, little witch?" He didn't know her name.

She opened her eyes slowly, the blue depths dark with pain. "I don't know." Her expression tightened. "I do know. I just don't know why he'd punish me for it now." She met his gaze. "He wants me to mount you."

Paenther jerked, his hands fisting. "*No*," he snarled.

Like hell she'd mount him. His body quaked with the remembered fury and bitter helplessness of all those times beneath Ancreta.

The dark-haired witch, so unlike Ancreta, sighed and tipped her head back, her gaze reaching the ceiling. Perhaps beyond. "I wanted to give you time to accept me, warrior. He's not going to allow it." Her voice broke as she met his gaze, suffering in her eyes. "I'm sorry."

She pushed herself to her feet, then stumbled back against the wall with a grimace before lurching forward, slowly, painfully. Blood matted her hair and streaked her face.

"*Don't.*" No way in hell was he accepting this. His fingertips began to tingle with the imminent eruption of his claws.

But when she reached him, all she did was curl her arm around his waist and lay her head on his chest, her face turned away.

He stared down at the top of her head, confounded. She never did what he expected. He felt her body trembling and felt the drip of hot tears onto his abdomen. If his hands had been free, he'd have been hard-pressed not to stroke her back. She was about to take him against his will, yet his overwhelming need was to offer her some small measure of comfort.

Sniffling, she stood and wiped her eyes, then moved down to the end of the stone and climbed up between his legs without meeting his gaze. Her misery was so sharp, it cut him.

She wasn't Ancreta. The fury at what she was planning to do to him . . . what she'd been *ordered* to do to him . . . began to lose its grip on his mind and slip away.

His body was flaccid. He'd found her pain anything but arousing. If she was going to use him, she was going to have to get him up first. But as she began to dip that ripe mouth toward his shaft, his body froze.

"Don't."

She looked up, defeat in every line of her body. "I have to."

"Use your hand."

Her brows pulled together as she watched him as if she wasn't certain she'd heard him right. Then she reached for him, closing her cool fingers softly around him. His breath hissed into his mouth at the incredible feel of her touch.

Slowly, she began to stroke him. With her free hand, she cupped his stones, squeezing gently and rolling them, rubbing them against one another. Blood surged between his legs. Within moments, he was erect and ready for her.

She wasted no time in lifting her dress to her waist and straddling him.

His mind balked, still fully mired in all those other times with Ancreta. But his body burned to feel *this* woman's body swallow his length as it had once before.

Taking firm but careful hold of him, she positioned him at her entrance and slowly tried to force him inside. But her body was tight and dry, and her jaw clenched against the obvious discomfort.

"You're not ready."

"It doesn't matter." Her voice was strained as she pushed him farther in.

His body longed to help her, to thrust up and inside, but he'd only hurt her more. "It matters. If you remember the way it was between us in the woods, you can't truly believe it doesn't make a difference if you're ready."

"You wanted me then."

Paenther groaned. "You're holding the evidence of my desire in your hand, witch." He met her gaze. "I hate what he did to you. I don't want to watch it happen again. Besides, I assure you, I *want* to be inside you."

Her eyes slowly began to darken. "Your words are helping."

"Good." He could tell. She was softening slightly, but his way was still far from clear. Goddess, but his body wanted to move. "What's your name, little witch?"

"Skye."

"Skye with the sky blue eyes. Touch yourself, Skye."

She looked at him uncertainly.

"Between your legs." His eyes narrowed. "Have you never pleasured yourself?"

She shook her head with a jerk.

"Touch yourself between your legs as you ride me, right at the front of your slit. Find the place it feels best, then stroke the flesh there. It should ready you."

Her gaze was enigmatic, as it was so often, but she did as he said, reaching down, her fingernail softly scraping his shaft as she found the place she sought. She gasped, and he knew she'd found it. Within seconds, her body opened like a slick, damp flower, easing his way.

What kind of a fool was he for *helping* his captor take him against his will? Yet, it was hardly against his will, was it? *Goddess*, she felt sweet.

Paenther threw his head back, lifting his hips to press more deeply inside her, then opened them to watch her hips rising and falling as if she were indeed riding him. Like in the woods, he felt an utter sense of rightness when he was buried inside her.

Skye watched him, her eyes growing heavy-lidded with rising passion, her full lips parting on soft, tiny gasps.

Power rose in the room, running not unpleasantly over his flesh. As the power thickened, her rhythm increased, her movements growing more rapid. She pumped him hard and fast, in and out until he was nearly out of his mind with lust and need and debilitating pleasure.

With a guttural cry, she threw her head back, coming, her inner muscles squeezing him in hard spasms until he was following her over, his body pumping his release deep inside her.

Skye looked up, and he followed her gaze to the dark orbs shooting with sparks of color as if they could barely contain the power inside. Her gaze lowered to his, her mouth softening.

"We did it," she said.

"We did." And what exactly had they done? To what dark purpose would the Mage put that power? Had he, in helping a sad-eyed witch, compromised his own mission? His own men?

Locked inside this cavern, he wasn't sure he'd ever know.

She rode him for a minute more, slowly, milking her pleasure, then finally pulled off him to sit at his side, pulling her dress down as she pressed back against the wall. With an unsteady hand, her chest still heaving, she ran her fingers through her hair, slowly meeting his gaze.

"Thank you." A soft, fleeting smile warmed her eyes, sending warmth cascading through his chest.

He felt the oddest, most inappropriate urge to smile in return. Goddess, but she affected him.

Her foot pressed against his hip, a light touch,

but contact all the same, as if she needed to touch him.

He felt the same disquieting need.

"Free me, Skye. Let's both leave this place before that bastard hurts you again."

"I can't. He'll never let me go."

"I'll protect you."

Her mouth lifted ruefully at one corner. "You've promised several times to kill me, warrior. I know a ploy for escape when I hear it." She shrugged and tilted her head against the wall behind her. "Even if I could trust you, no one can protect me."

"Why are you so important to him?"

"I have a way with animals."

He didn't understand at first. But then he remembered a story he'd once heard of rare Mage with deep ties to various aspects of nature.

"You're a Mage enchantress."

"Yes." She met his gaze again. "Which is why you're drawn to me. It's why we raise the power we do. Because of the animal inside you."

"Is that the only reason?" Did she really have no sense of her own allure? Hadn't she noticed he got hard every time she walked into the room? He was damned sure it had nothing to do with his animal. He and his animal didn't communicate. They never had.

She leaned forward and stroked his chest. "I don't know if it's the only reason I'm drawn to you, but it's the only reason that matters. I draw my power through the animals."

With that, she crawled off the stone, unbuttoning

the front of her bloodstained dress as she walked past his head to the far end of the room. He tilted his head back and watched as she tossed the dress aside, revealing a too-slender form of such delicacy it made him ache.

Reaching up, she turned on a crude water spigot and stood under the harsh rush of water. She picked up a bar of soap from the floor and washed the blood from her face, hair, and body, then turned off the water.

"The water doesn't flood the room?" he asked.

She grabbed a threadbare towel from a small pile on a rock in the corner and dried herself with it. "The floor's not even, and there are small gullies in the rock that run beneath the walls."

"How long have the Mage lived in this place?"

"Since the last war with the Ferals."

The war that came to a head with the Mage's capture of three newly marked Ferals—1738. After Lyon captured nearly a dozen Mage sorcerers and sentinels, and killed their high leader, the Elemental, he'd demanded peace. And gotten it. For 270-plus years, the two races had lived in strained harmony, basically ignoring one another. A cold war that was cold no longer.

He watched her drop the towel and pull a navy blue dress off one of the hangers. "How long have you been here?" he asked her.

"I don't know." She shrugged the dress over her head. "Time has no meaning in this place."

"Were you born here?"

"No. I was eight when Birik claimed me from

my mother, taking me as his apprentice. He's an enchanter, too, though his gift isn't nearly as strong as mine. He mostly just calls snakes." A small scowl marred her features, hinting at a temper he'd yet to see. "He taught me, *forced* me, to draw my power for his own use. I haven't been off this mountain since."

"What was happening in the human world at the time you came here, do you remember? Did you know?"

"They were sending men into orbit around the Earth. They were trying to reach the moon."

"The 1960s. You've been down here about forty years. You're still very young."

She quirked a brow, a glimmer of a challenge in her eyes that pleased him. "And you're older?"

He smiled, surprising himself. "Almost four hundred."

An answering smile broke over her face, bright and amused, but gone almost as quickly as it appeared. Yet in that fleeting instant, in the brief radiance of her smile, he felt as if he'd been sucker punched.

Skye pushed her sleeves to her forearms and came over to him, her natural grace back in full.

But when she stopped beside him, her gaze wouldn't quite meet his. With her hair wet, her features so achingly delicate, she looked as fragile as a sapling in a storm. A need to protect her rose fiercely within him.

Her pensive, fathomless gaze finally rose to his, pressing into his chest, into his heart.

"It's been a long time since I had someone to talk to. Someone who offered a little sympathy." She bent and laid a feather-soft kiss on his chest.

A pressure built inside him, squeezing at his heart.

"Thank you," she said softly.

He met her gaze. "You're welcome."

She turned and started toward the door.

"Where are you going . . . Skye?"

"To the woods." She glanced back at him with pensive eyes. "I need the woods." A sanctuary and the protection he couldn't provide.

As she disappeared around the corner, he stared at the empty doorway for a long, long time. A hundred dire problems pressed on his mind, yet all he could think about was her. Skye.

Without a doubt he'd been enchanted. The question was, by magic?

Or by the woman herself?

Hours later, Skye finally left the forest to return to the caverns, another doe by her side and a plump woodchuck in her arms. Though it was a day away from another midnight, she felt the need for their company. As she descended the cavern stairs, a pair of crows circled her head. Two more squirrels scampered around her feet.

She set the woodchuck down and slipped into the kitchen to fetch her Feral some food. She knew he had to be hungry though he hadn't asked for anything. Besides, she felt this soft need to bring him something. A gift in return for his kindness.

Not the gift he wanted, of course. She couldn't free him. But food she could manage.

She wrapped several thick strips of roast venison in two pieces of cheesecloth and slipped one wrapped package into each of the deep pockets in the seams of her dress.

With the woodchuck once more in her arms, she led her little troupe down the stone stairs that ran throughout the cavern. Spying Birik deep in discussion with two of the sorcerers and the Feral, Vhyper, her heart lurched. The doe, feeling her distress, pressed her head against her hip.

As always, she tried to pass without drawing his attention, but Birik's hand snagged her arm roughly, dislodging the woodchuck. The creature fell to the rock at her feet with a squeal and waddled behind her as Birik's flat eyes pinned her fast.

"It worked," he said coldly.

Skye nodded, holding the man's gaze for only a moment, before looking away. She fought not to tremble.

Vhyper laughed darkly. "I told you it would. Paenther's too much of a knight not to come to the aid of a damsel in distress." His gaze flicked to her hip. "I smell food. Taking him lunch? A treat for a performance well done?"

"Yes." She glanced at him briefly, seeing the same coldness in his eyes she saw in everyone's these days. Everyone except Paenther's. She liked that she knew his name, now. In Paenther's eyes she only ever saw heat. The heat of fury. Or passion.

Vhyper nodded, that cold humor lifting his mouth. He was a big man, taller than Birik by a good six inches. "You'll have him eating out of your hand." He turned that gaze back on Birik. "As I knew she would."

Birik pulled her closer, his hand tightening painfully around her upper arm. "It wasn't enough, enchantress."

She started, her gaze jerking up to his as understanding rushed over her. The power she'd raised with the Feral . . . wasn't enough? The orbs had been spitting with more power than she'd ever seen. How could it not be enough?

"I'll try again." Instead of dismaying her, the thought released a rush of heat low in her body.

"No. Leave him alone. I have something else in mind." He released her with a flick of his hand. "Go. Feed your pet. Then return to me."

Skye blinked, bewildered and not a little worried.

As Birik turned his back on her, she hurried away, her pulse too fast. He was planning something. What?

Her heart sank to her toes. Surely he wouldn't kill him. Surely not that. But she knew all too well Birik was more than capable of such savageness.

Her Feral couldn't die.

Yes, he was a rare and beautiful creature. And, no, she never wanted any of her creatures to die, but this was different.

He was different. Strong, powerful. A knight, Vhyper called him. A warrior of honor and courage, capable of treating even his enemy with gentleness when he'd been coerced into feeling pity for her.

For the first time in years, she was reminded there were those still in possession of a conscience. Warriors with goodness in their hearts.

With souls.

And she would not see this one destroyed.

Nor, selfishly, did she want to lose him. For so long she'd lived in the cold, she'd almost forgotten what warmth felt like.

His fury with her for capturing him had turned to fury over her beating. A precious gift. When she'd been hurting, he'd not only accepted her body but helped her take him without pain.

For so many years she'd been alone. Without sympathy. Without care. Those she'd loved, the friends, had all been sent elsewhere. Or changed, transformed for the strength of the Elemental's, Inir's, army.

Not in years had someone cared that she'd been beaten. Not in years had anyone tried to ease her misery.

Not until she'd captured a dark-eyed panther with hatred in his eyes and honor in his soul.

Now she feared Birik meant to take him from her as he'd taken everything else. All in the name of power.

Skye finally returned, smelling of roast venison. Paenther's stomach rumbled even as he watched her, drinking his fill of the sight of her. Her hair and dress were damp, as if she'd been caught in the rain. Her quiet, delicate beauty did something to him, flowing through him like a calming river even as it heated his blood.

Once again, animals surrounded her, though a different collection than before. As before, she ushered the smaller animals into a pair of cages and tied the doe with a rope at the wall. Then she came to him, her eyes at once troubled and lit with a warmth that slid softly across his heart.

"I brought you something." But as she pulled the wrapped venison out of her pocket, her gaze went to his wrists, sticky with his blood. Her brows lowered unhappily. "You've been struggling."

"Always."

Her eyes pleaded. "Accept your fate, warrior. There's nothing else you can do."

He shook his head. "Never quit fighting, little witch. It means the death of your soul."

Those troubled eyes of hers darkened as she unwrapped the meat in her hand. "I thought you might be hungry."

"I am."

She gave him a rueful frown and cocked her head. "Are you going to bite me again?"

"No." He thought of the way she'd curled around her injured arm after he'd attacked her, the blood soaking her dress. "I'm sorry for that. I thought you deserved it. I've changed my mind."

Her mobile mouth shifted into a semblance of a smile as her eyes softened. "I'm glad." She held the meat to his mouth for him to take a thick, juicy bite.

She stroked his chest with her free hand, nearly making him purr. Yet even as she touched him without wariness, he smelled fear in her. He could hear it in the racing of her heart.

"I won't bite you, Skye."

Her gaze flicked to his. "I believe you." She tried to feed him again, and he shook his head.

"You first. You're too thin."

"I'm not hungry."

He scowled at her. "I find that hard to believe." But those shadows in her eyes were darkening. "Tell me what's the matter."

She caught her bottom lip between her teeth and looked away. "Nothing."

"You're afraid."

"I'm fine."

"Are you afraid of Birik?" Her tiny jerk at the mention of his name told Paenther what he wanted to know. "He's threatened you again."

"No more than normal." She met his gaze, unhappiness etched into every line of her face. "This time he's threatened you."

"How?" Paenther's jaw clenched, his muscles flexing against his bonds. He was all for a battle, but to fight, he had to be free.

"I don't know. He said the energy we raised wasn't enough, but when I offered to try again, he said no. He had something else in mind. It can't be good."

Paenther captured her gaze and held it fast. "Get me out of here, Skye. I'll take you with me. You'll be safe from him."

"And where would you take me? Your people have been at war with mine forever."

"What difference does it make? He wouldn't beat you anymore."

She shook her head, fisting her hand on his chest. "I can't leave. I don't have a choice."

"We all have choices, Skye." He stared into her eyes, willing her to hear him. His life might depend on it. "Whether we choose to face them or hide from them defines who we are. Whether we choose to let evil live, or we fight to destroy it, defines our lives. Choose, Skye. *Choose*."

A spark of temper lit her eyes. "You don't understand."

"Skye . . ."

She pulled away from him. "You can't possibly understand! I *have* fought him. Over and over I've fought him, and all I've done is end up bloody and broken. He's too powerful! And his reach is too long. Even if I managed to get away, *and I wouldn't,* he'd hurt me until I begged to come back to him just to end the misery."

"I'll protect you."

"You can't!" She whirled and fled the room, his dinner still in her hand.

"Skye!"

He waited, praying she'd return, but she didn't. He cursed himself for a fool. She was his only hope of escape, his only company other than the animals chirping and whistling with agitation in the cages in the corner. He'd pushed her too hard, too fast, and scared her away.

He was still kicking himself for it sometime later when he heard heavy footsteps in the passage outside the room. The moment the pale-haired Birik stepped into the room, a green snake curled around his neck, Paenther knew this was it. The time had come.

Though for what, he didn't know.

The Mage studied him with dark curiosity. "Tonight's your big night, Feral. A night you'll never forget." The Mage reached for him.

Paenther fought to free himself, struggling against his chains, but there was nothing he could do to stop the cold press of the bastard's palm to his chest.

Or to stop himself from spinning into the net of enthrallment.

"Wake up, B.P."

Paenther heard Vhyper's voice as if from a distance. The hard kick to his ribs sent pain shooting through his body, propelling him into the thick, mind-sludge of partial enchantment.

Impressions bombarded his struggling brain. He could tell he wasn't alone with Vhyper by the murmur of other voices and the squawk of crows. Smells drove into his senses. Old blood, new fires, and violets.

Skye.

As before, he was on his back, but the rock beneath him felt different. Cool puddles of water gathered beneath his left calf and right shoulder. He tried to move, but he was caught as firmly as before, the chains clanking on the rock beneath his head.

Finally, his vision broke free. As he looked around him, he saw that everything had changed. He was on the floor this time, in a different, larger room within the cavern. A room that was dark except for a small shaft of moonlight breaking through from high above and the glowing embers of banked fires in vessels scattered around the room.

Though the floor was bare, the walls glowed with whitewash and graphic symbols he recognized as part of the ancient language of the Mage. Among the symbols, he knew only one. *Sacrifice.*

The rage that lived in his blood boiled over. He was not an animal to be chained and slaughtered! He struggled against his shackles. With a furious growl, he called on the power of the animal inside him and once again tried to shift. Like before, nothing happened.

"Fight it all you want," Vhyper drawled, standing at his side, his voice floating down from high above him. "You aren't going anywhere, B.P."

With his furious gaze, he searched the room. At one end stood nearly a dozen Mage sorcerers in ritual robes.

Ritual robes. Goddess, he smelled layers and layers of old blood in here. Was his about to coat these stones, too?

He searched for Skye and finally found her in the corner, stroking the agitated deer.

Vhyper squatted beside him, his forearm on his knee, his gaze on Skye. "She's a pretty little piece, isn't she, with those big doelike eyes? I told her you were a sucker for a damsel in distress. Wasn't that how Ancreta trapped you all those years ago?"

Paenther's eyes narrowed as he tore his gaze from the woman to look up at the man who'd once been his friend.

A malicious smile hovered at Vhyper's mouth. "I told her all she had to do was play the victim, and you'd be eating right out of her hand, giving her whatever she wanted."

Play the victim? A chill of foreboding rolled down his spine.

Vhyper shrugged. "Birik may have overplayed

his role a bit when he beat her. He's been doing a shitload of groveling to make it up to her, but I hear the ploy worked like a charm. You not only let her fuck you, but you helped her enjoy herself." He grinned and pretended to high-five him. "Way to go, B.P."

Paenther stared at him. He was supposed to believe that beating was an act? A lie to gain his cooperation? No way in hell. He'd seen the bastard's face. He'd seen the pain and bleakness in Skye's. No woman could be that good an actress.

That chill in his spine leached into his blood.

Except perhaps a witch.

With a bit of magic, she could make him believe he was seeing whatever she wanted him to see, couldn't she?

Hell. Denial roared through his head. Had he really been taken in all over again?

Or was Vhyper the one lying? How in the hell was he supposed to know? The only thing he knew for certain was, he couldn't trust either of them.

And if this night ended as he feared it might, it wouldn't matter. Nothing would matter once he was dead.

The smoke of the banked fires teased his nose. He stared up into his old friend's eyes, a growl grumbling deep in his throat as he saw no glimmer of the Vhyper he knew.

"Am I staked out for slaughter?"

A cruel smile slashed across Vhyper's face. "What fun would it be if you knew what to expect?"

"You've turned into a bastard, Vhyper."

"Oh, I've turned into a lot more than a bastard, B.P." Vhyper rose. "Looks like it's time to begin."

As the Mage circled the perimeter of the room, Skye stood. With quick, nimble hands, she pulled off her dress and tossed it aside as if perfectly at ease with her nudity among so many men.

He stared at her and knew he was watching a stranger.

Birik came up behind her and pulled her back against him, one hand covering her breast, the other diving between her legs.

Paenther's gut clenched with shock. His breaths became labored as he watched with disbelief as the bastard fingered her, working that supple body he'd lost himself in twice now, until she rocked against his hand, trembling. Enjoying it. *She was enjoying it.*

His mind exploded. She'd tried to mount him last night, cold and dry. *It doesn't matter.* Because she hadn't wanted him. Not *him.*

And he knew, he *knew,* what was going to happen. Birik wanted her to ride him again, but he had to prepare her himself since, clearly, *clearly,* she couldn't get there on her own. Not with a shape-shifter. Not with *him.*

Damn her.

But it was him she needed, him with his animal. So she'd played him with her sad eyes and pretense at vulnerability until he'd helped her fuck him.

Anger blazed through him, a fury as raw as it was ancient. A fury turned on himself as much as her. How could he have fallen for a witch's pretense of woe *twice*?

Birik finally released her. Without once meeting his gaze, she crossed to where he lay staked and stood over him, one foot planted on either side of his waist. In the shadows between her legs, her flower had opened, and the scent of her arousal blasted his senses, sending the blood flowing into his shaft in a throbbing rush.

Her eyes and expression were closed as she stood there, trembling, her heart racing. But no longer did her delicate beauty pull at him. It was all a lie. *She* was a lie. His chest ached, the flicker of warmth she'd sparked inside him sputtering beneath the mounting evidence of her deceit.

He struggled against his chains, determined to fight her every step of the way, though he knew with a despair born of bitter experience, his body would betray him. No matter how much his mind hated, his body would always struggle for release when buried inside a woman's sheath. He'd never been able to keep from coming when Ancreta had him trapped inside her.

And he stood even less of a chance with the witch standing over him now, whose scent drove him to distraction even when she wasn't aroused.

The witch began to chant, her melodious voice rising in volume until it echoed off the rock. Slowly, her lithe, graceful body began to move, gyrating to the rhythms of the chant, her small breasts softly swaying, raising the temperature of his blood.

In the corner, the deer cried out, then went suddenly silent. He looked at the witch's face, feeling a twist of empathy for the grief he expected her to feel, but her expression had turned as cold and lifeless as stone. Something shriveled inside him at this proof she was nothing more than a cold, calculating bitch, like all Mage witches.

Birik strode to her, a bucket in his hand. She didn't startle, didn't even flinch when Birik tipped it over her head, letting the blood run into her hair and over her bare shoulders.

She'd expected this. With a kick to his gut, he knew *this* was the reason she'd brought the animals into the cavern in the first place. To dance in their blood.

Hatred seared his mind. She'd had him so completely fooled.

With sick fascination, Paenther watched Skye slide her hands over her breasts and abdomen, slicking her palms. Then she squatted over him and took his swollen shaft in her hand, coating him with the sticky warmth.

He went feral, his fangs elongating, his claws unsheathing as he snarled, fighting his body's traitorous response to her as much as he fought the woman herself.

But she barely looked at him as she guided him between her legs.

As he had so many times with Ancreta, he tried to buck her off him, but the witch was too well coordinated, moving with him, refusing to be denied. She forced him inside her. Despite Birik's ministrations, her body was still too tight, but nothing on her face reflected the discomfort.

There was nothing he could do to help her. Nothing he *would* do even if he could. He wanted her to hurt. *Damn her.*

Slowly, she began to ride him, resuming her chant as around the room, the sorcerers joined their voices to hers until the sound pounded a thunderous beat echoed in Skye's movements.

A beat echoed by his own heart.

The chant pounded in his blood and in his shaft, the power rising until the hair on his head felt like it was trying to stand on end. Above him, Skye's short hair *was* lifting, as if she'd stepped into an electrical storm. Above her, the orbs he hadn't noticed before pulsed with dark light, growing.

As the power rose higher, the blue-eyed witch began to gasp, her gasps quickly turning to small screams of pleasure.

The pleasure had him in its grip, too, flowing through his chest and limbs, tightening every muscle, every blood vessel, as desire and pressure built in his cock to a fevered pitch. His body climbed to heights that appalled him until he was driving into her as desperate for the coming explosion as he'd ever been for anything.

His mind rebelled, horrified at the sexual fire

burning his body in the midst of such savagery. But the power in the room was driving him now, driving them both. And there was no fighting it.

With a scream, the witch came. As her hard, rapid contractions drove him to a blinding release, his gaze caught Birik's. The bastard stood over them, watching Paenther utterly lose control, his face a mask of deep arousal, his eyes alive with anticipation. Crawling with evil.

Paenther snarled. Hatred burned inside him as he spilled his seed.

A roar filled the room, turning the air hot and wild until it singed his lungs and scorched his skin. Pain ripped through his body on a sudden tide of fire.

A scream echoed through the walls from beyond, drawing Birik's shout of triumph.

Caught in the clutches of the pain, Paenther barely noticed when the chanting ended, and the men rushed from the room, leaving him alone with Skye. He stared up at her, at the face he'd once thought beautiful, now covered in blood, her eyes closed, her expression tight with pleasure . . . or pain. Hatred burned low in his gut as the sharp pain slowly died away except for a throbbing sting across his left eye.

Skye rose, lifting off him unsteadily as she tried to stand, only to collapse by his feet where she lay on her back, gasping.

He didn't know how long they stayed like that, lying in the moonlight and dying embers, amid the blood, their flesh rippling with the remnants of power.

Neither spoke. There was nothing to say.

Yet again, he wondered what Birik meant to do with the power they'd raised.

Birik finally returned, lightwicks floating above him. He strode to Skye and lifted her into his arms.

The bitch wrapped her arm around the Mage's neck as he carried her from the room, leaving Paenther chained and alone. With little hope, he strained against his shackles, pouring every-thing into freeing himself. Useless. He remained trapped as completely as any caged beast.

Outside the cavern room, a single bloodcur-dling scream ripped at his eardrums, followed by triumphant shouts and cheers.

Dread knotted deep inside his chest. Goddess help him. What evil had they unleashed?

Chapter Six

Paenther wasn't sure when they'd enthralled and transferred him, but as the fog cleared from his head, he found himself standing upright outside a glass enclosure deep within the caverns.

The clank of chains and the bite of cold shackles told him he was pinned fast to the wall behind him. Glancing down, he saw that he was wearing pants again. The leather pants he'd worn that disastrous afternoon he'd followed Skye into the woods. How long ago? He'd been out of it too much to know how long he'd been a prisoner.

Last thing he remembered, he'd been covered with blood. *The ritual.* Memory slammed into him, the force of his fury stealing his breath. His mouth tightened, his teeth grinding.

Goddess, but the witch had played him.

His furious gaze scrutinized the glassed chamber twelve to fifteen feet below him, trying to make sense of what he was seeing. In one corner, paint . . . or blood . . . had been splattered everywhere, copious amounts of it. His gaze narrowed as he tried to correlate the lit, bloody chamber below with the dark one he'd been in earlier, and failed. No, they were definitely not the same room. The fine hairs rose on the back of his neck. So what had happened here? And why was he chained so he could see it?

He sensed Vhyper even before the Feral rounded the corner to join him.

"Release me, Vhype," Paenther growled.

"You have to see this, B.P. No one's seen anything like it in millennia. Watch. The fun is about to begin."

On cue, four people stepped into sight in the room below, two men and two women, accompanied by a single Mage sentinel. Slowly, little by little, the people blinked and looked around groggily, as if coming out of enchantment.

"Are they human?"

"Yes. Watch."

The Mage left the room through a far door. Moments later, from an entrance below that Paenther couldn't see, another figure entered the room. A male, he thought, judging by the breadth of the shoulders, clad in some kind of filmy dark cloak, his back to Paenther. The man's hair was long and black and sparkled like diamonds. He didn't walk, but floated upright, a foot off the ground. And his cloak . . . A chill slid down Paenther's spine. Not a cloak at all, but the indistinct lines of his body.

The hair on Paenther's arms began to lift, his gaze narrowing. The air in the cavern dropped a good ten degrees.

This was no man.

A faint scent of rotting meat met Paenther's nose. His heart began to race.

The creature turned, revealing a bluish gray face badly contorted, as if made from melting wax, a single set of sharp fangs hanging from its mouth. As it raised its hands, daggerlike claws dripped from its fingertips.

Paenther's heart pounded with disbelief as he stared at the most fundamentally horrifying sight he'd ever seen.

A Daemon. A creature gone from this Earth for more than five thousand years, trapped all this time in the Daemon blade.

"The Mage have opened the blade," Paenther hissed. With the power Paenther had helped raise. *Goddess help them all.*

"Don't get your tail in a knot, B.P. The blade isn't open. Not entirely. We only managed to soften it enough to eke out a few of the wraith Daemons. The worker bees of the Daemon world. They're basically mindless feeding machines without Satanan here to control them, but it's amazing, isn't it?" His voice rose with excitement.

Paenther stared in fascinated horror at the creature of dark legend, a monster the Ferals had fought to keep from the Earth for thousands of years.

And failed.

"With the power you raise with the little witch, we'll free an entire army." Vhyper chuckled. "You've found your calling, B.P."

The words swirled in Paenther's mind until he had to swallow to keep the bile from rising in his throat. He had to stop this. He had to find a way to keep from freeing more of these things.

But his horrified gaze wouldn't turn away from the creature. Oddly, though the people were clearly agitated by the sight of all the blood, none of them were reacting to the Daemon itself. They didn't seem to see him.

Ah, goddess. Of course they couldn't see him. Just as humans couldn't see the draden.

One of the men looked up at the faces peering down at him. "What's going on here? What in the hell do you people want?"

"They won't be able to see him until he attacks them," Vhyper said, his voice sharp with anticipation.

The creature stopped in front of one of the women, lifted a single clawed finger, and ripped open her cheek down to the bone.

With a scream, the woman stumbled back, her eyes widening until they filled her face as she finally saw the creature who'd attacked her. Her scream turned to one of terror as she tripped and fell back onto the floor. Crying and whimpering, she scuttled back from a monster more hideous than any nightmare.

"He'll leave her like that," Vhyper murmured, as if to himself. "They feed on fear and pain. He'll make sure they all see him before he plays with them."

"How can you know this?"

"You've been out of it a while, B.P. We've already fed two of these fiends."

The blood. No wonder.

As one of the men rushed to the woman's side, the Daemon circled him, then turned his body horizontal in the air and bit through the man's hand, tearing it from his body.

A guttural scream rose from the man's throat.

Humans. They didn't regenerate lost limbs or missing body parts. His forehead burned with fury at the rank destruction. Needless, vile. . .

Paenther took deep breaths through his nose as Vhyper's words echoed in his ears. *With the power you raise with the little witch, we'll free an entire army.* Every night the blood and sex, his body used to free more of this evil.

He couldn't let this happen. With a growl, he struggled to free himself until his body with slick with sweat and his muscles straining. *He could not let this happen.*

But no matter how hard he tried to free himself, the chains held him fast. Just as the cage held the humans below. He tried to look away from the carnage, but couldn't. All four humans were screaming now. All were bloodied, searching for a way out. But there was no escape.

The Daemon sank his claws into the arm of one of the men, holding him fast. As the man pummeled him with his free fist, the Daemon pulled a strip of flesh from his skull, hair and all. Blood poured down the screaming man's face.

"What are you going to do with these things, Vhyper? Capture human after human to feed them? You must know you can't control them. You'll never contain them once they're free."

Vhyper grinned. "Who wants to contain them?"

Paenther forced his gaze elsewhere, sickened by the thought of these monsters set loose on the general population. All around the glassed walls, Mage watched with avid, excited expressions.

Except one. Huddled against the wall, not six yards away, was Skye, dressed and showered. Her hand covered her mouth, tears ran down pale, pale cheeks as she watched the horror unfold in front of her.

Was this another false display of emotion for his benefit? Or had she honestly not known what use Birik intended to make of the power they'd raised?

A growl rumbled low in his throat. It didn't matter. If he ever got his hands on the vile, traitorous witch. . .

He'd kill her.

*　*　*

Skye turned from the glass enclosure and fled down the cavern passage, falling to her knees and vomiting onto the rock. After the ritual, she'd fled to the woods and only now returned. She hadn't known. . .

Dear Mother, dear Mother, dear Mother.

What had they done?

She'd overheard Vhyper tell Paenther they were to do this every night. Free more of these . . . *things. This* is what Birik had been trying to raise the power for ever since Vhyper brought him the blade. Never had she dreamed her gift could be used for such evil.

Skye collapsed against the wall, her head back, tears streaming down her cheeks.

In so many ways, Birik used her. *But not for this.*

Please, Mother. Not for this.

She pressed her freezing palm to her clammy forehead, her chest heaving with agitation.

She didn't have a choice. She never had a choice.

But Paenther's voice rang in her head, mocking her. Goading her. *We all have choices, Skye.*

She cradled her head, covering her ears, but the warrior's voice, deep inside her head, wouldn't be silent.

Whether we choose to face them or hide from them defines who we are. Whether we choose to let evil live, or we fight to destroy it, defines our lives.

Sobs wracked her body as the humans' screams ripped through the caverns.

Choose, Skye.

She couldn't let this go on. She could not be the cause of so much suffering. So many deaths.

Choose!

Paenther didn't remember having been enthralled again, but he came back to consciousness to find himself once more on his back in the cell, Skye standing beside him, her cold, trembling hand on his cock as she tucked his distended flesh into his pants. His body still pulsed with the exquisite pleasure of sexual release.

His gaze speared her. She'd used him.

As if hearing his unspoken accusation, she nodded. "I had to unenthrall you fast, and this is the only way I know how." She faced him with fear in her eyes. "I know you hate me, and I know you don't trust me, but hear me, warrior, and hear me well."

The urgency in her voice and in her face set up a drumming in his blood.

"I didn't know what Birik intended. You told me to choose, and I'm choosing. I'm choosing not to allow another Daemon to be freed. I'm choosing to free you instead."

He stared at her, his jaw tight, afraid to believe.

"You won't get out of here without my help. If you attack me, you'll never leave."

"Free me." The sound of a single piteous scream punctuated the quiet of the caverns.

Skye flinched and nodded. "She's the only one still alive. Once she dies, the crowd will disburse,

and I'll never get you out of here. The two main
entrances to the caverns are in the open, but I know
of another one. You won't find it without me."

Like hell he wouldn't find his way out. *After* he
got what he'd come for. Vhyper.

She unlatched his ankles then, one after the
other, his wrists. His muscles were stiff as he
pulled his arms down from over his head and
swung off the rock and onto his feet with a rush
of savage satisfaction.

He stared down at her from his far greater height,
tempted nearly beyond reason to take out his fury
on her as he once had Ancreta. *Mage witch.* But
the rigid control that commanded his life held his
hand. He still needed her.

"Where's Vhyper?"

"I don't know, but if you try to find him, you'll
never get away. Your shackles are magic. Birik can
call you back through them from a great distance.
Throughout the caverns and the forests. Possibly
beyond."

He grabbed her upper arms, squeezing until she
winced.

"Remove the shackles."

"I can't! I don't have the magic." Her eyes be-
seeched him. "Paenther, there's no time! This will
be your only chance to escape. Save yourself. *Save
us all.*"

The need to get Vhyper out of there, to fight his
enemies, retrieve the Daemon blade, and kill the
Daemons, was a breathing, burning thing inside
him.

But if she was right, escaping now, before Birik realized she'd freed him, might be his only option. He'd rally the Ferals, and they would attack as one.

Paenther released her.

She hesitated for one pulsing, wary moment, then turned and fled for the door. "Come."

Skye led Paenther down the back passage. When she reached the dagger fields, she turned to the menacing Feral towering over her from behind. "Watch your head as you watch your feet. If one of the stalactites crashes, we'll be caught."

He said nothing, the only emotion in his eyes the promise of a slow, violent death. Her heart thudded, and she thought of running and letting him find his own way out.

But he'd never find it. And they'd be right back where they were tonight, freeing Daemons.

Choose.

She took a breath and rushed into the uncleared field of stalagmites, leading him through the open to a particularly dangerous patch where the floor and ceiling sloped together, converging until the rocklike daggers hanging from above and rising from below began to resemble sharp, interwoven teeth.

She'd climbed through here enough times to know the only path, but she was much smaller than he was. Still, as she made her way, no sound followed behind her. She turned to find him moving through the rock as sleekly and silently as the cat that lived inside him.

In the distance, the last of the screams died away, and the sound of excited voices rose. Her pulse began to pound. They were running out of time. Few ever came this way, but she wasn't the only one who knew the route. If anyone saw her with the Feral, they'd sound the alarm, and his chance at escape would vanish.

Her heart thudding, beads of perspiration rolling between her breasts, she finally led him out of the difficult patch of rock and onto a wide path. Around the next bend was the small opening that led to the forest and freedom. Even from here she could feel the night air wafting in, cool and damp with rain.

With a breath for courage, she turned to the angry Feral. "When you get outside, run and don't look back. The shackles are magic and will keep you from shifting. I don't know how far is too far for Birik to call you back." She stepped back between two stalagmites and pointed. "There, warrior. Around those rocks, you'll find the opening to the outside. Be safe. Run!"

Paenther's hand closed tight around her wrist, his expression turning ugly. "Do you really think I'd leave you behind, witch? When all I can think of is taking my revenge on you?"

Skye's knees went weak with fear. "Please, I can't leave. He won't let me leave."

Paenther jerked her off her feet and into the solid

rock of his chest, his free hand closing around her throat. "Your choices end here, witch."

As her mind went white with terror, his thumb pressed into the crevice beneath her ear.

Then all went black.

Chapter Seven

Cold rain drizzled over Paenther's head, running in rivulets down his bare chest and beating on the shackles he still wore as he ran through the dark, wet fields. He'd run several miles already but wasn't stopping until he had gone at least a few more. Around his shoulders, he'd draped the unconscious witch.

She'd told him the shackles could be used to call him back, and though he had reason to doubt everything she said, he was taking no chances.

Running from that place, and his chance to save Vhyper, was possibly the hardest thing he'd ever done. But he'd be no use to Vhyper or anyone else if Birik caught him and chained him again.

He wondered how long he'd been out of it between the blood ritual and the Daemon demonstration. He could have sworn it was night during the first, but as he'd escaped the cave, the sky had been purple with dusk. Had he lost another entire day? And how many more days on top of that since the witch dragged him down to her lair?

He followed the now-dark road but took care to remain out of sight of it. Half-dressed, wearing shackles, and carrying an unconscious young woman, he'd draw far more attention than he wanted from the humans and would be easy prey for the Mage if they came after him. His first goal was to find a phone and call Lyon.

And find a knife. He had yet to attract draden, but it was only a matter of time. There were no swarms this far from the Radiant, thank the goddess, but the occasional rogue draden could be found anywhere. Sooner or later, if there were any in the area, they'd find him.

As he approached a dark farmhouse, he decided a little breaking and entering was his only alternative.

He laid Skye within a cluster of trees on the hillside and pressed his thumb into her slender neck to make sure she stayed fully unconscious. He stared down at her damp, delicate face, emotions warring inside him. He hated her for reeling him in, for making him believe she was in need of his sympathy and protection when she was really just a conniving bitch. But even as he knew what she was, her fragile beauty tugged at him.

Paenther scowled and rose, turning away from the siren who enchanted him even in her sleep.

What he'd told her was true. If it was the last thing he did, he'd get his revenge.

He approached the house with catlike stealth, frustrated he couldn't actually shift into his cat. No scent of dog reached his nose, which boded well for keeping his arrival a secret. When he found the back door unlocked, he slipped inside, palmed a kitchen knife from the wood block on the counter, and grabbed the phone.

He punched in Lyon's number, praying his chief would answer the call.

"Hello?"

"It's Paenther." He kept his voice low on the off chance there was actually someone in the house.

"Thank the goddess. Where are you?"

"Good question." Looking around, he found a magazine lying on the counter and read off the address.

"Tighe and Jag have been in the mountains looking for you for the past two days."

"Tighe's clone?"

"Is dead. Tighe's fine."

Paenther closed his eyes, sending a prayer of thanks skyward. "That's the best bit of news I've gotten in days. What about Foxx?"

"He's here. What's the situation? Do you need additional backup?"

"No. The attack is going to have to wait. I'm wearing Mage shackles and can't go near the place without risk of enthrallment."

"Then I'll send Tighe and Jag to pick you up."

"Roar, I'm not alone. I've got the witch who captured me. We have some unfinished business," he added darkly.

Lyon was silent for several moments. "The last thing we need is another witch in this house."

"She needs to be interrogated."

Silence, then a low growl. "Bring her in, but I want her hands tied at all times. And you'll have to be cleared of any possible enchantment when you get in. All of you. You want me to call Evangeline?"

"Yes." Evangeline had been his sexual partner of choice for decades. Their relationship had never extended beyond the sex, though that was his fault. He had no softness to give a woman anymore, thanks to Ancreta.

"I'll call the Shaman. I believe he knows a binding spell to keep your witch from practicing her magic. And he may know of a way to get you out of those shackles. Hold on, Kara's got Tighe on her cell phone." He repeated the address Paenther had given him. "They're about an hour north of there, B.P. He'll find you. We'll regroup here."

"Agreed."

Paenther replaced the phone in its cradle, left the house as quietly as he'd arrived, and went to retrieve Skye. As he climbed the hill to the trees where he'd left her, he heard the low growl of a dog. His heart lurched. He'd left Skye unconscious, unprotected.

But the dog, a medium-sized mutt, was curled up beside her. As if protecting her.

"Go!" he shouted softly to the dog. The animal

jumped up and barked at him. Paenther went feral, baring his teeth. The dog turned tail and ran.

Even unconscious she drew the animals. Looking down at her, at the dress plastered against her too-slender body, he couldn't deny he struggled against the same need to protect her. When he thought the mutt had hurt her, he'd been furious.

Paenther scowled. Even unconscious she wove her spell around him. Protect her, *hell*. All he wanted to do was hurt her.

Except that wasn't true.

Maybe once he was free of the shackles, he'd be able to see her clearly at last. He'd be able to see the cunning, calculating bitch who'd played on his sympathies and pretended to be beaten and vulnerable so he'd fuck her and help her raise the power to free those abominations.

He settled onto the ground beside her, leaning back against one thick oak trunk, where he had sight of the road and could watch for Tighe's white Land Rover.

Reaching for her instinctively, he stopped and pulled his hand back, fighting the urge to pull her onto his lap and hold her against the rain. Even knowing what she was, he felt this need to touch her, to hold her.

Which made him hate her even more.

He would get his retribution. Goddess help him, he would. She'd rue the day she'd turned those sad, blue eyes on him and pulled him under her spell.

* * *

"Panther-man," Jag drawled, thrusting out his arm and slapping his forearm to Paenther's as each man grasped the other's wrist in the traditional greeting. "Glad to see you made it out of there, Geronimo."

Paenther nodded, then turned to Tighe. As one, they embraced. Little emotion ever escaped past the fury that consumed his life, but he felt a relief to see his old friend that went all the way to his soul.

"You finally got that clone."

"Hell, yeah." Tighe pulled back. Sharp, warm emotion glittered in his eyes. "We've been looking for you for days."

He didn't have to say the words for Paenther to know they'd feared he was dead.

"How long have I been gone? I lost track of time in that place."

"About six days." He nodded at Skye, still lying asleep in the grass. "Is that the witch?"

"That's her."

Tighe scowled. "Do we really want to bring another one of those things in the house?"

"I'm not leaving her behind. But we need to tie her hands. Got any rope?"

Tighe flicked his hand at Jag. "Give me your belt."

Jag grunted but unfastened the belt on his camouflage pants and tossed it over. Paenther knelt in the wet grass beside Skye and tied her arms behind her back. Mage generally couldn't enchant a Feral or Therian without the direct touch of their hand. This one had claimed she couldn't do even that, but he didn't trust her.

As he slung her over his shoulder, an attractive brunette slid out of Tighe's SUV and joined them. When Tighe slid his arm around her shoulder, Paenther lifted a brow. He'd heard Tighe had taken a human as his mate, but he'd thought it was only to keep her from betraying him while he used her to capture his clone.

"This is Delaney, B.P."

The woman extended her hand to him, and he shook it, impressed by her fearless, straightforward attitude. He wasn't exactly the most docile-looking of males. None of the Ferals were.

Paenther nodded to her. "It's dangerous out here for a human."

The woman smiled, her sharp gaze meeting his own. "Turns out I'm no longer human. No longer mortal, anyway."

Paenther's surprised gaze swiveled to Tighe.

Tighe grinned. "It's true. But it's a long story. Let's get—"

"Draden," Jag warned. "A tiny little flock of them."

Sure enough, half a dozen of the fiends were descending from the sky. Paenther grabbed the knife he'd taken from the farmhouse and plucked out the hearts of the ones that came near him as his friends dispatched the others.

"Let's get out of here before more find us," Tighe said, closing his switchblade. Paenther carried the unconscious witch to the SUV and laid her in the cargo area in back, then climbed in beside Jag while Delaney took the front seat beside Tighe. If Skye woke, he'd be ready to grab her before she could touch anyone.

The last thing he needed was her enchanting more Ferals. Not when he suspected he was still under her spell.

Even before she was fully awake, Skye's heart began to pound like a hammer on an anvil. She was lying on her side, yet moving, the low hum of an engine tight against her ear. *A car.*

This couldn't be happening. Birik would never let her go. Yet clearly, somehow, she'd escaped the cavern.

In a rush of memory, it all came back. She'd tried to free Paenther, and he'd grabbed her, knocking her out.

He'd captured her.

As his last words rang in her ears, her stomach cramped with fear. *Do you really think I'd leave you behind, witch? When all I can think of is taking my revenge on you?*

Skye began to tremble, perspiration dampening her back. Slowly, carefully, she opened her eyes to find herself swallowed by a darkness punctuated by flashes of light from the windows above.

"How's Foxx?"

Paenther's voice rumbled close by, the sound strangely comforting even as it filled her with dread. He was furious with her, convinced everything she'd told him was a lie. Vhyper had told her as much.

If she could ever convince him she wasn't his enemy, that she hated Birik more than he did, she felt in her heart he'd help her again, just as he had that night Birik attacked her.

But if not. . .

Her mouth turned to dust. If not, she was going to suffer.

"Foxx is fine," a male voice replied from the front of the car. "He avoided capture though they managed to slam him with some kind of confusion spell. He couldn't remember where he'd lost you."

A third man grunted. The one directly in front of her. "It took three fucks to clear him of the magic."

"Watch your language around my mate, Jag," the man in front warned.

A low sound of warm feminine laughter erupted, also from the front, a sound Skye might have found pleasing if she weren't so frightened.

"Six years with the FBI. Believe me, I've heard worse. I've *said* worse. But I'm still having a hard time believing sex cures magical enchantment. That sounds like a line if I ever heard one. Right up there with, *But honey, it'll make your acne go away.*"

"It's during—" the man began.

"I know, I know," the woman replied. "It's during the moment of sexual release that the mind and body are most open." She made a sound that was half humor, half sigh. "I don't really doubt it's true. It's just one of a hundred things I'm having trouble wrapping my human mind around."

"You know, D, after being in the car with a witch . . ." The man's voice trailed off suggestively.

The woman laughed, that same sultry burst of air. "As if you needed an excuse." Her voice was rich with warmth and deep with affection.

Skye blinked into the darkness. How long had it been since she'd heard such affection between two people? She and Lucian had spoken to one another like that once, years ago. She'd barely been full grown when they'd fallen in love behind Birik's back. But then Inir had come and Lucian's eyes had turned as cold as the others' and he'd decided hurting her was more fun than loving her.

"We're all going to need a good fuck after riding with the witch," the one called Jag drawled. "Ever taken two cocks at once, FBI? I'm not real particular which hole I shove mine into."

The driver's growl turned deep and vicious. The car swerved, rolling Skye onto her back as the smell of blood suddenly filled the air.

"Tighe, *drive*," Paenther barked.

"Then rip his throat out for me," Tighe snarled.

"Jag . . ." Paenther's voice was as hard granite, yet laced with a deep frustration. "That's too far, even for you."

"Just making conversation." No hint of remorse warmed Jag's words. If anything, a note of smug satisfaction rang in his tone. But she felt the animal inside him, the jaguar, and heard him howl softly as if in pain.

Instinctively, her mind reached out to him,

trying to offer comfort. But the animal turned on her, hissing.

Jag growled low in his throat swinging around to stare down at her with malice in his eyes. "Your witch is fucking with my animal."

Skye scrambled to sit up, pressing her back against the hatch door, the beat of her heart turning erratic. Paenther might wear shackles that kept him from shifting, but the other men in this car didn't. And the animals inside them were huge, fierce felines, every one.

Paenther turned as well, his face shadowed, his displeasure palpable.

She tensed out of long habit, bracing for the strike of a fist.

None came.

"Stop it, Skye. Stop screwing with their animals."

She stared at him, at the anger in his eyes. Anger, but no violence. At least not yet.

"I . . . didn't mean to," she said quietly.

"She has a way with animals," Paenther said coldly. "She slaughters them."

Skye opened her mouth to object, then closed it again as Paenther continued.

"And dances in their blood."

She pressed her lips together, the knot in her chest tightening. She couldn't argue that she danced in their blood. And while she never killed her creatures, there was no denying she led them to the slaughter. Even if it destroyed something inside her every time.

How could she ever convince him that she did none of it willingly? He'd already made up his mind against her. She felt his animal sense her and give welcome, his silent purr a balm to her quaking heart.

But Jag's animal was still hissing and a third cat—a tiger, maybe?—didn't seem to be much happier about her presence. Why? Animals always greeted her. Why not these? Was the men's animosity toward her affecting the animals inside them? Or maybe she simply didn't have a way with animals that were also men.

Except the one inside Paenther.

As Jag turned back around, she met Paenther's warning gaze, briefly, before turning to look out the windows. There was nothing she could do, either way. She couldn't control their animals any more than she could control the men themselves.

Fear lived and breathed inside her as her distracted gaze took in the vast array of vehicles, and the buildings lit with a thousand lights. For the first time in her adult life, she was free of the cavern.

Free of the slaughter.

The realization swept over her on a deep tide of relief and anxiety. Her precious creatures were safe, at last. She wasn't. Birik's reach was long. She'd thwarted him, escaping without meaning to, and there would be hell to pay. The thought of it trembled inside her, but not even fear could dull the warmth in her heart of knowing her creatures would never again suffer because of her.

Whatever happened, she could not allow the Ferals to send her back.

The scenery passed, the office buildings giving way to houses and rolling roads, and finally to a long, circular driveway that told her they'd reached their destination. Feral House, she'd heard it called. The home of the Feral Warriors.

It sat at the back of the drive, a magnificent three-story brick house with black shutters at the windows and dormers tucked under the roofline. The windows were ablaze with light, giving the house a look of warmth and welcome that reminded her with bitter longing of the house, the Mage stronghold, where she'd lived as a child.

Any appearance of warmth was an illusion. There would never be any welcome at Feral House for her.

Along the edges of the drive were parked an array of cars, everything from low-slung sports cars to unremarkable sedans.

The car came to a stop, the hum of the engine going silent as the men and the woman flung open the doors and escaped into the night, slamming the doors behind them.

Skye scooted toward the seat backs as the door behind her lifted. Paenther's hard and shadowed face stared down at her as he reached in and gripped her arm, hauling her out of the car and depositing her on her bare feet. She stood in the light coming from the windows of the well-lit house, her hands tied behind her, trembling. As the cool breeze tugged and pulled at the skirt of her dress, she watched Paenther reach up and pull down the hatch, the muscles of his bare arms and torso flexing.

He was a beautiful creature. Strong. Powerful. If he decided she needed to die, she'd be dead in the heartbeat of his choosing. He turned and came to her with a dangerous catlike grace that drew her even as it scared her. Never had she wanted to be this man's enemy.

He grabbed her arm again without meeting her gaze, his jaw hard as granite, and led her up the brick walk as if she were a prisoner on her last journey. She wondered, briefly, despondently, if she'd ever again breathe the night air.

The couple she assumed were Tighe and his mate waited for them to catch up. Tighe was handsome in a classic sort of way, with his short blond hair and hard, unfriendly eyes. The woman was beautiful, with her dark hair and confident bearing. She watched Skye with an assessing, curious gaze.

"Interesting eyes," she murmured. "Are those copper rings what make them Mage eyes?" She turned and looked up at her husband.

"They are, but some Mage can hide the copper. This one did when she trapped Paenther." The raw disgust in his voice flayed her.

Finally, after so many years, she was among others with souls. Others capable of honor and self-sacrifice. Of love and kindness. But none of that kindness would be turned toward her. Because she was a Mage. The enemy. And the Feral Warriors were well-known to be merciless to their enemies.

Paenther ushered her through the front door and into the warm interior of an extraordinary house. There were luxuriously appointed apartments within the caverns where she'd lived all these years, the apartments of Birik and his sorcerers, but she rarely visited them and never willingly. She'd preferred her own rustic cell, or the woods, where she'd been left alone.

But her gaze focused on the grandeur before her with wonder. The foyer glowed brilliantly with light, nearly blinding her as her gaze took in the beauty of the high, three-story room. Stairs curved upward from either side, while high above them hung a huge crystal chandelier the likes of which she'd never seen. The walls were covered in richly decorated papers, gilt-framed paintings of flowers and animals positioned elegantly upon them. The largest of the paintings was on the floor beneath her feet, a portrayal of a forest filled with naked men and women and all manner of creatures that no longer existed, if they ever had.

Skye jerked at the sound of footsteps and looked up to find three people rushing into the foyer— two more large Ferals striding purposefully, towering over the blond female between them.

"Paenther!" the woman cried, smiling with such relief, Skye wondered if this were Paenther's mate. "We were so worried." But as she started forward, the largest of the men, a man with a commanding face and thick waves of golden hair, held her back.

"Lyon . . ." the blond complained.

"Easy, Kara. He's caught a witch."

Kara's blue eyes swung to her, flaring with wariness and no small amount of hostility. The female pressed herself back against the big man as his arm went around her protectively.

This man was clearly the woman's mate. Strangely, foolishly, Skye was glad.

The woman's wary gaze returned to Paenther. "I'm glad you're okay."

"Thank you, Radiant."

Holding the woman against him, Lyon reached for Paenther and clasped arms with him, his expression deep and warm and moving. "I'm glad to have you back, B.P."

The man beside him greeted Paenther in the same way. He said nothing, but the relief in his pale eyes was clear. When he released Paenther, he looked at her, his eyes going cold as a snowy day as he plucked at his goatee.

"She's tugging at my animal."

"And mine," Lyon said, pinning her with a look sharp enough to cut before lifting his gaze to Paenther. "The Shaman's on his way. I want her locked up until he gets here."

"Agreed."

"Evangeline and Genovia are on their way as well. I want everyone in that car cleared immediately." Lyon's gaze swung to Tighe. "You and Delaney can clear one another."

Tighe grinned as he pulled the dark-haired woman against him, the dimpled smile turning his hard face rakish as he visibly inhaled the scent of her hair. "If I have to."

The woman elbowed him gently, making him laugh.

Lyon's gaze swung to the man with the cold eyes. "Kougar, you and Jag keep an eye on Paenther until we know whether he's still enthralled." His gaze came back to Paenther. "Get rid of her cantric, if you haven't already."

Skye blanched. All Mage were implanted with the braided copper circle upon maturity. The cantric acted as a magic focuser and accelerator. Usually it was implanted deep in the flesh of the buttocks, where it wouldn't be seen except by another Mage. But hers wasn't in her buttocks.

"You can't," she said quietly.

"The hell we can't." Lyon turned on her with eyes filled with such venom she reared back, right into Paenther. His arm went around her middle, pulling her tight against his chest.

A deep, lion's growl erupted from Lyon's throat. "You're ours now, witch, and we'll do whatever we damn please. The death of one Mage won't upset the balance of the natural world." Lyon lifted that hard gaze to Paenther. "Lock her up. I'll call you and Jag when the women get here. As soon as you're cleared, we'll meet in the war room."

Paenther released her, took her arm again, and pulled her down the hall to a doorway, then down a long, long flight of stairs.

"Paenther." She swallowed hard. "I'm not your enemy. If I were, I wouldn't have helped you escape."

His hand tightened around her upper arm. "I don't want to hear it." His voice was like ice.

"I hate Birik as much as you do. More! I hate him more."

He jerked her, making her lose her balance, but his too-tight grip kept her from falling. "*Silence.*"

With a mounting feeling of dread, she did as he commanded. Reaching the bottom of the stairs, he led her down a long passage lit by electric sconces hung on the walls. They walked past a dark room before Paenther led her into a large, well-lit room with ultramodern workout equipment at one end.

She wondered if they'd rigged up the exercise machinery to turn this into some kind of torture chamber, but Paenther never slowed as he pulled her through the large room until he reached a glass wall at the far end. Set into the glass was a door.

Paenther pushed her through into a long, narrow passage that appeared to have been cut out of the rock. The stone was cold beneath her feet. Finally, the passage opened to a wide, rustic prison block, each cell separated from the next by thick stone walls.

Her stomach cramped at the realization that this was to be her fate. For how long? Would she ever again see the light of day?

So many times, Birik had imprisoned her. But

she'd always known all she had to do to be set free was cooperate. The power to free herself had always, ultimately, been in her hands.

This time, nothing was in her hands. Her breath caught on a hard lump of fear. Revenge, he'd said. She was used to pain. But taking the abuse from this man, who she knew possessed kindness, threatened to break her. Her body began to tremble.

Paenther pulled her to a halt in front of one of the cells and opened it. "Leave us," he said to the two men who'd followed them down.

"No can do, Hiawatha," Jag drawled.

Paenther glared at him. When he spoke, his voice was hard. "Go back to the gym and shut the door. Both of you. The witch and I are going to have a . . . *discussion*. And I won't have an audience."

If his words hadn't told her he meant to hurt her, the tightening of his grip on her arm did. Her mouth went dry, and it was suddenly all she could do not to try to fight her way loose from his hold.

But she'd never get loose, never get away. And the punishment would only be worse if she tried. That was the way it had always been with Birik.

The air didn't seem to want to go into her lungs.

The pale-eyed man slapped Jag on the back. "Come." To Paenther he said, "Don't kill her. Yet."

As the two huge males walked away, Skye fought the tears that tried to clog her throat. It was so much harder taking cruelty from a man who'd once been kind. Lucian's betrayal had broken her as Birik's attacks never had.

Paenther released her arm and pushed her into the cell.

Skye whirled to face him, desperate to try to make him understand. "Please, Paenther. Nothing I did was because I wanted to. Except free you."

"Shut up, Skye."

"He controls me. I don't have a choice. I never have a choice!"

He grabbed her and pushed her around, pressing her face-first into the rock wall until the cold stone bit into her cheek.

"Shut up!"

She felt his hand tugging at the hem of her dress and closed her eyes against the burn of tears. He grabbed her buttocks, his fingers digging into her painfully, over and over, first one side then the other.

"Where is it? Where's your cantric?" His hands began to grip her thighs, bruising her.

"It was embedded in my heart when I was eight."

His hand stopped abruptly. "That's impossible."

She swallowed hard, remembering the words of his chief. *Get rid of her cantric.*

"Paenther, *please.*"

He tugged and pulled at her wrists, and suddenly her arms were free of the binding. Gripping her shoulders, he turned her around roughly, his eyes hard as flint.

"Take off your dress."

She stared at him. He wasn't going to kill her. Not yet. *Of course not,* she thought bitterly. He'd yet to take his revenge.

With shaking hands, she reached for the hem, pulling the fabric up and over her head in a single tug. Nudity didn't bother her. She was far too used to it. Instead of tossing the dress to the floor, she pulled it against her chest like a shield. No, nudity didn't bother her. It was why he wanted her naked that terrified her. What punishment did he intend to visit on her body?

Her heart began to pound in hard, erratic thuds. Trembling, she met his hard gaze.

Fire burned in his eyes. And the promise of pain.

As many times as Birik had hurt her, she knew this would be worse. Because Birik was without a soul. He got no more pleasure from hurting her than he did anyone else. In a strange way, it wasn't personal. And because of that, the pain he inflicted never touched her mind or her heart.

But Paenther wasn't like Birik. She knew he had kindness in him. She'd felt it. Been warmed by it.

Whatever punishment Paenther chose to mete out would be very, very personal.

When he hurt her, she was going to bleed all the way to her soul.

Chapter Eight

"It's payback time," Paenther snarled. Leaving Skye in the cage, pressed against the wall with her dress clutched to her chest, he grabbed a small coil of rope off the wall. He was so damned mad at her. He knew what she was! Yet she simpered and pleaded and tugged at his sympathies. Playing him. She was still playing him! "It's time I rode you as you rode me, witch. But you like it bloody, don't you? I wonder how you'll like it when the blood's your own."

With the knife he'd taken from the farmhouse, he started cutting lengths of rope and tying them to the eyebolts fastened at the base of the walls at regular intervals for just this purpose. When he'd tied the last length, he rose and stared down at her as she stood covering herself in a pretense of modesty, trembling.

Creamy shoulders sloped from a long, graceful neck. A swell of bare hip peeked out from behind the dress, heating his blood.

"Quit pretending, Skye. I know what you are. Lie down. It's time you felt what it's like to be the one staked, your legs spread for another's pleasure."

Goddess, the thought of parting those silken legs, of finally, *finally*, being able to touch her fully, sent blood throbbing deep and low.

"I know what it feels like." Her voice vibrated with fear and echoed with hollowness. "Those chains weren't put on that rock for you."

His gaze snapped to hers as her words registered. That rock where he'd lain, strapped for six days. Her dresses hanging on the wall as if that miserable bit of rock were *her* cell and not his.

Shit. He would not feel sorry for her! It was what she wanted. Just an act.

But as he stared at her, at those copper-and-blue eyes, he'd be damned if he could see any cunning. She had to be enchanting him, because all he saw in her was a terrible bleakness. And it chilled him to the bone.

What if I'm wrong about her?

As she watched him, a sheen of tears began to glisten in her eyes. Tears just like the ones that had streaked Ancreta's cheeks as she'd run to him that day, her gown torn, her heavy breasts on full view. She'd kept her eyes downcast so he wouldn't see the Mage copper in them, but those tears on her cheeks had slain him. And gotten him captured.

Tears. Just like Ancreta, Skye was playing on his sympathies.

"Lie down!"

Her jaw clenched, her head jerking in a tiny, defiant movement.

He closed the distance between them, pressing his hands on the wall on either side of her head. Her chest heaved, her body shook, but she didn't plead, she didn't cower. Instead, she closed her eyes on a hopeless sweep of dark lashes. "I'm not what you think."

Her scent enveloped him, stirring his blood. He wanted her beneath him, yet everything inside him demanded revenge on her for enthralling him, for leading him into that hellhole. For making him feel sorry for her so that he'd help her . . . *help her* . . . use him.

A single tear broke free from the cage of her lashes, and she quickly brushed it away with her bare shoulder. The light caught the teardrop. Somehow that single, glistening drop on her perfect shoulder damned him.

He fought the tug of pity, that misguided need to protect her all over again.

It was a lie!

He grabbed her face, making her look at him. "Open your eyes, witch. I bought this act once before. The poor little victim. I know better. Open your eyes!"

To his surprise, her lashes flew up, temper heating the tears. "I don't know what you want from me! How could my fear of you possibly be an act? Even if I were as soulless as you think I am, I'd be afraid right now. Any woman would. I can't fight you."

"Yet you defy me when you refuse to lie down."

She looked away, then back, glaring at him even as her bottom lip began to quiver. "I won't help you rape me."

His stomach cramped. Never, in more than four hundred years, had he taken a woman against her will. He'd killed others for doing just that.

Dammit. She was a witch! Just like Ancreta.

No. She wasn't.

Ancreta had tortured him for the joy of it for months. Skye had never hurt him.

He released her and whirled away, slamming his fists into the stone of her cage. That was the problem. In all the time she'd had him at her mercy, she'd never once caused him an ounce of pain. Even after he attacked her.

If the witch in here with him were Ancreta, he'd have no trouble hurting her just as she'd hurt him all those months with her eyes filled with malicious glee.

But Skye wasn't Ancreta. He hated her for her lies, for making him think she was being abused so he'd fuck her. He despised the way she'd led the animals in her care to slaughter. Most of all, he hated the way she'd made him care about her, forcing this need in him to protect her.

But as far as he remembered, she'd never done anything to cause him pain. How could he get any satisfaction from hurting her in return? Even her fear was making him ill.

Yes, she'd taken him against his will, but he couldn't pretend there was any similarity. When she'd impaled herself on him during that ritual, he'd been furious. But she hadn't hurt him. Until the power rushed through him afterward, the physical act itself had brought him only pleasure.

That wouldn't be the case if he forced himself on her. Not unless she was wet and ready. Goddess, he could do that. He wanted to do that, to stroke her and touch her until she was writhing with need beneath his hand.

That he could force on her. A need she didn't want.

Retribution.

But he couldn't shake the thought of her on that stone, chained as he'd been. For whose pleasure? Birik's?

Fury burned through him, but it was a fury against her attackers, not against her.

Shit.

For all he knew, every thought in his head was being manipulated by her deft enchantment.

He stormed out of the small cell without a backward glance, locking the barred door behind him. It was past time he got himself cleared of this damned magic. And the only way to do that was with a good sexual release. Evangeline's warm and willing body would have to do. But, goddess, the only one he wanted was the very one who'd enchanted him in the first place.

Skye.

* * *

As Paenther climbed the stairs from the underground chambers, his fingers curled around the cold metal manacle biting into his opposite wrist. Dark fury twined with the rage that was as much a part of him as the magic that allowed him to shift. A magic chained as thoroughly by these damned shackles as he'd been chained to that rock.

His fingers dug into his flesh, trying to claw beneath the metal. He wanted the damned things off! The witch claimed they were magic, which meant they could be doing things to him. Goddess knew what.

The shackles alone were stopping him from racing back to that cavern to grab Vhyper before he couldn't find him again. Vhyper's soul was still in his body, Paenther was sure of it. Trapped by the evil that had already stolen too many.

If it was the last thing he did, he'd get him out of that cavern and free of the dark control.

Paenther strode into the foyer to find Evangeline waiting for him, watching him with hunger in her eyes. She'd dressed for him, her ripe curves well displayed by the low-cut red dress that hugged her body and left her long, shapely legs bare. Her dark hair tumbled loose around her shoulders just the way he liked it.

"Where's Genovia?" he asked.

"Jag's already taken her upstairs." She held out her hand to him, a slow, knowing smile lifting her mouth.

He made no move to take her hand. For the first

time in decades that smile, that ripe, lush body, stirred nothing inside him.

Skye's fault. Ironically, the only way to eliminate the web of enchantment she'd spun around him was to take Evangeline anyway. And he would. Dammit, he would.

In a minute.

"Do you want something?" He walked past her into the living room, a room as flowery and gilded as the rest of the house, and grabbed the bottle of scotch from the bar, pouring himself a drink and kicking it back in a single swallow.

"I want you," the woman said softly, leaning against the doorframe, her arms crossed beneath her ample breasts. She watched him with shrewd eyes, her gaze flicking down to his crotch and his decided lack of erection. "But you don't want me today. What's happened, Paenther?" There was no rancor in her tone. No hurt.

Theirs was a relationship built on sex and nothing more. On physical pleasure and needs met. He liked and respected her and was always careful to bring her as much pleasure as she brought him. But what they had together ended at the bedroom door.

"I've been enthralled. I'm probably still under her enchantment."

Evangeline nodded. "Which is why Lyon called me." She straightened and held out her hand again. "Come, warrior. Let's get you cleared of that magic. Then when you're interested again, I'll pleasure you a second time, if you like."

Paenther watched her, seeking the rush of heat that should have accompanied her words. But it was frustratingly absent. Still, she was right. The sooner he got the witch's magic out of his system, the better.

Without touching her, he led her upstairs to his bedroom, his own private sanctuary. The previous Radiant, Beatrice, had insisted on sharing her love of art with all the Ferals. Paintings of Indians on horseback covered two of his walls. But the large, rough-hewn furniture and collections of now-antique guns and arrowheads were all his.

He closed the door and watched the woman slowly strip out of the dress until she wore nothing but a pair of tiny lace panties and a bra, which left little to the imagination. Evangeline was soft and curvy, and sexy as hell. At least, he'd always thought so. But as he imagined removing those scraps of lace and having his way with the womanly parts beneath, he felt nothing. His body refused to rise.

He gave a snort of disgust.

Evangeline frowned. "She really has you under her spell, doesn't she?"

With a growl, he closed the distance between them, turned Evangeline in his arms, pressing her back against his chest as his hands covered her full, ripe breasts. Too ripe. His hands itched to cup a pair of small breasts on a too-slender frame. "Dammit."

Evangeline eased out of his arms. "Close your eyes, Paenther. Maybe that will help. Close your eyes and think of her."

"Evie . . ."

"Do whatever it takes to get aroused, warrior. We have to clear you of her magic."

He leaned back against the door and did as she suggested, closing his eyes. The moment he did, Skye's face rose in his mind as he'd first seen her. The excitement in her eyes as she'd looked up from perusing the magazine and caught his gaze. He thought of the way she'd looked as he'd driven himself into her in the woods, her head thrown back in ecstasy.

His body rose and heated at the thought. He felt soft hands on his crotch, unzipping his pants, taking his heavy shaft into a warm palm. He arched into the touch, heat coursing through his body.

The scent of jasmine filled his senses, and he stilled, everything inside him rebelling. Jasmine, not violets.

He didn't want jasmine. He didn't want . . . Evangeline.

The only one who could slake this hunger was Skye.

He opened his eyes to look down at the woman preparing to take him into her mouth. Her hair was too long. Her body too lush, too ripe.

His body went soft. With a growl of disgust, he moved away from her, zipping himself back into his pants as he prowled the room like a caged and wounded animal. Dammit! He might as well still be shackled and chained to the witch's rock for all the freedom he had from her.

"What do you want me to do, Paenther?" Evangeline asked carefully.

"I don't know." He had a beautiful, practically naked, *willing* woman in front of him, and direct orders from his chief to find sexual release. And he couldn't take her. He didn't want to be inside her. Not between her legs. Not in her mouth. He didn't even want her touching him.

Goddess, that witch had him screwed up.

"If you're not going to let me clear you, Paenther, you'll have to do it yourself. And I'll have to watch to make sure you do. We can't have the enchantment keeping you from getting cleared."

Shit.

Standing where Evangeline's scent didn't overpower him, he closed his eyes and thought of Skye. Of the day he kissed her for the first time, still thinking she was human. He'd ordered Foxx back to the country store a second time, needing to see her again. He hadn't expected her to be there, but she'd been waiting. And when she'd slid into his arms and pressed her mouth to his. . .

Fire erupted inside him, heating his body. As she swept her tongue into his mouth, all thought of gentleness flew from his head. He took her mouth, plundering, conquering with his tongue as he pulled her tight against him. She tasted like raindrops and smelled like violets, and all he could think of was being inside her.

Her arm slipped from around his neck and moved down to slide over that distended part of his anatomy, telling him her thoughts were as carnal and desperate

as his own. He slid his palm down her thigh, then up
again, lifting the skirt of her dress until he found the
hem. He reached beneath, his fingers skimming her
warm flesh, his hand slipping between her thighs, finding her hot, damp core.

The woman wore no undergarments.

A smile pulled at his mouth as he kissed her hard and
slid a single, shaking finger deep inside her tight wet
sheath.

Paenther opened his eyes and strode to the
bathroom, leaving the door open as he pulled
his throbbing erection out of his pants and began
pumping himself off over the sink. His mind remained on Skye.

Foxx had interrupted them, or he might have
taken her right there. Right then. He'd been so
hard for her. And she'd been so ready.

Damn the witch!

In his mind he saw her again as she'd ridden
him on the stone that first time, fingering herself
as he'd directed her to.

Goddess, she'd been glorious as the passion had
begun to ride her, as the cries had escaped that
slender throat.

And when she'd come. . .

His body tightened as the memory of her
orgasm brought on his own. With a low groan, he
pumped his seed into the sink, the release satisfy-
ing in only the most basic way. Grabbing a towel,
he cleaned himself off, then zipped up his pants
as he glanced at Evangeline watching him from
the doorway, heat in her eyes.

No matching heat rose in his body. A flare of panic ran beneath his breastbone. He'd cleared himself of the magic. It should be gone!

Reaching for Evangeline, he pulled her into his arms and released her just as quickly, wanting her even less than he had before. Skye's slender body rose in his mind, her scent the only one he craved.

"Shit!" He stormed past Evangeline, into the bedroom, the ever-present rage boiling his blood.

Behind him, a feminine snort of disbelief. "She's enchanted you, all right, just not with magic. You're into her for real, warrior."

Paenther swung to face his scantily clad companion. "I have not fallen for a witch!"

"Maybe not emotionally, but physically, you want her bad. Bad enough that no one else will do."

Paenther felt the rush of feral anger, his teeth and claws elongating, his mind spoiling for a fight. One of his brothers was about to get bloody.

"Ease down, warrior," Evangeline said without fear. "It'll go away, Paenther. You're not the first male to want a female you shouldn't have. You won't be the last. Sooner or later, you'll get over her."

Paenther clenched his jaw hard and nodded. "Sooner, not later." He pulled himself back, retracting his fangs and claws. The best way to end this unholy infatuation was to avoid the witch altogether. The only reason he'd brought her back here was to interrogate her and find out what she knew. Once they'd done that, there was nothing to keep them from destroying her. Then he *knew* he'd get over her.

Striding back into the bathroom, he shut the door, stripped, and took a hot shower, washing the smell of the caverns and the witch off his skin. As he dried himself, he made his decision. He'd give her into Roar's keeping. Let his chief decide what to do with her. Because, enchanted or not, he obviously wasn't thinking clearly when it came to this particular witch. And there was too much at stake for him to make any more errors.

Paenther dressed quickly, in a clean pair of black leathers and a black silk shirt, buckling his knife belt around his waist.

The witch was no longer his concern.

If only, for one damned minute, he could stop wanting her.

Chapter Nine

Skye stood within her prison cell deep below Feral House, once more dressed, her back against the wall. Her body quaked as she struggled for breath, fearing what Paenther would do when he returned, dreading Birik's retribution. How many times had Birik told her if she ever escaped him, he'd make her long to return . . . or long to die?

If only she could escape them both. But where would she go?

Home. She'd go home.

Tears heated her eyes as the longing for her mother nearly overwhelmed her. But she didn't know how to find her. Her world had been so contained, so secure, she had no frame of reference within the human world to lead her back there.

No idea what human town they'd lived near, or even what state. No way to contact the people she'd loved.

And no way to know if they, too, had lost their souls and were now part of Inir's army.

She brushed at the tear that rolled down her cheek. It didn't matter because she'd never be free. Escape was impossible. The Feral Warriors would never let her go. She wasn't sure they'd even let her live once she'd told them what she knew about Birik and the Daemons.

The memory of what she'd witnessed doubled her over until she thought she would be sick again. The terror of those poor people still pulsed through her blood, their screams ringing forever in her head. The foul smell of the Daemon himself felt permanently burned into her nose.

She pressed the back of her fist against her mouth. All the more reason she could never let Birik catch her again. He would only try to use her power to free more of those things. Even if he didn't get Paenther, too, he'd search for another way until he succeeded in freeing more.

And she'd die before she helped him set loose another of those monsters.

Slowly, she sank to the floor, cold from the bleakness of the future before her. Her old life was over. And she had none to replace it. She could never go back. Yet trapped in the Ferals' prison, there was no way to go forward. Was this it, then?

She pressed her head back against the wall, tears falling freely as Paenther's words replayed in her head. *Whether we choose to let evil live, or we fight to destroy it, defines our lives. Choose, Skye.*

She snorted softly. She had no choices.

But she'd made *one*, hadn't she? She'd freed Paenther and accidentally removed herself from Birik's control in the process. And it had been the right choice, no matter what happened to her.

When the Ferals came to interrogate her, she'd tell them everything she knew. Maybe, in some small way, she could help them defeat Birik and his Daemons. Maybe in some small way she could make up for all the suffering she'd caused with her gift.

Then, if they still felt they had to destroy her, so be it. What was one life when so many would die, when so many creatures had already died, because of her?

With a hard shudder, she pulled her knees up, wrapping her arms tight around them.

So be it.

But, dear Mother, I don't want to die.

As Paenther descended the stairs with Evangeline, Lyon opened the front door to the Shaman. To all appearances, the man who stepped into Feral House was little more than a boy, a fifteen-year-old dressed in costume—a ruffled white shirt and black breeches from a bygone era. He nodded to Lyon, then looked up to meet Paenther's gaze, his eyes ancient in his youthful face.

The Shaman gave a brief nod. "Warrior."

"Shaman." A growl rumbled in Paenther's throat. "Get me out of these shackles."

"I'll do what I can."

When he reached the foyer, Paenther motioned the Shaman into the living room. Like every room in Feral House, the walls were covered in original oil paintings, most dating from the midnineteenth century.

While Paenther took a seat on one of the deeply cushioned chairs, the Shaman pulled up a footstool and took hold of one of Paenther's arms, pressing his slender fingers around the manacle. Closing his eyes, he began to chant, murmuring words under his breath from a language Paenther had heard him use before, one he himself didn't know. Minute after minute passed, long, tense minutes where Paenther forgot to breathe, his mind and body concentrating so hard on willing the Shaman's magic to work.

When the Shaman opened his eyes and pressed his lips together unhappily, Paenther wanted to yell his fury.

The Shaman shook his head. "I'm sorry. It's strong, strong magic, warrior. I'm going to have to do more research to see if I can find another way."

Paenther closed his eyes, wrestling down the fury inflamed by his frustration. He needed to be able to shift! As long as he wore these shackles, he remained a prisoner to the Mage.

He speared the Shaman with his gaze. "The witch is in the prison. Lyon wants you to bind her magic."

A flash of venom tightened the Shaman's mouth as he nodded. Like his own, the Shaman's fate had long ago been decreed by a Mage attack. He'd been a youth at the time, and the attack had ended his growth into manhood. Though he was one of the oldest Therians alive, he looked like a young teen and always would.

Paenther rose and led the smaller man into the foyer, where he found Lyon waiting, his arms crossed over his chest, his expression grim as he eyed the manacles still on Paenther's wrists.

"No luck." Paenther's tone was clipped.

"Bring the witch to the war room as soon as the Shaman's bound her."

Paenther nodded. "Then, Roar? She needs to be someone else's concern. She's still got her claws in me."

Lyon looked at him sharply. "I thought you got yourself cleared."

"I did. That's why I know someone else has to see to her after this."

Lyon eyed him thoughtfully, then nodded.

Paenther led the Shaman down the long flight of stairs and through the underground chambers. When they reached the prison cell, Skye rose with that fluid grace of hers and faced him, her back straight, her chin raised. In her eyes he saw a mix of courage and hopelessness, as if she expected the worst but was prepared to face it all the same.

That errant tug she had on him had him wanting to reach out to her, to reassure her nothing bad was going to happen to her. But he couldn't reassure her even if he wanted to. Mage witches didn't live long in Feral House. For good reason.

"She's not tied." The Shaman stepped back. "I'm not going near her unless she's tied."

Skye pressed her lips together and turned her head. Paenther opened the cell and grabbed one of the lengths of rope he'd originally intended to stake her out with. Skye put her hands behind her back, allowing him to tie her without effort.

As he looped the rope around her wrists, his body began to react to her nearness as it always did, rising, hardening as if he hadn't just jerked himself off. The cat in him wanted to rub its cheek against her soft hair, to rub his body against her softer curves. His hands itched to slide over the parts of her only his eyes had ever touched.

He gripped her wrists harder than necessary. Just the touch of his flesh on hers had desire flowing through him, raw and hot. *Goddess*, what she did to him. She turned her head, and it was all he could do not to press his mouth against the long, silken length of her neck. To lick, to nibble.

With a growl of deep frustration, he finished tying her and stepped out of the cell, allowing the Shaman to take his place. The Shaman watched her with all the warmth one might reserve for a hissing cobra. Repugnance darkened his eyes as he circled the witch, chanting the binding spell.

Skye looked down at her bare feet.

Sympathy rose from some misbegotten place inside him. So what if everyone loathed her? She was Mage. He would not feel sorry for a witch.

The Shaman stopped abruptly. "You haven't removed her cantric."

"I couldn't find it. She says it's buried in her heart."

"That's impossible." He motioned Paenther to him with a quick tilt of his head. "Hold her for me while I check."

Skye's gaze snapped up to his, her eyes sharp and wary.

He knew what she was thinking. "The Shaman doesn't have to use a knife to find your cantric, witch. Calm down." Moving behind her, he took hold of those slender shoulders, feeling a strength in her bones that he wouldn't have expected. Maybe she wasn't quite as delicate as she looked.

His mind played with him, reminding him of the inviting appeal of those shoulders when they'd been bare a short while ago. Would the skin taste as sweet as her kisses? He imagined pulling her dress aside, baring one shoulder for his mouth.

With a growl, he fought back his body's obsession with this woman.

The Shaman, only as tall as Skye, stood in front of her and ran his hands in front of her chest, an inch from her dress. Slowly, his hands stilled, the one coming to rest directly over her heart. The Shaman closed his eyes as if hearing a tune that played only in his head.

"It's in her heart, as she says. You'll not remove the cantric without taking the heart."

Killing her. "How did she ever survive its placement in the first place?"

"I imagine she was a child."

Paenther nodded, remembering what Skye had told him. "She was eight." Eight. That bastard Mage had cut open an eight-year-old little girl to insert a copper ring in her heart. He could have killed her.

The Shaman nodded. "That would explain it. Magic has unpredictable consequences in children. In this case, she apparently survived what an adult would not. The heart grew around the cantric." He resumed his chanting. Two more circles around her and he moved out of the cell. "She's bound, but . . ." He shook his head. "I can't guarantee she's no longer dangerous. Be careful, warrior."

Oh, she was dangerous, all right. All he had to do was get near her, and he wanted her. Hell, all he had to do was think of her.

He took hold of her upper arm and steered her out of the cell.

As he did, she looked up at him. "I can't hurt you. I don't have that kind of power. And I wouldn't hurt you if I could." Her words were as intense as her eyes, spinning a dangerous web around his mind, trying to soften his resolve against her.

"Why should I believe anything you say?"

"Because it's the truth."

And what was the truth? Who was she? A dangerous enemy? A victimized innocent? Or perhaps just enough of both to throw him off his guard and doom the Feral Warriors and their mission once and for all.

* * *

With deep trepidation, Skye followed Paenther through the foyer from the basement, trying to take her mind off the impending interrogation.

The painted wood floor was cool and smooth beneath her bare feet. She barely remembered the feel of shoes, it had been so long since she'd worn any. Birik had never provided anything but the basics for her—dresses and a minimal amount of food. In the days before Inir came, back when she was young and still had friends, they'd tried to slip her treats—a doll, a small necklace, a pretty pair of panties—but Birik invariably discovered the gifts and destroyed them.

Paenther steered her down the hall. Her pulse began to race. A bead of perspiration slid between her breasts. Even before they reached the room where the Ferals waited, she heard the deep rumblings of male voices and felt the stirrings of the animals inside them. Mostly large animals, jungle cats and canines, along with a single bird of prey.

Paenther ushered her into a large, wood-paneled room dominated by a huge oval table and the men themselves—more than half a dozen huge males. With them was the woman she'd seen in the foyer. Kara. All eyes turned her way, a mix of curiosity and animosity in every pair.

The animals leaped to greet her, then one by one began to growl and hiss, mimicking the hostility of the men in which they resided.

Three of the big men strode forward, watching

her with wary eyes but looking at Paenther with deep, heartfelt relief.

A sharp-faced man with arched brows grasped Paenther's arm with both of his.

"Hawke," Paenther murmured.

"You had us worried, buddy." He held Paenther's forearm for a long moment. "Glad you got away."

"Me, too."

As Hawke stepped back, a second man, the largest in the room, grabbed his arm.

"Wulfe."

"Welcome back, B.P."

The third man, Skye had seen before. A young man with a shock of unkempt red hair. Foxx. He'd been with Paenther each time she'd seen him at the Market, before she'd captured him.

Paenther gripped the young man's forearm, then released her to clasp his shoulder. "I'm glad you're okay, Cub. But that's the last time I'm listening to those instincts of yours."

The younger man groaned. "I guess she didn't turn out to be so good for you after all."

"You could say that."

"Have a seat," Lyon barked.

Paenther seated Skye on an empty chair at the near end of the table. With her hands tied, she didn't have the luxury of leaning back as the others did. But she wouldn't have been able to relax anyway. Not in this room, with the men throwing hostile looks her way every few moments.

Lyon, sitting at the head of the table at the far end, vibrated with tension. He turned to the

Shaman, who had followed them in. "Is there any possibility that Paenther is still enthralled?"

"There's always the possibility. I feel no evidence of enthrallment, but he still wears the shackles. I can't say for certain what they're doing to him. The witch may be using them to control him in some way."

Lyon's intense gaze swung to Paenther. "What happened, B.P.? And what do we have to do to end this threat once and for all?"

As Paenther filled them in on the capture, Vhyper, and the Daemons, Skye watched him, glad for the opportunity to turn away from the unfriendly eyes in the room and drink her fill of the man at her side.

Paenther commanded a power unrivaled by any man in the room, with the possible exception of the chief himself. A power she felt every time he came near her. A power that lit fires in her blood.

As he talked, turning from his chief to the other men and back again, his black hair swung about his shoulders, and the scars across his eye rippled and moved. His was a face of incredible beauty and depth, exotic with its high, pronounced cheekbones, yet ruggedly, vibrantly handsome.

Anger tightened his voice as he spoke, yet the panther spirit inside him rubbed against her mind, like a tame cat might her ankles, as if wholly unaware that much of his anger was directed at her. Paenther seemed to be the only one of the Ferals whose emotion toward her was not in tune with his animal's.

She felt as if she had a friend in the room. Unfortunately, that panther spirit could never help her if the others—even the man he shared a body with—turned against her.

"Witch," Lyon snapped, jerking her gaze to the other end of the table. "What are Birik's plans?"

Skye sat straighter, feeling all eyes turn on her. "Birik doesn't tell me his plans. All I know is he craves power. The kind my gift provides him. I heard the same thing Paenther did, that Birik wants more Daemons. An entire army. And he intends to use us to get it. Even if he doesn't get Paenther, he'll find a way to use my power to free more of those things." She met the Chief of the Ferals' gaze, her fingers curling into her fists until her nails bit into the flesh of her palms. "You can't let that happen. You can never give me back to him."

Lyon eyed her, his eyes narrowing as if he didn't believe her.

She tried to make him understand. "I was as much a prisoner of that place as Paenther was. I don't ever want to go back. But it's not what I want that matters. All that matters is that Birik not succeed." She stared at the Chief of the Ferals, willing him to know the truth of her words. "You must never allow him access to my power again." Though she couldn't bring herself to say the words out loud, the thought was clear in her eyes. *If you have to, destroy me first.*

The room was silent. Beside her, she felt the tug of Paenther's strong presence and turned to find him watching her with dark, unfathomable eyes as if he couldn't quite figure her out. Sometimes she almost felt like he believed her. Like he saw the truth.

Almost.

Two people slipped into the room, the couple from the car, hand in hand, looking both well pleased and sheepish.

"Sorry," Tighe said. "We got a little carried away."

Lyon nodded, then turned back to Skye. "How many Mage in the cavern?"

"Twenty-seven including me."

"How many ways in and out?"

"Three. Two main passages and a little-used back passage, which was the one I led Paenther through to escape. But I don't know if you can get through the warding on the mountain to reach the cavern. I know it's impossible for humans to breach."

"She's fucking with my animal again," Jag snarled, his brows low and menacing as he rose from his chair and started toward her.

Skye tensed.

"Jag . . ." Lyon warned.

Paenther stood, putting himself between her and the angry warrior. "She can't help it. Animals are drawn to her."

Jag scowled. "Mine's not *drawn* to her. It's getting itchy. Annoyed. And so am I."

"Sit down, Jag," Lyon said. "We've got to understand what's going on before we deal with the witch."

His words did nothing to calm Skye.

And little enough to calm the angry Feral. Jag scowled. He didn't reach for her, but neither did he return to his seat. Instead, he paced like a caged animal, ready to bite off the first hand thrust into his cage.

Paenther remained standing at her back.

"How did the Mage regain their ancient magic?" Lyon demanded of her.

"They didn't."

"Do you think we're fools?" The Chief of the Ferals' voice was deceptively soft.

"No, I think you may be the only ones standing between the world and true evil. The Mage haven't regained their ancient magic. They've acquired dark magic."

Lyon's gaze narrowed, but in question now rather than hostility. "Explain."

Skye clasped her hands, knitting her fingers together behind her. "I don't know the entire story, but I've heard rumors that the Elemental, Inir, was infected by dark spirit years ago. He was only a sentinel at the time, but within a few months he rose through the ranks to become the high leader. I do know . . . he changes people. I think he changed Birik a long time ago. Before he claimed me. I saw the changes myself when Inir came to the cavern years ago."

"How many years?"

"I'm not sure. I'd reached my full height, but not my maturity. It was probably eight or nine years after I'd arrived there. Thirty or so years ago.

He did something to the Mage. I think he stole their souls. They serve the purpose of the High Daemon now."

The room went deathly silent. Growls slowly erupted.

"Satanan hasn't risen," Lyon said.

"No." Skye shook her head. "Inir's intent is to free him."

The Shaman nodded, leaning forward. "Dark spirit always seeks to free evil. Some believe the dark spirit left in the world is part of Satanan himself, tiny bits of his consciousness left behind when he was imprisoned."

Lyon's eyes narrowed as he stared at Skye. "So you have no soul?" The cords in Lyon's neck were beginning to stand out.

Skye's pulse ratcheted up another notch. "I alone was left untouched by Inir's sorcerers. Birik feared I'd lose my ability to call the animals if they changed me. He feared he'd lose the source of my power."

"Yet you're able to hide your Mage eyes," Paenther said behind her. "That's a magic Mage haven't had in millennia."

She turned and looked up, meeting his piercing black gaze. "Birik gave me that ability in the form of a short-term spell to enable me to capture you. I can no longer hide them."

"Our first target is Birik and the cavern stronghold."

Skye turned back to the table as Lyon addressed his men. "I want Vhyper and the blade out of there, and those Daemons destroyed." Lyon looked at the Shaman. "What's it going to take to free Paenther from the shackles?"

"I don't know."

"Work on it. I need him." Lyon turned back to the table. "But we can't wait. Kougar, Wulfe, and Hawke, you'll leave for the Blue Ridge immediately. Once you've located the cavern, we'll regroup and move on it, full strength."

Foxx leaned forward, his face eager. "And me. Let me go, Lyon. I've already been out there. I'll recognize the area."

"You remembered shit, Cub," Jag said. "Or have you forgotten?"

"Lyon?" Foxx persisted.

The Chief of the Ferals shook his head. "You stay here, Foxx. You were touched by magic once out there, I'm not sending you again." He turned to Hawke. "Go. I don't know what she's doing to our animals, but I feel it, too. The sooner you're out of here, the better. Foxx and Paenther can fill you in further over the phone."

Hawke nodded as all three men rose and left.

Skye watched them go, wondering why the animals were becoming so agitated. And there was no denying they were. All but Paenther's. Why? She was doing nothing to antagonize the Ferals themselves and certainly nothing to harm their animals. Why would they be getting more and more angry?

Jag began snarling, glaring at her.

"You take your life in your hands, witch," Lyon warned.

"I don't know what I'm doing." She was beginning to shake. "It's not on purpose."

Jag started around the table toward her again. Paenther moved to block his access to her, but Jag didn't back off this time. Instead, fangs sprouted in his mouth, claws erupted from his fingertips, and his eyes turned the color of a jungle cat's.

Paenther tensed, his arms opening at his sides as if preparing for a fight. *"Back off,* Jag."

"If you can't make her stop fucking with our animals, *I* will."

To Skye's horror, the terrifying creature Jag had become leaped at Paenther, his claws out. She ducked, fearing they were going to land right on top of her, but Paenther met the attack with one of his own. The two men, both part animal, tumbled to the ground, clawing and ripping at flesh in a tangle of teeth and claws and massive limbs.

"Enough!" Lyon roared.

The fight went on for about ten more seconds before the two bloody combatants rose to their feet and retracted their fangs, eyeing one another as if ready to go at it again.

Her heart pounded.

"No one touches her but me," Paenther snarled.

Skye felt something warm and raw stir in her chest as she realized he was protecting her. From his own men.

"Get her out of here, B.P.," Lyon snapped. "I don't know what the hell she's doing, but I'm about to leap out of my own skin. Lock her up in the prison, then come back. We have some decisions to make."

Paenther's jaw clenched, drawing his cheekbones in high relief. Finally, he nodded once and turned to her, barely looking at her as he pulled her from her chair and steered her out of the room, retracing the path back to the prison.

"What in the hell did you do to them?" he asked tightly as he led her down the long stairs.

"Nothing. I don't understand what happened. Animals always react to me, but it's with friendliness, not anger. Your panther was the only one who didn't go nuts in there."

Paenther said nothing more as he led her back to the prison and locked her up. Then he turned and left without a backward glance as she watched his bloody and retreating back disappear into the passage.

He'd protected her. And, so far, he hadn't been able to bring himself to hurt her. There was goodness inside him. And honor. She'd thought it before, and she believed it even more, now.

But that didn't mean she was safe from him. As long as he was convinced she was his enemy—and the strange reaction of the animal spirits to her wasn't doing much to convince him otherwise—she was in deadly peril from the very strength she admired. Maybe, whether they meant to or not, the Mage and the Ferals couldn't help but harm one another. Even if harming these men was the last thing in the world she wanted to do.

She sat on the hard floor against the back wall, her hands still trapped uncomfortably behind her back. While she feared what the Ferals might ultimately decide to do with her, she feared Birik more. Because she *knew* what Birik would do.

And it was almost midnight.

Chapter
Ten

Paenther rejoined the group in the war room minutes later.

"We're spread too thin. I'm enlisting the aid of the Guard," Lyon said as Paenther took his seat.

Jag scoffed. "The Guard is just a bunch of Therians. What in the hell can they do?"

Lyon growled. "They're damn fine fighters, *just* Therians or not. They won't be of much help in fighting the draden, but they can help in other ways. A small team is on its way over to discuss the situation as we speak."

Paenther half listened to the discussion, shaken by how violently he'd reacted to Jag's threat against Skye. It infuriated him. He should be clear of her magic, but she obviously still had her claws in him.

Lyon placed his hands palm down on the table and looked at Paenther. "Until those shackles come off, you'll be guarding Feral House. I don't want you leaving."

Great. Now I'm essentially under house arrest. Yet he couldn't argue the point. Lyon was right.

"Tighe and Foxx, you take first shift with the draden. You'll rotate with Jag."

Paenther looked at Lyon. "Since when do we need three men guarding the house?"

"Since one of them brought a witch home and still wears the shackles to prove it. I won't compromise the safety of our Radiant, or the other women in this house."

He turned to the others. "If that's it, we're through."

When no one said anything more, they all rose.

Paenther scowled, hating the situation the Mage had put him in. Even his own chief couldn't trust him. Worse, he couldn't trust himself.

Kara came to him, her blue eyes warm and determined. "I'd like to give you a shot of radiance, Paenther. After all you've been through, I think you could use it."

Paenther inclined his head with deep respect and deeper affection for this petite woman with the heart of a lioness. "I'd be honored, Radiant."

"*Fuck.*" Jag grabbed the back of a chair.

Lyon and Tighe, too, seemed to be in some kind of pain.

"What's happening?" Paenther demanded.

"Your witch," Tighe said, through gritted teeth. "I think the pain is hers."

Paenther leaped for the door and took the stairs to the underground chambers four at a time, running the rest of the way back to the prison. No sound reached his ears as he approached her cell, but as he came even with it and his gaze took in the sight of her, his chest seized, his mind going gray as a winter sky.

She lay on her back in a pool of blood, her arms still caught behind her, her back bowed in agony. Deep cuts marred her lovely face, neck, and hands. Scores of them.

Fury roared through his blood as he grabbed for the keys to her cell with shaking hands. As Lyon and the others raced in behind him, he whirled on his chief, his lip pulling back in a snarl. *"I'll kill the man who did this."*

Lyon came to stand beside him as Paenther unlocked the door of the cell. "Look at her legs, B.P."

Through a haze of rage, Paenther stared, uncomprehending. Cuts erupted along the lengths of her legs as if a ghost wielded an invisible blade. The bloodstains on her dress grew, encompassing her abdomen and hips, arms and thighs, though no cuts appeared in the fabric. They were coming from within her.

"What's doing this?" he demanded, pulling the door open and rushing inside. As he knelt beside her, blood-caked lashes rose slowly, painfully. "What's happening, little witch?"

She tried to speak, but her voice broke on a word, forcing Paenther to lean closer. "Birik." Her face and body contorted, but her mouth fought to form the words. "The moon . . . ritual."

"The slaughter?"

"Yes," she gasped. "My punishment . . . for not . . ." Her mouth went still as a wicked cut slashed across it.

Paenther stared at her, at the slashes wreaking havoc on her flesh with quicker and quicker frequency. Her meaning slowly penetrated the furious fog encasing his brain.

Birik was punishing her for not performing the ritual. As if she had any choice when she'd been stolen away.

That *bastard*.

The slashes were coming so fast that it was as if five men attacked her at once. The pool of her blood spread.

Her suffering tore at him. It shouldn't matter to him. *She* shouldn't matter to him. But she did.

"How do we stop it, Skye?"

"Can't. It will . . . stop." Her words told him clearly she'd been through this before. *How many times?*

Her eyes rolled back, her body bowing against the agony. Yet she made no sound, suffering in silence until finally she collapsed into unconsciousness.

In his mind's eye, he saw her again as she'd lain in a heap on the floor of the cavern, bloodied and broken from Birik's attack. He'd kill him. If it was the last thing he did, he'd kill that son of a bitch. Fury roared through his body, a fury born from the depths of his abhorrence for the abuse of innocents.

He stared down at her, at the beauty nearly obscured beneath the bloody cuts that crisscrossed her face. And he finally accepted what his gut had been telling him from the beginning. This witch was different. She was innocent of the cruelty and treachery he'd suffered from Ancreta.

Innocent.

"We may finally know the purpose of that cantric of hers," the Shaman said behind him.

Paenther glanced at him over his shoulder, taking in the small audience that had followed him down. "What do you mean?"

"I've been wondering why anyone would embed a cantric in a heart, and I've come up with one reason. So the one in whom it was embedded cannot ever be free of it."

"What are you saying?"

"I think it's there to control her. Punishment, she called it. That Mage loaded spells into her cantric to punish her for doing the forbidden, or for failing to do the things he wanted her to do."

Like perform the moon ritual.

"Then he put the cantric where she could never remove it."

"Seems like a drastic measure," Tighe said.

"I agree." The Shaman shook out the lace cuffs of his sleeves. "It makes you wonder just how hard she fought him for him to resort to such a measure."

"Was she a slave, then?" Tighe asked. "To her own people?"

Paenther's hands fisted at his sides. "To one person, I think." *Birik.* Goddess, he didn't know what she was. He didn't know anything anymore. She'd shown all the signs of a woman abused. But then during that nightmare of a ritual, she'd seemed completely involved in the slaughter and the sex, taking him inside her against his will, and he'd believed what Vhyper had told him, that it was all a ploy to gain his cooperation. But when he thought back on that night, he remembered how tight she'd been even after Birik had attempted to ready her. He'd assumed that proved her interest in him had been faked. Now he was beginning to realize their mating had been as against her will as it had been his own.

Paenther looked down at the ravaged, delicate beauty as if seeing her clearly for the very first time. *Eight years old.* She'd fought Birik like a panther cub. Why?

But he knew. She'd fought him over the animals.

He looked up at Lyon. "She's an enchantress."

"What's an enchantress?" Kara asked.

The Shaman answered. "The enchantress is one of the truest of the nature spirits the Mage evolved from. There are few left. I've seen them attract birds or butterflies. Occasionally bees. For this one to affect *your* animals is extraordinary."

"What function did she perform for the Mage, B.P.?" Lyon asked.

"I'm not sure. She called animals from the forest, five or six at a time. Birik sacrificed them, drenching her in their blood while she . . . performed . . . a ritual. It was through the power of that ritual that Birik was able to free three wraith Daemons from the blade."

The Shaman frowned. "Sacrifices are used to call forth dark power. Killings like that would go against the very nature of a true enchantress."

Paenther nodded. "Hence the punishments loaded into her cantric." It was suddenly so clear. And yet not clear at all. Just because she hadn't wanted to kill the animals she took from the forest didn't mean she held any love for the Ferals and Therians, the natural enemies of her people.

"Why are our animals reacting to her like they are if she supposedly attracts creatures?" Tighe asked.

The Shaman turned to him thoughtfully. "I'm not sure. They may simply be reacting to your own rampant distrust of what she is. Or they may sense something in her they don't like. Be very careful. There's no telling what else has been loaded into that cantric. She could be a danger to you without ever meaning to be."

Lyon grunted. "You think he could try to use her as a weapon."

"I'm saying anything is possible. Just be very careful."

Paenther looked up at the smaller man. "Is there a way to clear the cantric of its magic?"

"Not as long as the one who wove the spells still lives."

"He lives. For now."

When he was sure the cutting was done, Paenther pulled out a knife and cut the ropes off her wrists. Then he scooped her into his arms and stood.

"Putting her in a different cell?" Lyon asked.

"No. She's staying with me."

Lyon's mouth tightened. "You heard what the Shaman said. Just because she's fought Birik in the past doesn't mean she's not dangerous now."

"I heard. But I owe her this."

"How can you owe her anything? She's a witch, B.P."

He met his chief's gaze. "I haven't forgotten. But she's earned an open mind, and I intend to give it to her."

"You can do it down here."

Paenther shook his head, turned and walked away. Logically, he knew Lyon was right. She was still potentially dangerous, whether or not she meant to be.

But the protectiveness he'd been struggling with since the first time he saw her had gone into hyperdrive.

"B.P. . . ."

"See you in the morning, Roar."

As Paenther carried her into the showers off the gym, he accepted the probability of what his gut had been telling him for some time, now. That she wasn't his enemy. That she had never been his enemy. That she had, in fact, been every bit as much a captive of Birik as he'd been. For so much longer.

Stepping into the open showers, he turned on one of the faucets. When the water ran warm, he tucked Skye's head against his shoulder and stepped under it, fully clothed. For a long time, he stood beneath the warm spray and held her, thinking of all the things she'd told him, all the evidence of abuse he'd seen. And the deep sadness that seemed to be etched into her eyes.

Yet not once had he seen her cower. And while she must have known Birik's fury would be terrible if she freed her Feral captive, she'd done it anyway. He might have saved her from Birik's immediate retribution, but he'd forced her to suffer another.

Her strength in the face of such violent mistreatment had made it possible for him to believe Vhyper's assertion that she'd been a willing and cunning participant in her own beating. Yet deep down, even then, his instincts had balked at the claim. There had always been something innocent about her. Something achingly vulnerable.

Now he thought he understood.

He laid her on the bench across from the shower and peeled her soaked dress off her body. His shocked gaze took in the sight of hundreds of fading cuts. Across her breasts and nipples, through her pubic hair and tracing like latticework across her stomach and thighs. How she'd taken such pain without screaming, he didn't know. Had that been another of Birik's many lessons?

She'd been eight when that bastard implanted the cantric in her heart. *Eight.*

He stripped off his own torn clothes and scooped her back into his arms. Grabbing a bar of soap, he sat on the tile beneath the spray, his legs crossed in the style of his tribal ancestors, and gathered Skye onto his lap. Carefully and thoroughly, he washed the last traces of blood from her skin as the cuts slowly disappeared.

Once she was clean, he wrapped her in a thick, fluffy towel and wrapped a second around his waist, then carried her up to his bedroom.

He pulled on a pair of sweatpants and dressed her in one of his silk shirts, then tucked her into bed. As he climbed in the other side, she stirred, her dark lashes fluttering up weakly.

As he met that copper-ringed gaze, a sharp memory of other, malicious copper-ringed eyes rose in his mind, and the old hatred flared.

Her lashes swept down.

"Skye . . ." He reached for her hand, curling his fingers gently around it. "Don't fear me, little one. You're safe tonight."

In answer, she rolled onto her side toward him and reached for him, her palm resting on his chest. The simple expression of need, of comfort, even from the man who'd treated her as his enemy, moved him greatly.

As sleep reclaimed her, her hand slipped away,

so he gathered her up and pulled her into his arms. Just as she'd done in the cavern, she curled around his body, her head on his chest. Paenther held her against him, his arm tight around her, as pressure welled in his chest, a terrible tenderness that eased the rage that lived in his soul.

What exactly was he going to do with her? Even if she was, as he was beginning to suspect, nothing like Ancreta, she was still a powerful Mage. A witch controlled by a man without a soul.

If the Shaman was right about her cantric, she could turn on them without meaning to. Could he really risk the Ferals and their mission for her?

No. And yet. . .

He knew deep down he would never allow anyone to hurt her again.

Chapter Eleven

For a few delicious moments, Skye thought she was dreaming, her body warm and comfortable, a hand rubbing her back with long, gentle strokes. A dream from another time. Another place. But the hand at her back wasn't her mother's. The sound beneath her ear was that of a strong, masculine heartbeat. And the scent that filled her nostrils was lush and male.

Paenther's.

She tensed, her mind scrambling to make sense of her situation. Beneath her cheek, she felt warm flesh, damp from long contact with her own. Clearly, she'd been sleeping on his chest just as she'd done in the caverns, except this time he was holding her.

How could this not be a dream? How was it possible that the dangerous Feral who'd come close to raping her was now rubbing her back with a gentle touch? Even as the notion seemed ridiculous, the feeling of being cared for, even for a moment, was so sweet that it welled up until tears burned in her eyes.

She didn't want it to end. Trying not to move, she fought back the tears, not wanting to weep on his chest and give herself away. The memory of how she got there came back to her slowly. How she'd sat in that prison cell knowing midnight would come, then felt the first invisible blade tear across her cheek. She shivered at the memory of what had come next.

The hand left her back to cup her head gently.

"I know you're awake."

With a sigh, she lifted onto her elbow, swiping away the errant tears, feeling both awkward and wary. Why was he being nice to her now when he'd come so close to hurting her before?

Pushing herself up until she was sitting beside him, she avoided his gaze, instead taking in his long legs encased in soft gray pants, and the hard, muscular planes of his bare chest. She studied the golden armband curling around his arm before finally lifting her gaze to his face.

The moment she did, their gazes locked. Paenther's body tensed, something harsh and ugly flaring in his eyes.

Skye flinched and turned her head against the blow, an instinctive move. Her heart began to thud.

"Skye." His voice was low and pained. "I'm not going to hurt you." But when she felt him move, her heart raced faster. She squeezed her eyes closed, fighting against the instinct Birik had beaten into her, and forced herself to turn back to him.

He was sitting up, now. *Too close.* But there was no violence in his expression. Of course, there was rarely any in Birik's, either, before he struck her.

With a low sound of self-disgust, Paenther turned away and climbed from the bed, padding to the window with the quick, sinuous grace of a jungle cat. He stared out the glass, his hands fisted on the window frame.

"I saw the copper in your eyes, and for one moment, it took me by surprise, Skye. I've had some bad experiences with Mage eyes. But I'm not going to hurt you."

"Unless you decide I'm your enemy."

Paenther didn't reply to that. He didn't have to. They both knew it was true.

Paenther turned and met Skye's gaze, but remained by the window, giving her space. Inside him, the old rage started to rush back in, a rage he'd thought had been permanently carved into his soul until a delicate Mage witch made it disappear every time she slept curled around his body. It had happened in the cavern and again last night. He'd woken a short while ago feeling almost at peace.

But the respite hadn't lasted last time, and it wasn't lasting this time either. Almost as soon as she sat up, the peace had started to fade. As always, he gathered the fury in an iron grip and bound it within his icy control. The last thing he wanted to do was frighten her more.

Even from here, he could hear her heart pounding like it was trying to escape her chest. He'd scared her with the flash of hatred he hadn't even given voice to. A hatred that hadn't been meant for her. And she'd reacted with a look in her eyes like the one she'd had the night Birik had crashed into the room and beaten her half to death.

"Why did he punish you with the cutting?" he asked quietly even though he was certain he knew.

"Because I didn't perform the moon ritual."

"The sacrifice?"

She nodded, drawing up her knees and wrapping her arms tight around them as if she could protect herself that way. In the middle of his large bed, dwarfed by his shirt, she looked small and terribly fragile.

"How often does he make you perform that ritual?"

"Every night." Her tone was bleak.

Every night?

"I find the animals during the day, and he kills them at midnight while I raise the power he wants."

He felt his fists tightening and forced himself to loosen his hands. The thought of her riding that white-haired bastard as she'd ridden him made his skin crawl with something akin to jealousy.

But the thought of him taking her like that at eight made him crazy.

"Has he always been your . . . sexual partner?"

Her body jerked. "No. Sex has never been part of that ritual. Not until you came. Usually, I just dance."

The rush of relief nearly weakened his knees. *"Thank the goddess."*

She looked at him, her gaze probing. Uncertain. "Why?"

"How long have you been doing that ritual for him?"

"Since I got there."

"Since you were eight?"

"Yes."

"That's why."

She stared at him, then looked away, as if suddenly fascinated by the paintings on his wall. There was something about her, a sudden brittleness that made him feel like the wrong word would make her shatter.

And he knew.

"He hurt you anyway, didn't he? When you were young." She didn't react, and he didn't push. "You don't have to tell me, Skye. I just want to understand you better."

Slowly, she turned back to him, in her eyes a strange mixture of pain and strength. She met his gaze, held it, as if trying to comprehend him instead.

"Why do you want to understand me?" *Why are you being nice to me now when you nearly raped me last night?* She didn't have to say the words for him to hear them.

Paenther pushed away from the window and leaned his shoulder against the wall, crossing his arms over his chest.

"You've been a contradiction to me from the start. The forthright siren with the sad eyes who led me into the woods, took me into her body, then enthralled me. The gentle witch who was beaten bloody for not forcing herself on me. My instincts have told me all along that you weren't like the other witches I've known. That you were innocent. That's why I couldn't hurt you, even though the part of me that has always hated the Mage wanted to."

He looked up at the ceiling, remembering last night with a crushing ache. "When I saw the cuts, Skye . . ." When he looked down, he found her watching him with an odd combination of wariness and tears in her eyes. "When I saw the cuts, I knew my instincts were right. Whatever else you might be, you were every bit as much a captive of that place as I was. I judged you without knowing you. I saw the copper rings around your irises and expected the worst from you. And even when I didn't get it, I chalked it up to enthrallment or subterfuge."

He shrugged. "For the first time, I'm listening, Skye. I want to know who you are. And I'll try my damndest to judge you on that and not your race."

The edges of wariness in her expression softened. She brushed away the single tear that had escaped her eye while he spoke and met his gaze. "The first time he raped me was two weeks after he took me from my mother."

Goddess. "I'm sorry." He suddenly wasn't sure he wanted to hear this after all, but he wouldn't turn away from her now. Not after he'd begged her to talk to him. "Why did she let him take you?"

"She tried to hide me, but I wouldn't let her."

"You *wanted* to go with him?"

"No." She released her legs, digging her fingers into her hair and raking it back. "Going with him was the *last* thing I wanted." Her words were hot and vehement. "I don't know how he found out I was an enchantress, but he just showed up one day. I detested him on sight. Even then, I think I sensed he was without a soul. He told me to come to him, and I refused, so he grabbed me. One of my dogs attacked him. A small one, unfortunately. The big dogs were all outside."

She wrapped her arms tight around her legs again, pulling into herself. "He killed her with his magic."

"Again, I'm sorry."

She shrugged one slender shoulder. "It was probably a good thing. It told me all I needed to know about him. That night, the leader of our clan, the archsorcerer, told my mother I had to go with him. Birik was too powerful, too dangerous to attempt to cross. But after I went to bed, my mother came to me and told me to run. I'd befriended a human girl a couple of years before in the neighborhood on the other side of the woods and had played with her a couple of times. She wanted me to go there, thinking the humans might hide me."

Skye shook her head, meeting his gaze with re-membered fear in her eyes. "But I was afraid Birik would destroy my friend and her family as he'd destroyed my dog. And he would have, I know that now. So I hid in the woods by the house that night so my mother wouldn't try to take me away and endanger herself. When morning came, I went to Birik and told him I was ready to go."

She turned her head, pressing her cheek to her knees. "I don't know if my mother ever forgave me for that." Her voice was soft and low, as if she were speaking to herself. "She was so upset."

"She forgave you. Whether or not she under-stood why you did it, she never blamed you, Skye. She only wanted to protect you."

Skye lifted her head to look at him, her mouth turning wry, a glimmer of thanks in her eyes. "I hope you're right. I don't know if I saved anyone in the end. My entire clan may be soulless by now."

"You never saw your mother again?"

"No. I never heard from any of them. They disappeared from my life. I've often dreamed of escaping Birik and going back, but I don't know where they are."

She pulled her knees closer to her chest, her eyes taking on a faraway look. "After we left my clan, Birik took me to the caverns and taught me the chant and the dance of the enchantress that raised my power. They were kind of fun, though I didn't like dancing without clothes on. It was too cold, but he insisted I be sky-clad. Then he took me outside and told me to call the animals. Dozens came. In hindsight, I think it made him angry that I could call them so easily when all he could call were snakes. But he selected a beautiful doe and her fawn, and we led them back into the cavern. I was happy. I'd been scared and lonely, and the creatures comforted me. He promised me I could bring them to watch me dance that night."

His stomach rolled. "He slaughtered them in front of you."

Her mouth compressed, and she nodded. "I went crazy. I refused to dance. I tried to run away, but he beat me. Every night he dragged me back to the ritual cavern, but I refused. He tried one thing after another to punish me. He ripped me out of the plush little room his people had prepared for me and locked me in the cell where you were chained. Then he took away my clothes and stopped feeding me, but still I refused to dance.

"Finally, one night, he'd had it with me. He grabbed me by my hair and dragged me all the way up the stairs to the room where he held the rituals, the stone stairs tearing up my bare back. But I still wouldn't do what he wanted, so he threw me to the floor, followed me down, and raped me. Then he ordered the sorcerers to do the same, one after another, and they did. For hours."

Paenther's scalp crawled with horror at what she'd endured. Fury pounded in his ears, his teeth bared as he imagined ripping every one of those bastards apart with his panther's fangs.

"After each rape, he told me to dance, and I refused. My creatures were standing there, watching me. For them, I never gave in."

He stared at her, in awe of her courage, her sheer determination. *At eight.* "You were a stubborn little thing."

To his amazement, she smiled. It was a small smile. A lopsided one that didn't reach those sad eyes, but it was a smile all the same.

"That night I chopped off my hair so he could never again drag me up the stairs. I've never let it grow long since. For all his power, he couldn't make me dance, and it infuriated him. He chained me in that cell, like he chained you, and used me for weeks, promising it would stop when I danced. Finally, one of his sorcerers came up with the idea of the cantric."

"Putting it in your heart like that could have killed you."

"I was of no use to him the way things were. With the cantric in my heart, the battle was no longer between him and me. It was mine alone. Every night . . ." She closed her eyes on a shudder.

He tried to image that child, that stubborn, determined little girl, suffering that cutting, and it almost brought him to his knees. "Is that the only punishment?"

"No, though I don't know what all he loaded into it. I shouldn't have been able to leave the mountain. Every time I've tried in the past, I've hit a wall at the outer warding, then been consumed by so much pain I couldn't move. I don't know how you got me out of there."

"You were unconscious. If you suffered, I didn't know it." His brows drew down as another thought occurred to him. "How did you get down to the Market? Did the warding extend that far?"

"Only recently. After Vhyper arrived, Birik became intrigued with the idea of seeing what kind of power I could draw from Ferals. Vhyper and I created sparks between us, but they weren't the right kind."

Something coiled in his chest. "Did Vhyper hurt you?"

"No, not really. He kissed me, and I hated it. I've never had an affinity for snakes, nor for the soulless."

"He's not soulless." The words came out hot and fast. But as he watched Skye visibly tense, he forced himself to calm his voice. "His soul is still there. And I'm going to find a way to free him."

She met his gaze. "I hope you do."

Paenther nodded once. He would. "Anyway . . ." he prompted.

"Anyway, Vhyper assured Birik other Ferals would come. He knew you'd come looking for him. So Birik extended the warding to include the Market." A fleeting smile flickered across her face. "It was the first time since I was a child that I'd been able to touch the outside world. I spent two days in that place, watching the television, looking at the magazines, and drooling over the junk food before the day you finally arrived."

"Drooling? You didn't buy any?"

"I didn't have any money."

That simple statement told so much, confirming that she didn't have the power of a witch, to control the mind of a human and take what she wanted. Then again, he suspected she wouldn't have taken even if she'd been able to. Stealing wasn't in her nature any more than the slaughtering of innocent creatures. He wasn't sure how he knew that, but he'd bet money on it.

"How did Vhyper know I'd wind up at the Market?"

"It's the only public building on the mountain."

Paenther considered that. "I won't send you back there."

"I don't want you to." The strength in her eyes hardened. "I meant what I said to Lyon. I won't be used to free more Daemons." Fire leaped in her blue-and-copper eyes as she released her legs and rose to her knees. "I'm not your enemy, Paenther. I'm not the enemy of any of your people. I *hate* Birik. I *hate* what he's doing, and I'll do *anything* to help you stop him. Anything. I know you can never completely trust me, but trust me in this. Please?"

He pushed away from the wall and went to her, as drawn to the fire of her conviction as to the woman herself. She didn't back away when he sat on the edge of the bed in front of her, mere inches from her knees.

"I do trust you." He reached for her hand and took it in his. "But I want you to trust me, too. Trust me when I tell you I don't hurt women, not without certain cause." His thumb brushed the back of her hand, his fingers, caressing the soft flesh of her palm, sending tendrils of excitement snaking along the edge of his flesh. "It may take me a while to get past the copper in your eyes. It's been a symbol of all I've distrusted for too long to forget easily."

With his free hand, he reached for her face, glad she didn't turn away. As he slid his fingers along the silken line of her jaw, awareness rippled through the air between them. "But I won't hurt you, Skye."

To his surprise, she lifted her hand, her soft palm mirroring his, sliding along the edge of his jaw. Her eyes softened and glistened, tightening the band of tenderness around his heart.

"No matter what happens," she said softly, her fingers lifting to stroke his cheek, making him ache with the need to take her into his arms. "No matter what you ultimately have to do with me, I want you to know you're the finest man I've ever met."

He wanted to object. The only thing he intended to ultimately do with her was protect her. But he couldn't make that promise. Not when there were still so many unknowns about her role in all this.

Besides, her words made his conscience rebel. "How can you think that when I've hurt you?" Not only had he torn a chunk from her arm, but he'd scared them both by what he'd almost done to her in the prison.

"You never hurt me without reason. Never for the fun of it." Her fingers slid into his hair, sliding through the locks, making him want to purr. "Even when you scared me, even when I thought you were going to hurt me downstairs, I understood why. What I did to you, capturing you, was reprehensible."

"You didn't have a choice."

She looked away, even as her fingers dug more deeply into his hair as if she needed to anchor herself. Her eyes, when they looked up again, were deep wells of regret. "I did have a choice, though. I almost told you to run that day, the day I led you into the woods. I was terrified of what would happen to you if I captured you. Birik had assured me I'd be able to keep my Feral, that he didn't mean to kill you, but I knew he'd do whatever he wanted. His word means nothing. But I also knew that if I let you go, Birik would only capture another Feral for me."

Her gentle thumb stroked his cheek. Her fingers moved, their tips trailing across his mouth, sending tendrils of lush excitement heating his blood. Her gaze flicked back to his, her eyes luminous, reflecting the heat he felt in his own.

"I didn't want another Feral, Paenther. I wanted you. It was selfishness that made me lead you into the woods that day. I wanted you inside me. And I wanted to keep you."

Her admission probably should have angered

him, but all it did was inflame him more. Because the truth was, from the moment he first laid eyes on her, he'd wanted her, too. His hands slid into her soft hair and he pulled her to him and kissed her, a tender kiss meant to cherish instead of dominate. A kiss he wanted to share instead of take.

His lips moved over hers slowly, sensuously, as he savored the heady brush of flesh against sensitive flesh. When her tongue darted out, he nipped it lightly then stroked it with his own, pulling it into his mouth. Passion erupted, stealing his breath. He needed her beneath him, her legs spread. And it would be so easy. So easy because he knew exactly what she wore under that shirt of his. Nothing. Absolutely nothing.

With a few deft strokes of his fingers he could make her want him as badly as he wanted her. She was his prisoner, now. He held all the power.

And for that reason, he held back. He wouldn't take advantage of her. Not when so many already had.

But, goddess, he *wanted*. His mouth opened fully over hers, his tongue sweeping inside her mouth, drinking the taste of raindrops. Her soft hands slid around his neck and into his hair as she kissed him back, her tongue quick and strong, parrying every thrust.

His breath became ragged, lifting in time with hers until they both sounded like they'd been running hard and fast. He thought he'd happily drown in the taste of her, in the scent of violets.

Her hand slipped down to his bare chest, her touch almost rough as it grazed his nipple, then lifted to his shoulder and down his arm, caressing his skin, molding the muscle beneath her hand.

Over and over, he told himself this was just a kiss. Just a kiss. But the heat built, second by second. If there had been power orbs in the room, they'd have been spitting with light. What was it about her that sent his passion spiraling into orbit and had him flaming like the sun?

His hand moved down to slide over one small, perfect breast. Her nipple pebbled, pressing against his palm through the silk of the shirt. His body surged, hard and throbbing with need. *Take it slow.* But he had to touch her. He had to feel that flesh beneath his palm.

Knowing better than to reach under her shirt if he wanted to retain any scrap of sanity at all, he unbuttoned her from the top instead, two buttons, then three, until his hand slipped freely inside. As his palm cupped that perfect mound, he gripped the back of her head with his other hand and kissed her hard, desperately, inhaling her. *Needing her.*

The feel of her hand on his shaft jerked him out of his insanity even as it threatened to send him over the edge for good.

With a strength born of all he'd watched her suffer, he forced himself to let go of her and take gentle hold of her wrists, pulling her hands to his mouth.

She looked at him, her eyes searching his, heat

and uncertainty swirling in their depths as he kissed her palms, one after the other.

"You don't want me touching you there?" she asked, no feigned innocence in her eyes. Her uncertainty was all too real.

"I'm not going to take advantage of you."

Her delicate brows drew together. "How does my touching you mean you're taking advantage?"

He squeezed her hands softly. "You've had to give yourself to too many people, for too many years."

"That's not true. I've never given myself to anyone. Others have taken. But you're the only one I've ever wanted, Paenther. The only one I've ever touched like that."

Her words tightened the band around his chest and only inflamed his desire more.

She pulled her hands from his, then rose to her knees and cupped his face, looking down at him from her slight advantage. Her eyes held soft vulnerability and raging heat.

"Do you want me?" she asked huskily.

He gripped her waist because he couldn't keep his hands off her. "That's not the issue."

"I think it is. Your body's ready for me, Paenther. I felt it. But I won't push you. I know how you feel about the Mage."

He tightened his grip on her. "It has nothing to do with your being Mage. I want you, little witch. I'm throbbing for want of you. I just think we should take it slower. You deserve that."

Her expression softened, and she leaned forward and kissed him lightly on the cheek, her arms curving around his neck as she turned and brushed her cheek to his, like a creature starved for touch. Exactly what she was, he realized.

He pulled her tight against him.

"I want what we had in the woods that day, before you knew what I was." Her words, against his ear, were but a whisper. She was starting to tremble. "It's never been like that before. Or since. I want you to touch me like that again."

She pulled back where she could face him, looking into his eyes with a trust and a tenderness that slew him. "Please, Paenther? We may never get this chance again. And I need to be close to you."

She was shooting his good intentions to hell, but he was beginning to understand. Yes, she'd been used, but the worst thing Birik had done to her was isolate her. From kindness and comfort. From tenderness and touch. She'd had her animals, briefly, before they were slaughtered each night. But she'd lacked the touch of her own kind.

He remembered the way she'd crawled up beside him on the stone slab. Even after he'd attacked her and torn a chunk from her arm, she'd curled around him in sleep. She'd almost never been in that room that she hadn't been touching him.

She might not be Feral, with his own animal need for physical contact, but she was more at one with the animal world than most. And she clearly hungered for that contact.

With him.

The softness toward her expanded inside him, swelling, giving birth to a tenderness he wasn't sure he could contain. Without a doubt, she was casting a spell over him, weaving a net around his heart. A net he wasn't entirely sure he wanted to escape.

"You want me," he murmured against her temple. His hand slid down her hip, to the hem of the shirt that covered her.

"Yes, Paenther. *Yes.*"

His fingers curved around her warm thigh, then started a soft, sensual climb to her heat.

Chapter
Twelve

Skye curled her hands behind Paenther's neck as his warm fingers slid up her bare thigh and curved around her hip. She'd begged him to touch her again, to take her in the most basic way. Her body quaked with anticipation even as her heart swelled with a raw affection for this man who had so many reasons to hate her yet treated her with more caring, more gentleness, than anyone since her mother.

She pulled back, her gaze caressing the strong lines of his face, those high cheekbones and the feral slashes across his eye, then dipped to his mouth. Her own lips parted, longing to feel his again.

As if reading her mind, he leaned forward. She met him halfway, melding her mouth with his, shoving her tongue into his mouth even as he shoved his into hers. She craved his kiss and his touch. Three times he'd come inside her, but only one of those times had he been free to touch her. Only that time in the woods when she'd captured him, and it had all happened too fast.

"Lift up," he murmured against her mouth, as his hands gripped her hips on either side and lifted her off her heels.

Skye pulled back from his kiss, watching his dark, passion-filled eyes.

"Spread your knees for me, Beauty. Let me touch you."

Thick, damp heat gathered low inside her as she did what he asked, her gaze locked on his as she curved her hands over the thick muscles of his bare shoulders to steady herself. She held on to him as his hand traveled from her hip to her stomach, then slowly down.

As her breath caught with frantic anticipation, his other hand slid inside her shirt and covered her breast, setting fire to the sparks already consuming her. She gasped, her fingers digging into his shoulders as his own finger and thumb plucked at her nipple, drawing hot gasps of pleasure from her throat until she was leaning into his touch, silently begging for more.

The hand on her stomach slid down into her curls before sliding lower, straight to the source of her heat. As a single finger teased the hot core of her pleasure, her hands slid into his hair, and she grabbed his head, holding on against the torrent of sensation. His finger stroked between her legs, flicking the center of her heat over and over until she was moaning and rocking against his hand. Then his finger slid deep inside her, curling against her inner walls, circling the edges of her sheath, around and around, harder, faster, until she felt she was spinning in the eye of a storm.

"Paenther."

A second finger dove inside her, both shoving deeper still as she pressed her hips down, groaning with pleasure.

Paenther's head dipped, his mouth on her breast. No one had ever touched her like this. No one had ever tried to give her pleasure at all. No one but Paenther.

As he sucked on her breast, one hand pressed against her back, holding her close as the fingers of the other pressed deep into her body until she was moaning, lost in the whirlwind of sensation.

Paenther's warm mouth released her breast, moving slowly to her chest and her shoulder. He pulled her closer as his mouth went to her neck. His hand slid into her hair, and he cradled her head, tilting it away to give him full access to her throat.

A thrill of danger danced down her spine at the thought of how vulnerable she was. If he changed into the half animal who'd ripped open her arm, he could kill her. Then again, with his vastly superior strength, he could have killed her at any time.

She trusted him. For now, in this moment, she trusted him.

As he kissed her neck, she rode his fingers, gasping, straining toward release, certain the pleasure couldn't get any sharper. His hand slid around the back of her neck as his kisses moved to her ear, and she shuddered with delight.

He pulled his fingers out of her suddenly, and she groaned. *"Paenther."*

"Shhh, Beauty. Patience." He grabbed the hem of her shirt and pulled it off over her head in one impatient tug, then moved away to remove his pants with a sensuous feline grace. His body was a study in male perfection. She'd seen him aroused before, but the sight of him now, thick and long and wholly erect, took her breath away. He was twice the size of any Mage. And she was more than ready for him.

With a low, animal growl, he swept her into his arms, deposited her in the middle of the bed, and followed her down. She looked up into his face, waiting for him to come to her, but he didn't move. For long moments, he looked into her eyes, their gazes twined. She felt herself falling into the black depths of his eyes, spinning head over feet. The sweet pressure in her chest grew until her chest hurt.

She adored him.

If only he could be hers.

Paenther's knuckles brushed her cheek as he stared down at her, then he dipped his head and claimed her mouth, and the passion exploded all over again.

His soft hair caressed her cheeks as his hand slid down her hip, to her thigh, and back up again with barely controlled passion. She curled her arms around his neck and held on, but her Feral wouldn't be caged, not even within her arms. He nuzzled her cheek and dipped to her neck, then broke her gentle hold and trailed kisses down her chest, between her breasts, over her belly button, and lower.

The light brush of his warm breath tickled her inner thighs as he dropped damp kisses all the way down to her knees. Then he swung around with that animal grace and knelt between her legs, staring at the flesh between with open hunger.

Skye shivered with anticipation, a smile tugging at her mouth. "What are you doing?"

He met her gaze with a look that was positively sinful. "Enjoying the view." With his hands, he pushed her knees apart until she was fully open to his sight. He reached for her with both hands, his fingers sliding over tender flesh, plucking and tugging until her body wept with need. "Beautiful," he whispered.

She expected him to cover her and slide himself inside her. Instead, he slid his hands beneath her hips and lifted her. "Paenther, what . . . ?"

"Hook your legs over my shoulders, Beauty."

"*Why?*"

The look he gave her was pure cat. "So I can pleasure you. So I can pleasure us both."

Her cheeks flamed, but she did as he asked, ready to trust him with anything. Even this. As she wrapped her legs over his shoulders, he pulled her hips up and closed his mouth over the very core of her.

The intensity of the pleasure made her cry out.

He lifted his head an inch, spearing her with his dark gaze. "Do you like it?"

"*Yes.*"

His tongue stroked her, sliding inside her, then out again until she was writhing against his mouth, crying for release. Her hands gripped the sheets as she held on against the building tempest. His lips closed over the sensitive heart of her, the place he'd helped her discover with her fingers that night after Birik beat her, and she did cry out. The pleasure was almost too sharp. Almost.

He sucked that small bit of flesh into his mouth and teased it with his tongue over and over, driving and coiling the tension in her body until she shattered on a cry of pleasure, her body pulsing and throbbing, desperate to be filled.

As Paenther lowered her back to the bed, she held out her arms to him, her hips rocking with unabated need. For him. Only for him. "Come inside me, Paenther. Please. I need you inside me."

He didn't disappoint her. He slid into her arms and entered her body, his thickness filling her with a delicious stretching pressure. She pulsed around him, thrusting her hips to drive him deeper, needing to be one with this man.

He held himself up on his forearms, capturing her mouth in a drugging kiss as he drove into her, over and over, filling her again and again with a beauty and a warmth. A completeness of body and spirit.

The pressure built inside her, coiling tighter, deeper, until finally the tension released on an explosion of such strength, such richness, it was as if she'd never come before. As her body clenched over and over, Paenther thrust into her hard two, three times more, then on a hard groan of completion, dropped his head to her shoulder.

Tender feelings nearly overwhelmed her as she wrapped her arms around him and stroked his damp back.

If only we could stay like this. Forever.

Finally, Paenther pulled out of her and stood up, scooping her into his arms, startling a smile out of her.

"What are you doing?"

"Getting a shower. Then I'm finding you something to eat. You need flesh on these bones, woman."

He carried her to the bathroom at the back of his room and turned on the water but didn't step in.

She lifted her head from his shoulder. "What are you waiting for?"

"The water to warm up."

"A warm shower," she murmured with pleasure. "The water in my room in the cavern never ran anything but cold."

He kissed her temple. "No more cold, Skye. I'll keep you warm." Finally, he stepped into the shower with her, gently lowering her to her feet beneath the warm spray. But as he turned to get the soap, she slid her arms around him and pressed her cheek to his back, overwhelmed by the force of her emotions.

Tears began to run freely, mingling with the water from the shower. No one had ever cared for her like this before.

She'd fallen in love with him. But he could never be hers. They had no future because they belonged to two different worlds.

No, that wasn't completely true. He belonged to the world of the Ferals.

And she belonged nowhere.

Chapter
Thirteen

Paenther ushered Skye down the stairs, his stomach rumbling for food, his body nearly sated, his mind and heart in turmoil. The woman at his side was a Mage witch. Yet he couldn't deny that he was starting to have feelings for her. He was beginning to honestly care about her.

And how screwed up is that? She's my prisoner, for goddess sake.

Yet he'd discovered a surprising strength in her despite all she'd been through. A softness. A sweetness. And an achingly deep loneliness. She hungered for touch and affection and wasn't afraid to return them. Her arms had gone around him in the shower, and she'd clung to him with a need he was certain had little to do with the body and everything to do with the soul. He'd turned around and pulled her into his arms and held her, just held her beneath the warm spray for a long, long time. Until she'd pulled away and begun kissing his neck and his shoulders and his chest, making him hard and ready for her all over again.

He'd taken her in the shower, holding her as she wrapped her legs around his hips. As he'd pushed himself inside her for a second time, she'd thrown her head back with a sound of pleasure that had moved him more than he wanted to admit.

He'd pressed her back against the warmed tile and thrust into her, over and over, until he'd felt her inner muscles contract around him in a hard, pulsing release. As she'd gasped, he'd followed her for a second time, then stood there, buried inside her, wondering how he'd fallen so completely under her spell.

He was still wondering about that. *What in the hell am I going to do with her?*

They reached the foyer, and he glanced down, unable to keep from looking at her. Yet every time he did, he felt an ache in his chest. Her scent, a blend of his own shampoo and her natural violets, wove through his body, heightening his senses, sharpening the ever-present edge of desire that never seemed to go away.

He never looked at her that he didn't feel something strong and visceral, but ever since he found her bleeding from Birik's curse and had peeled away his rampant distrust, those feelings had been growing increasingly warm. Increasingly deep.

She was lovely, there was no doubt about it, even in his sweatpants, pants he'd had to cinch at her waist with a belt to keep them from falling off her too-slender frame. She wore one of his shirts, a soft navy flannel he'd been known to wear draden hunting in the winter. She'd rolled the sleeves three times and they now bunched midforearm, revealing delicate wrists. She was missing shoes, but he'd have to beg a pair off Kara or Delaney. There was no way she could ever keep a pair of his on her feet.

Even dressed like a street urchin, she carried herself with the natural loveliness of a dancer.

As if feeling his gaze on her, she lifted her hand and tucked a short, stray lock of dark hair behind her ear, then turned to meet his gaze. A soft smile lit her eyes, doing funny things to his insides. Yet he couldn't look at her without seeing the copper in her eyes. And the sight of it dug at him, cutting him with dark memories, whispering of treachery and subterfuge. Foxx had fallen hard for Zaphene. He'd been ready to make her his mate. Yet it had all been a lie. His feelings had been manipulated by Zaphene's magic.

Even though he was convinced Skye wasn't anything like Zaphene, every time he saw those copper rings, doubt whispered in his mind.

He forced the dark thoughts aside, determined to protect Skye from them just as he was determined to protect her from everything else that might hurt her. He lifted his hand and stroked the back of her damp hair, and she leaned into his touch, calming the doubts.

His hand returned to the small of her back, and he ushered her toward the dining room and the scent of roasting meat.

"Are you as hungry as I am?"

"I'm not sure," she said cryptically.

The sun shone brightly into the dining room through the wide, spacious windows, the crystal chandeliers sending ribbons of color dancing over the papered walls. Beatrice's tastes had run toward the palatial. Nowhere was it more obvious than the dining room. The decorating of the house had always been the domain of the Radiant, but though he sensed Kara didn't particularly share her predecessor's tastes, she was too practical and too wise to insist time and effort be expended on the frivolous when their situation was becoming more dire by the day.

If Birik and his master, Inir, managed to find a way to free Satanan, the world as they knew it was over.

Only two men sat at the table eating from the platters of meat already laid out. Foxx and Jag. The others would join them soon enough, as soon as the scent reached the upper floors. Then again, both Lyon and Tighe had mates, now. A warm and willing female in one's bed tended to trump food. At least for a while. And, at the moment, they were the only other Ferals at Feral House.

As he led Skye toward the mammoth table set before the windows, both men looked up. Jag's eyes, as always, were sharp with antagonism. But so were Foxx's. And Paenther wasn't sure why. Until Foxx turned his gaze on Skye, and it trebled.

Out of respect, both stood and greeted him, but it was clear neither was pleased by his bringing Skye with him. And what did they expect him to do? Tie her up and take her food to her?

If she'd been any other Mage witch, that was exactly what he would have done. But she wasn't any other. She was Skye.

He led her to the far end of the table and pulled out a chair for her, putting several chairs between her and the other two Ferals. As she sat, Pink pushed through the swinging kitchen door carrying another platter between her feathered hands. Pink was the size of a person, but her legs were those of a flamingo and her hands and face, though human-looking, were covered in pink feathers instead of skin.

The servant nodded to Paenther with friendly deference as she sat the platter on the table, but when her gaze landed on Skye, her bird eyes went cold. Without giving him a chance to offer an introduction, the bird-woman turned and headed back to the kitchen.

Paenther stared at Pink's stiff, retreating back. Not one member of this household was willing to give Skye a chance. Was it simply because their enmity and prejudices toward the Mage ran so deep?

Please, Goddess, don't let it be because they see the truth I'm blinded to.

He looked down at Skye. She met his gaze with a wry, unhappy twist of her lips. No, he wasn't blinded. They were the ones who couldn't see. His heart had never lied to him. And in Skye, his heart recognized a kindred spirit. A fighter who'd been forced to bend but had never broken. A captive willing to risk terrible punishment to keep others from suffering the terrifying, agonizing deaths they'd witnessed at the hands of the Daemons.

As Pink returned with a pair of pitchers of water and juice, he grabbed two empty plates from a stack in the middle of the table and started piling the fragrant meat on the first. His gaze swung to Skye. "Do you like pork?"

"I . . ." She jerked her head in a small, agitated movement. "No."

Paenther finished loading up his own plate, set it down in front of him, then sat at the end of the table beside her.

"Is there anything here you'll eat?"

She looked at him with misery in her eyes. "I don't eat animals."

Understanding flowed over him. Of course not. She was drawn to them and them to her.

"Are you connected to them even in death?"

"I don't know. It's probably just my imagination, but I can't bring myself to eat them."

As Pink set the pitchers on the table and started to turn away, Paenther stopped her. "Skye's a vegetarian, Pink. Do we have anything that's not meat?"

"I just put cinnamon rolls in the oven for Delaney and Kara," the half-flamingo, half-human servant said stiffly.

He turned to Skye with question, but the glimmer of excitement in her eyes and the fleeting smile on her lips told him all he needed to know.

"Thanks, Pink," he said without turning, unable to draw his gaze from the beauty at his side.

"You like cinnamon rolls," he murmured, his own lips turning up.

Her swift nod and widening eyes pleased him. "I haven't had one since I was a child."

He cut a bite of meat. "Forgive me for eating in front of you, but . . ."

She shook her head. "Eat."

As he dug into his meal, he watched her. "What do you eat in the caverns?"

Her hands gripped the empty plate in front of her, her fingers tracing the edges. "In the summer, I eat berries from the bushes in the woods, and mushrooms when I find them. Sometimes the cook has bushels of apples or nuts brought in, and I'll eat those. Once a month, he bakes bread. Otherwise, all there is to eat is meat."

"I didn't realize any Mage were exclusively meat eaters. The ones I've known were not."

She shrugged. "The meat was already there."

With a stab of empathy, he understood. "They cook your animals. The ones killed during your sacrifices."

Her mouth compressed. "Yes."

He remembered the way she'd stroked the creatures with loving gentleness, and the way they'd clung to her. No wonder she couldn't bring herself to eat them.

No wonder she was so damned thin.

"The current Ferals are all predators," he told her. "Before Kara's arrival, Pink fixed almost exclusively meat, but Kara prefers a variety. And Pink has a soft spot for Kara. Cinnamon rolls are starting to make a regular appearance."

"What is she?" Skye asked quietly. "Pink. She looks like an animal, yet she's not one."

He looked at her curiously. "You don't feel an animal inside her like the other Ferals?"

Skye shook her head slowly. "No."

He was sorry to hear that. "We've always believed her animal had been destroyed but never had any way to know for sure. I'm sorry we were right."

"What happened?"

"She would have been a Feral Warrior, though a decidedly nonpredatory one. The flamingos were always a weak line. When the last of the warriors died, the animal leaped to the strongest of that line. Unfortunately, he entered the fetus of a baby girl. A fetus that was about to split into twins."

"The animal became trapped?"

"Apparently. The girls were born half-flamingo, half-human. Pink's twin was killed in hopes the animal would be free to rejoin within Pink, but it didn't work. She's never believed any animal lived inside her. Apparently she's right."

"She can't shift?"

"No. She is as she's always been. She lives with the Ferals because even without her animal, she needs radiance to thrive."

"And she needs a safe place to live out of the sight of others."

Paenther nodded. "Yes."

A movement in the doorway had them both looking up. Tighe and his new mate strolled into the room. Delaney wore black pants and a white shirt, a gun strapped to her waist. Her sharp, dark gaze lit on Skye with interest.

Tighe's expression turned into a scowl. His arm slid around Delaney's waist. "Let's grab our breakfast and eat outside. It's a nice morning."

Skye looked down at her empty plate as if she'd been slapped. Again, Paenther found himself feeling bad for her. Whether or not the animosity was deserved, living with it so constantly had to be getting on her nerves. It was sure as hell getting on his.

Delaney turned to Tighe, her gaze utterly serious. "Is she that dangerous? Do you think she'll hurt me if I sit at the table with her?"

Tighe growled low in his throat. "If I thought she'd hurt you, she'd already be dead."

The woman's serious expression dissolved into a smile. "Then I'll eat in here. I'm curious about her."

Tighe frowned. "D . . . you're too damned curious about everything." But as Delaney slipped out of his hold, he let her go. "Don't touch her. They usually enchant through touch."

Paenther rose as he watched the woman approach, her manner forthright and fearless, interest to the point of excitement glittering in her eyes. She reached for the chair directly across from Skye, but Tighe nudged her down one. With a roll of her eyes, she turned to Paenther and thrust out her hand.

"Good morning, Paenther."

With amusement, he shook her hand. "Good morning, Delaney."

As Paenther greeted Tighe in the traditional manner, Delaney took her seat, leaning forward with her arms folded in front of her. The gaze she leveled on Skye was neither friendly nor antagonistic but purely assessing.

"We haven't been properly introduced. I'm Delaney Randall."

Paenther watched Skye meet the other woman's gaze with wariness and a touch of vulnerability that tugged at him. No doubt, she expected more animosity. But she lifted her chin and met Delaney's gaze head-on.

"I'm Skye."

"Do you have a last name?"

Skye shook her head. "There aren't enough Mage to warrant two names unless we live among the humans."

Delaney nodded, glancing at Tighe and Paenther as they took their seats. "Same with the Therians, right?"

Tighe's wary gaze moved between the two women, clearly reluctant to be drawn into this discussion.

Delaney's none-too-subtle jab of her elbow to his arm elicited a grunt from the warrior and a stiff reply. "Most Therians take two names because they *do* live and work among the humans. The Ferals don't."

Delaney's gaze swung to Tighe. "Then why does your driver's license say you're John Tighe?"

Tighe lifted a brow. "You've been in my wallet?"

She grinned at him. "I'm FBI. You know full well I'm snooping around every chance I get."

Tighe hooked his arm around her neck and pulled her close for a quick kiss to her temple.

"And I'm going to have to put up with this for eternity?" His voice was low, the look in his eyes full of such love that Paenther lost the last of his doubts about why his friend had taken the woman as his mate. Tighe had clearly found his match.

"We've all taken John as a first name for the purposes of the licenses. Among other aliases."

Delaney rolled her eyes. "It's a good thing I'm on your side, now. I'm learning way too much." She turned to Skye. "So, you're really a witch?"

"I'm a Mage, although female Mages are often called witches." Her mouth turned rueful. "Few of us have hooked noses with warts on the ends, though."

The touch of wry humor in her voice surprised him.

Delaney's eyes lit. "So you don't fly around on a broomstick?"

To his amazement, an answering smile twitched at the corners of Skye's mouth. "No broomsticks. Unfortunately, no flying. I *wish* I could fly."

"Me, too. What about that . . ." Delaney lifted her finger to the end of her nose and wiggled it.

The small burst of laughter, sweet and genuine, that erupted from Skye's throat almost seemed to startle her as much as it did Paenther.

"Bewitched!" The delight in Skye's eyes entranced him. "I loved that show when I was a little girl. The way Samantha could make things appear and disappear with the click of her fingers or a wiggle of her nose. Even Tabitha could do it!"

"Oh my God, did you ever see the episode where Tabitha . . ."

As the smell of cinnamon rolls began to fill the dining room, Paenther met Tighe's gaze as the two women talked about a television show he'd never seen, nor had ever cared to. Tighe was looking decidedly unhappy with the enthusiasm with which his mate was embracing the conversation with the witch. His friend's wary gaze turned back to Skye and stayed, like a man prepared to defend his mate against a wild and dangerous beast.

As much as he hated that Skye had to endure the constant distrust, he couldn't blame Tighe. Few Therians ever found a mate worth binding themselves to for an eternity. None of the other current Ferals ever had except those chosen as the mates of the Radiants. Lyon for Kara and Wulfe for the now-deceased Beatrice. While Lyon seemed happy with the choice, Wulfe never had even though those pairings were supposed to be as perfect as any pairings ever made.

Now there was Tighe.

Paenther shook his head, watching the play of possessiveness, unable to fathom caring so deeply about one woman that he would be willing to forsake all others for eternity. But as his gaze turned back to Skye, to the fragile pleasure lighting her face as she talked about the old television show, he could . . . almost . . . understand. Every now and then, a woman had a way of changing everything.

Her eyes positively danced as she leaned forward, deeply engrossed in her discussion with Delaney, a self-deprecating smile lifting her lips.

"I used to complain bitterly to my mother about the unfairness of being a real witch and not being able to do any of those cool things."

Delaney watched her intently, her smile bemused. "You can't do *any* of those things? Then what can you do?" Her gaze rounded on Tighe. "There has to be a reason everyone's so afraid of you."

The delight slowly drained from Skye's expression. "The Mage I grew up with could do little more than simple spells and charms, lighting lightwicks . . ." Her hand lifted and twirled in the air. "Floating candles, basically. And increasing the yield of the garden or healing minor sickness. Some had other gifts, the gift of foresight or the ability to read another's mind. None of those was any real danger to the Therians except for the ability to enchant and capture the mind of another with the touch of a hand. A dangerous trick since the victim can be stolen away without effort and made to do anything the captor wishes. But not all Mage possess that ability. I never have."

Paenther stilled. "You captured me."

She met his gaze with a lift of her brow, a decidedly impudent twist to her mouth. "I did." Even as she held his gaze, color began to stain her cheeks. "But it took considerably more than a touch."

The memory of just how she'd captured him, of how he'd slid inside her, had his blood heating all over again.

"I hadn't heard this part," Tighe said, his voice a low rumble. "By the look passing between you, I take it she . . . uh . . . opened your mind for you?"

"She did."

"Without enchanting you first?"

"She hid her Mage eyes, if that's what you're asking."

"It's not like you to get distracted by a female."

Paenther knew that all too well. And yet . . . As Skye looked up at him, as their gazes met, he felt her reach deep inside him and stroke that tight knot in his chest. "I hadn't met *this* female," he said softly.

The soft smile that curved her lips had him longing to reach for her, to stroke her face and bury his nose into the curve of her neck, immersing himself in her scent.

Tighe growled low. "Did you ever consider that she's enchanted you?"

"Of course she's enchanted him," Jag snarled from the other end of the table. "She's been fucking with my animal since she got here. All fucking night!"

Paenther turned, slowly, meeting the hard anger in the other Feral's eyes. It had been a mistake to bring her into the dining room. But he'd be damned if he was going to steal her away before she'd had a chance to eat. She deserved better than that.

"What in the hell is *she* doing here?" Lyon stood in the doorway, Kara at his side.

Paenther groaned, then rose to greet his chief. But Lyon didn't move forward. Instead, he pushed Kara behind him as if protecting her.

Paenther's jaw clenched. "She needs to eat."

"She's not even tied."

"I thought the Shaman bound her magic," Delaney said evenly.

"We have no way of knowing if it was effective."

Jag snarled. "I can tell you right now, Chief, it wasn't. *She's fucking with my animal!*" Jag began to light as if he were . . . *shifting.*

Chaos erupted as the sleek jaguar materialized in Jag's chair. The chair crashed backward as the animal twisted and leaped to the floor.

"What the hell?" Lyon demanded.

It's her! Jag's angry voice rang in Paenther's head

as he was sure it did in all the Ferals'. A shifted Feral was able to speak telepathically with whomever he chose as long as that person was relatively close by. *I didn't intend to shift. I felt her pulling on me, and suddenly it was happening.*

The cat came around the table slowly, his walk stealthy. Deadly. *I'm going to rip that bitch's throat out.*

Paenther shoved back his chair and stood, Skye at his back. "Like hell you are. It's not her fault, Jag."

No? She works her magic, and it's not her fault? Who's to blame, then? Lyon? Kara? Maybe Santa Claus?

Jag's muscles bunched to spring.

"I can't shift," Paenther told Tighe even as he grabbed Skye from her chair and pushed her against the wall, shielding her with his body.

"I can." In a flash of lights and striped fur, Tighe shifted into his tiger and leaped at the same moment the jaguar did, colliding in midair, right over the table. The pair crashed on top of the platters of food, sending dishes, crystal pitchers, and silverware crashing to the floor.

Paenther pulled Skye to the other side of the room as the two big cats fought in a way strictly forbidden by the code of the Ferals.

"Jag, shift. Now!" Lyon ordered.

But the jaguar's only reply was a furious growl as he sank his fangs in the tiger's shoulder and was batted back by a huge, powerful paw.

Lyon turned on Paenther. "Get her out of here, or I'm going to kill her myself!"

Paenther snarled, pulling Skye hard against him, but he couldn't argue. Whether she was doing this on purpose or not, the result was the same.

"The Prisons, B.P.," Lyon yelled, as Paenther pulled Skye from the room. "I don't want her anywhere near the others."

In the hallway outside the dining room, Paenther grasped Skye's trembling hand and saw the fear in her eyes. A fear that echoed deep in his soul. Because whether she was doing it intentionally or through the cantric embedded in her heart, he could not allow her to endanger his friends.

As he led her down the long stairs to the prisons below, he felt his choices narrowing to a dismal few. In a terrible twist of irony, he'd found that rarest of creatures, a kind and gentle witch. Yet thanks to the treachery of her own kind, she was still dangerous.

And a dangerous witch, caught in the Ferals' trap, had only one kind of future. Bleak.

Chapter Fourteen

Skye turned to face Paenther as they reached the prison deep below the house. She was shaking, her stomach tight with misery after what had happened in the dining room. The jaguar inside Jag had been acting increasingly desperate to reach her. Not drawn to her. Not leaping to greet her as the panther was. He'd almost been acting as if he were being pulled against his will, turning him angry. Viciously so.

"I didn't do it on purpose."

Paenther looked down at her, his mouth hard, his eyes grim. "I didn't say you did."

"But you have to think I was responsible."

"I don't think it's you but your cantric that's to blame."

"Why? I mean, why would Birik load a spell

into my cantric that would drive a Feral crazy? He couldn't have expected me to free you, let alone be kidnapped by you in return. It doesn't make any sense."

He opened the door of a cell across from where she'd stayed . . . and bled . . . at midnight. Someone had cleaned up the blood.

He ushered her inside, then followed her. There was a wooden bench in this one, and she sat on it as Paenther stood beside the door, his arms crossed over his broad chest, his body still. No expression crossed his face.

"It might not make any sense, but the only alternative I can see is that you're doing these things intentionally."

"I'm not."

He watched her closely. "I believe you."

She closed her eyes, absorbing the sound of those words.

"But that means it's the cantric." He moved, coming to sit beside her on the bench. "Or something else we haven't thought of."

As he stretched his long legs out in front of him, she turned to him. "What are you going to do, Paenther?"

He turned to meet her gaze. "What do you mean?"

"With me?" She knew her survival was at stake. She *knew* it. And knew he did, too. "I want to help you stop Birik. More than anything in the world, I want that. But I don't know how."

He reached for her, hooking his arm around her

shoulder as he pulled her against him. "I know. I don't know how, either."

"You can't let me go for fear Birik will catch me and use me to free more of those things. But Lyon won't let me stay here, will he? Not when I'm causing so much distress to your animals."

"Maybe your staying down here is enough for now. We'll figure out something, Beauty."

With a gentle squeeze, he released her, then stood and turned to look down at her. "Stay here. I'm going to get you some food."

"I'm not hungry."

He cupped her face with hand. "I'll be right back." Then he locked her in and disappeared down the long passage, leaving her alone and trembling.

For all her adult life she'd longed for kindness. For goodness in another. She'd finally found it and fallen head over heels in love with a good man.

But love was never enough.

Paenther strode through the underground of the house, hating that he had nothing more to offer Skye than platitudes. Lies. Words of hope, some called them.

Hope was good, of course. Vhyper's words, repeated every day of their incarceration three centuries ago, had kept him sane, kept him believing he'd make it. *"We are going to get out of this, we three. Together. Do not doubt it. Do not ever doubt it."*

The words had turned out to be a lie for Frederick, the third of their group. He'd died in that dungeon, bleeding to death from a wound An-creta had inflicted on him just for the fun of it. She'd cut off his foot to see how long it would take to grow back. It hadn't.

The three of them hadn't gotten out of there together. Frederick had never become the jaguar Feral he was marked to be. It was nearly two years later that Jag had finally dragged his surly ass into Feral House and set about turning every Feral against him. They'd thought he'd never show up. To this day, nearly three centuries later, most wished he hadn't.

Frederick, with his quiet strength and dry wit, would have rounded out their team well, but he'd never gotten the chance, despite Vhyper's words of hope.

But sometimes words were all you had.

As he reached the main floor, he saw Lyon at the front door greeting three strangers, two men and a woman. The chief's gaze swung to Paenther, and he motioned him over.

"The Guard, B.P."

The Guard hailed mainly from Europe, trained in the British Isles, and were known to be fierce fighters. He was interested to see the leader of this team seemed to be the woman, a petite female in a trim pantsuit and high heels with flaming shoulder-length red hair.

Paenther shook hands with each of the three. The men both spoke with English accents, but the woman, Olivia, possessed a hint of a Scottish brogue.

As Lyon turned to usher them into the parlor, Jag came storming into the foyer. "That witch has to go! I feel like I've got her magic crawling all over me," he growled, then stopped short as he saw the visitors. His gaze zeroed in on Olivia, his gaze raking her from head to toe and back again. "You'll do."

"Jag . . ." Lyon warned, but the surly warrior slid his arm around the redhead's shoulders. "How about you come upstairs and spread your legs for me, Sugar," he drawled.

"How about I don't." The words purred from her mouth, but her eyes had turned hard as steel.

Jag didn't seem to notice. His hand dropped from her shoulder to grasp her breast. "I'll be good."

"I'm sure," she murmured as she lifted one of her high spiked heels and drove it down hard on his instep.

"Fuck!" Jag leaped back, lifting his injured foot. The look he turned on the woman was pure venom.

Olivia turned so that she could keep Jag in her sights, but glanced at Lyon and lifted one well-arched brow. "As you were saying?"

Paenther struggled to keep a straight face.

"Did I just see what I thought I saw?" Tighe said coming up behind him.

"You did."

Lyon eyed the woman with a bemused look. "I was saying I appreciate your willingness to help. I'll be pairing your warriors with mine, allowing my team to cover more ground."

The redhead gave a decisive nod, glancing at Jag, then back at Lyon. "We'll be ready. As many of us as you need."

"You're one of the fighters, then?" Lyon asked.

"Of course. Do not let my size fool you, warrior. Many have done so to their regret."

Admiration lit Lyon's eyes, and a hint of amusement as he glanced at Jag. "I don't doubt that. I'll be happy for your help. All of you," he said, his words encompassing the other two men.

Tighe chuckled low and glanced at Paenther. "Think Lyon will pair her with Jag? She could sure teach him some manners."

Paenther grunted. "A hundred bucks on the redhead."

Jag glared at the pair of them, growling. All of a sudden his skin began to sparkle with lights. The next moment, a furious jaguar prowled the parlor.

Fuck! Jag's yell roared through Paenther's head.

Lyon scowled and glared at Paenther. "See to your witch."

Paenther nodded and left the room. Tighe accompanied him back to the kitchen, where he was determined to find Skye some food.

"Hawke called while you were downstairs. They're on their way back."

"What happened?"

"They found the farmhouse where we picked you up without any trouble, and Wulfe located your scent. He followed it about four miles, then lost it. They spent all night searching but can't find anything that looks like a cave."

"What about the Market?" They turned the corner into the dining room, where Foxx, Kara, and Delaney were helping Pink sweep up the mess. On the sideboard sat a platter of cinnamon rolls still half-full.

"They can't find it." Tighe picked up one of the rolls and took a big bite. "Mmm, not bad."

Paenther grabbed one of the unbroken plates and loaded it with four rolls.

"They were starting to feel disoriented, so Lyon ordered them back here, stat."

"Magic."

"Yep. Gotta be."

"Dammit. I can find my way back in there. I know I can. As soon as I get these damned shackles off."

"Any word from the Shaman this morning?"

"None. If he doesn't come up with something soon, I may not have any choice but to cut off one of my hands to see if it works." He couldn't shake the memory of Frederick bleeding to death after Ancreta cut off his foot, but Frederick had been two years without radiance. He'd turned mortal, as all newly marked Ferals did if they didn't find Feral House within a couple of years.

It wouldn't happen to him. His hand would grow back. He hoped.

Tighe grimaced. "And if it doesn't work?"

Paenther met his gaze. "If the Mage find a way to free Satanan from that blade, a missing hand is going to be the least of my worries."

He took the plate and started back down the

stairs to the underground, but as he neared the bottom, a strange sensation began to crawl over his scalp, as if something were dripping into his head and spreading, taking root.

The plate of cinnamon rolls slipped from his fingers and crashed to the floor. Voices whispered inside his head on a thick, cold mist as his skin crawled with recognition.

Enthrallment.

The mist rushed in, and he knew no more.

Skye rested her head back against the wall, trying to make sense of what had happened upstairs. A dull queasiness played in her stomach, a fear that if she didn't figure out a way to stop whatever it was and convince the Ferals she could be of help to them, she was in serious danger.

Paenther would protect her as long as he could. But if his chief decided she was dangerous, there would be nothing he could do.

It was as if the animals inside the Ferals were both drawn to her and repelled by her. She'd thought it was simply a matter of confusion on the animals' part by their warriors' animosity toward her.

Unfortunately, that didn't explain what had happened to Jag. She'd felt his animal's pain, in a different way than she'd felt it before. What was worse, Foxx's, Lyon's, and Tighe's animals had all been exhibiting echoes of that same pain that morning. As if something were wrong with them. Her gift should never cause a creature pain. Even if she wanted to hurt them, she couldn't. Not when the Shaman had bound her magic.

She stilled. Maybe that was the problem. Maybe the Shaman had changed her gift in some fundamental way. As soon as Paenther returned, she'd ask him.

The sound of footsteps carried to her. Paenther's footsteps. Her skin heated. Her heart fluttered with anticipation, her chest expanding and filling until the warmth was nearly too much to contain. How had Paenther become her entire world in such a short time?

But as he turned the corner, she sensed something was wrong. His walk was tense. His expression hard. And he'd come without the food he'd promised her.

"What's the matter?" she asked as he unlocked her cell, his gaze fixed on the task.

"We have to go."

"Why?" She wiped suddenly damp palms on the pants Paenther had loaned her. Had Lyon already ordered her to be destroyed?

Swinging the door open, glancing back over his shoulder, he reached his hand out to her. She placed her hand in his and followed him through the passage and into the gym.

"Can you tell me what happened, Paenther?" Her heart was beginning to race with fear.

He didn't reply. When they reached the hallway that led to the stairs, he instead led her to a pair of double doors. Releasing her hand for just a moment, he unlocked the doors and swung one open only enough for the two of them to slip through, then he closed it behind him.

He grabbed her hand and led her up the wide set of steep stairs. Daylight filtered in from above, lighting their way and glinting off spiderwebs and dust motes.

"Where do these go?" she asked softly. But again, he didn't answer. "Paenther?"

Her heart lurched. Alarms began to ring in her head. "Paenther, look at me." She tried to jerk her hand from his grasp and couldn't. "Look at me!"

Finally, he turned his head, and met her gaze with the eyes of a stranger. Eyes dulled by magic.

He was enthralled.

Birik had come for them.

Chapter Fifteen

Skye tried to yell for Lyon, but Paenther slammed his hand over her mouth before she made a sound. She struggled against him, but he dragged her up the stairs effortlessly, unlocked the door at the top, and pulled her into the harsh sunlight.

Birik couldn't be calling Paenther all the way from the mountains. He must have come for Paenther himself or sent one of his minions. Now they waited for them, calling to Paenther through his shackles.

No, she would *not* go back there! Every time she closed her eyes, she saw that Daemon again, ripping those poor people to shreds. Worse, much worse, was the thought of Paenther chained again, back under Birik's control.

Her mind screamed. Birds took flight, rattling

the trees around them. Dogs howled in the distance, feeling her distress. Her magic being bound seemed to have no effect on her ability to call the animals.

Paenther dragged her through the tree-filled backyard, one hand over her mouth, one hand firm on her arm. She struggled, desperate to get away, but he only lifted her off the ground and carried her as if she weighed nothing.

She had to do something! She couldn't let this happen.

But the only ones who'd ever come to her call were animals. And not even a large dog was likely to be able to stop this man.

She stilled. But there were other animals in these woods. Animals that were also men.

Praying the Ferals' animals would hear her distress, she opened her mind and heart and sent her plea out into the wind.

Within moments, animals began to appear. Squirrels scampered through the underbrush, a groundhog waddled out from behind a nearby bush, and birds of every kind and color appeared, landing in nearby trees.

Dozens of creatures came to her call.

But the animals she needed to hear her, the only ones who could stop Paenther and keep them from becoming prisoners all over again, weren't among them.

Lyon shook hands with each of the Guard and finally their lead, Olivia. "Where are you staying?"

"At the Bethesda Therian enclave," she replied with that hint of a Scottish brogue.

Lyon nodded. "I'll be in touch." Just as soon as he figured out what to do with Paenther's damned witch. He reached for the door and stopped mid-move as his beast leaped within him, lifting his head on a roar of distress. A second later, a strange blast of energy hit him. The power rushed over him, *power he hadn't called*, and he felt himself shifting. He struggled against the magic and failed.

Son of a *bitch*.

His line of sight dropped as he shifted into his animal form, a large, full-maned African lion.

One of the Guards crowed. "Brilliant!"

What the hell? Tighe's voice roared in his head. *I just shifted. And I can't shift back!*

Lyon growled angrily from his lion's throat. *That witch has got to go.*

"Tighe!" Delaney's voice rang down the stairs. As the huge tiger ran into the foyer, his mate raced toward them.

"I just saw Paenther and Skye out our window. He's carrying her off through the backyard, his hand over her mouth. She's struggling."

Something's seriously screwed up here, Tighe muttered.

Lyon had to agree. *Olivia, I'd appreciate it if you'd stick around. We may need you.* To Tighe he said, *Let's go.*

Delaney ran for the back door and threw it open, then stood back as Lyon ran through, the tiger close behind him. As he ran into the yard, he called to his mate.

Kara, lock the doors and stay in the house. We've got a problem.

He heard her groan. *I wish I could say that's a surprise. Be careful, Lyon.*

Always, little Radiant.

Through the trees, he caught a flash of color. Paenther and the witch. As Delaney said, it appeared Paenther was dragging her against her will.

The little witch bitch is at it again, Jag drawled, joining them in his jaguar form.

Where's Foxx?

He left for the store a little while ago. Hopefully, he was out of reach of that blast.

Lyon had to agree.

The cats ran on all fours, their sleek animal bodies eating up the distance in a handful of seconds. It was rare for Lyon to run free in his full lion form, and the power of its body filled him with a rush rivaled only by the joy he found in Kara's arms.

The cats circled around the fleeing pair and cut them off. *Stop, B.P.,* Lyon demanded, but the Feral only tried to push around him. *Paenther!*

His eyes don't look right, Roar, Tighe said.

And they didn't. They were unfocused. Paenther was almost certainly enthralled. Yet the witch wasn't leading him away. Instead, she seemed to be fighting him with every ounce of strength she possessed. When had his well-ordered world turned into such a mire of chaos?

We're going to have to take him down, he told Tighe. *Don't kill her until I know what she's done to him.*

Agreed.

As Tighe blocked Paenther's escape, snapping and growling, Lyon circled around. Bunching his powerful lion's muscles, he took a running leap, hitting Paenther full in the back with his forepaws, then flinging himself sideways before he could injure his friend.

The witch rolled free.

Kara, love, we need rope. Olivia, we're going to need your help.

As Paenther hit the ground, the massive tiger leaped on him, pressing him down with his weight.

The witch rose and backed away.

Delaney, don't let her escape. Shoot her if you have to. Lyon speared the witch with his lion's gaze. *What have you done? Why can't we shift back?*

The Mage shook her dark head, her blue eyes wide and confused. "I don't know."

You're failing the test, witch. Give me one good reason why I shouldn't kill you right now.

Tears glittered in her eyes as her hands lifted in a helpless gesture, then dropped to her sides. "I can't."

The wrenching honesty of her whispered words combined with her courage in the face of his threat stayed his hand and saved her life.

But for how long, he didn't know.

Skye stood at the door of her cage, her temple resting against the cold steel as she watched Paenther in the cage across from hers with pained eyes. He was standing in the middle of the cell, vibrating with fury.

"Release me!" he shouted, but in his eyes she could still see the fog of Birik's enthrallment.

It had taken all three of the Therians, Delaney and Kara, and the four shape-shifters in their animal forms to wrestle Paenther into the house, back to the prisons, and into his cage. His clothes were torn and bloody, though the wounds from the cats' teeth and claws had already healed.

Outside the prison cells, the huge cats paced.

The Therians had left a short while ago when Wulfe, Hawke, and Kougar returned. Now the three Ferals stood eyeing the scene with grim expressions.

Lyon came to stand in front of her, his magnificent, maned head shaking back and forth, the anger rolling off him in waves.

If you value your life or his, tell me everything that happened, witch.

Skye straightened, meeting the lion's amber gaze and did as he asked, telling him all she knew. "All I could think to do was call to your animals."

"So that's why the yard suddenly filled with birds," Delaney said. She was standing beside the tiger, stroking his fur. "It looked like something out of a creeper movie."

Skye looked at the lion. "I'd hoped your animals would hear me so you could stop him. I don't know why calling you would make you shift."

Delaney released the tiger and started toward

her, but the tiger swung his head, blocking her way.

"Tighe." Delaney groaned. "Can't you reverse it, Skye?"

"I've tried everything I know to do. I sent the other animals away, but doing so had no effect on the Ferals."

Even her gift had turned on her.

Paenther heard the voices as if from a distance interspersed with the growls and roars of the Ferals' animals.

Delaney's voice rang sure and clear. "Jag shifted accidentally at breakfast, but he was able to shift back after a few minutes."

"Has Jag spent more time around the witch than the rest of you?" the Shaman asked.

"Skye spent the night in Paenther's room," Kara said. "And Paenther's room is next door to Jag's."

"This is clearly the witch's doing," the Shaman muttered. "The question is how is she doing it? Jag, let me touch your head."

Slowly the fog of enchantment encasing Paenther's head began to lift, and he became aware of his surroundings. He was standing at the bars of one of the prison cells, his hands tied behind him. Feral animals paced just outside his cell, while Wulfe leaned against the wall, and Delaney stood with the tiger.

The Shaman had his hand on the jaguar. "Interesting. I feel the enchantress's call trapped within strong ropes of magic. Magic that's not hers."

Paenther's gaze caught on Skye leaning against the back wall of the cell opposite him, as if she would get as far away from what was going on as she could.

Skye. "What did you do to me?" He said the words quietly, but her eyes widened and she flew to the bars of her own cage, her gaze reaching for him.

"You're back."

He shook his head, trying to clear it. "What happened?"

What do you remember? Lyon's voice sounded in his mind.

He thought about it for only a moment. "I was getting Skye's cinnamon rolls. I dropped them."

Wulfe grunted. "I wondered why there were sweet rolls on the stairs."

You were enthralled, B.P., Lyon said. *The witch claims your shackles are to blame, that Birik called you through them.*

"From the mountain?" he asked incredulously.

No, the Shaman thinks he or his men were nearby. Within a mile. Hawke and Kougar have gone to look for them.

"May I touch one of your shackles?" the Shaman asked calmly.

Blinking slowly, Paenther turned around to allow him to grasp the metal encircling his wrist. His teeth ground together as he held control over the old torment of ungodly rage.

The Shaman grunted. "The magic that's binding you in your animal forms is coming from the shackles rather than the witch. I believe it may be acting as a magnifier for the enchantress's natural gift. She calls animals without always trying."

So we can't reclaim our human forms until those shackles are disabled? Jag's voice was ripe with disbelief.

Lyon roared. *Find a way to remove them, Shaman.*

"Trust me, warrior, I've been trying. I'm getting nowhere. I have a way with magic, but I'm not a Mage."

Paenther pulled his hand from the Shaman's grasp. "Cut these ropes off me and give me the knife. I'll get rid of the shackles."

What good is a knife going to do? Lyon asked.

"I'm going to cut off my feet and hands and pull them off. Someone else will have to do my right hand."

Like hell. There's no telling if that will work.

"There's one possibility," the Shaman said. "Though I think it's a long shot."

Name it.

"Mind-skinning."

Paenther groaned silently. Yeah, that was going to feel good. "If you think it'll work, do it."

"I actually have strong doubts that it will work. The very magic we're trying to break will likely keep me from reaching into your memory. But I've yet to find another option."

What exactly are you skinning his mind for? Lyon demanded.

"The spell that was used to lock the shackles

on him in the first place. If I can get that original spell, I might be able to fashion a counterspell."

Lyon growled his displeasure.

The Shaman shrugged. "Do you have a better idea?"

"I do." Skye gripped the steel bars of her own cage. "I once wore those shackles."

All eyes turned toward her as her unspoken offer became clear. Somewhere in her head was the counterspell.

"No," Paenther ground out. "It's too painful."

Skye protested. "It's better than you cutting off your hands and feet."

"They'll grow back."

"I can do this, Paenther."

"It's going to hurt."

The Shaman shook his head. "This may not hurt her at all. Mage minds are built differently. It certainly won't hurt her as it did Kara. Kara's memory had been intentionally blocked. I had to strip away the layers of magic to reach what we needed. I shouldn't have to do that with the witch. I'll simply be accessing a memory no longer within easy reach of her conscious mind."

"See?" Skye cocked her head at him. "Easy."

He didn't like it. What if the Shaman was wrong? He trusted the man implicitly when it came to all things Feral or Therian, but the man hated the Mage. What if he hurt her, intentionally or not?

And yet . . . he clenched his teeth against the pain as he stared at the lion, tiger, and jaguar pacing in front of his cage. A cage he wasn't likely to get far from after what just happened. There was so much more at stake here.

"You're not doing it unless I'm with her."

Agreed, Lyon said. *Wulfe?*

Wulfe took a key off the hook and opened Paenther's cage. He pulled a switchblade from his pants pocket, and Paenther turned to allow him access to his ropes. As the ropes fell free, Paenther turned and greeted his friend properly, then pushed past him to go to Skye.

The moment he entered her cell, she slid into his arms. He pulled her tight, cradling her head against his shoulder as his hand burrowed into her hair.

"Tell me what happened, Beauty." As she quickly caught him up, he held her, stroking her, feeling her tremble. "Easy, little one." But he couldn't blame her for being afraid. Not with the beasts pacing outside her cage, eyeing her as if they meant to make her their next meal.

They wouldn't, of course. They'd damn well better not even be thinking about it. With a low growl, he dipped his head and captured her mouth, claiming her. Marking her in front of his brothers. *She's mine.*

The kiss eased his soul, and it was with reluctance that he drew back, cupping her face gently, briefly, before he turned on the Shaman with a fierce, animalistic growl.

"You hurt her, you die."

Skye touched his arm. "Paenther, it's okay. I can handle it."

"I've seen what you can handle." His hard gaze never left the Shaman. "But he has a deep-rooted prejudice against Mage, and I'd hate for it to creep into his actions here."

To his credit, the Shaman met his gaze with perfect calm. "I vow to you, I'll not intentionally harm her. I've never mind-skinned a Mage, warrior. I cannot be certain of the outcome. In any way."

Paenther growled, but nodded. "Do it."

The Shaman turned to Skye. "Lie down."

Paenther held her hand as she lowered herself to the stone floor. As the Shaman knelt at her head, Paenther squatted at her side, stroking his thumb over her fingers where they curled around his.

The pain tore at his flesh, but his only concern was for Skye. He held her tight as the Shaman gripped her head in his hands. He'd been there when the Shaman skinned Kara's mind. The pain . . . *goddess, the pain*. He'd already seen Skye in pain when he still thought she was against him, and every time it had nearly killed him. He wouldn't be able to stand it again. Not when she was coming to mean too much to him.

As the Shaman began to chant, Paenther steeled himself for the first wave of agony to hit her.

"How far back, witch?"

"Skye," Paenther snapped. "Her name is Skye."

"How old were you, Skye?" the Shaman asked.

"Eight."

The thought of her stretched out on that rock like he'd been, *abused* . . . Paenther's hand clenched hers. Birik was going to die.

Her hand spasmed around his, her mouth tightening as her entire body went rigid.

"It hurts," he growled.

Skye squeezed his hand. "It's okay."

"Like hell."

"I'm going to open your memories of that time, Skye. They may swallow you at first, pulling you back there, but we'll bring you forward again when it's done. It's up to you to find the spell. Find it and repeat it. Are you ready?"

"Yes."

The Shaman resumed his chanting, different though equally unintelligible words, then stopped abruptly. "We should be there."

Skye's body went rigid.

"How old are you, Skye?" the Shaman asked.

"Eight." Her voice had changed. It was higher. Younger. As he watched her face, her bottom lip began to quiver, tears springing into her eyes. "I want my mother."

She sounded . . . eight. For one horrible moment, he glimpsed the little girl she'd been.

"Skye," the Shaman said, his tone surprisingly gentle. "Are you still wearing the shackles?"

"Yes."

"Has he put the cantric in you, yet?"

"I'm not . . . big enough for a cantric." Her eyes went wide with fear. "He's coming. I hear him coming." Her voice broke. "He's going to hurt me again."

Paenther felt her frantic grip on his hand and stroked her head, hating, *hating*, the man who'd done this to her. "He's not going to hurt you again, Skye. Never again."

The Shaman glanced at him, then spoke to her. "Skye, you're a little older now. I want you to come forward a few days. To the day he removed your shackles."

Her skin was cool but damp to his touch as Paenther stroked the short hair off her forehead.

"Are you wearing the shackles, Skye?"

"I don't need them anymore. He's taking them off."

"Repeat the spell, Skye. Repeat the spell Birik used to remove your shackles."

Softly, almost too softly to hear, she began to chant in ancient Mage in the voice of the girl she'd once been. The Shaman took her free hand and curled it around one of Paenther's manacles.

Magic began to dance at his wrists and ankles, a prickly, uncomfortable sensation that slowly began to burn. The metal shackles turned to gold, then bronze in a shimmer of light, the air filling with the smell of heated metal and burning flesh. His flesh.

With a sudden, blinding burst of light, pain roared through his body. He stumbled back against the wall, his vision turning black as the fire from the shackles spread, racing up his arms and legs to consume his entire body in a white-hot rush of agony.

"Get her out of here!" Lyon's human voice roared through the prison block.

"No!" Paenther reached blindly for Skye, feeling her strong, slender arms wrap around him as if she could keep him from stumbling. He locked her against him as he felt the strong hands of one of his brothers.

"Easy, B.P.," Tighe said.

Skye's small hand stroked his back. "You need to sit down."

His voice cracked with pain. "What did you do to me?"

"Nothing." Skye's voice sounded small. Injured. "The shackles are gone."

"Gone?" He reached for his opposite wrist and found . . . nothing. "I'll be damned."

"Kara's going to give you radiance, B.P." Lyon's voice reached out to him from a small distance. "You have to let go of the witch."

"Not the witch. *Skye.*" He was finally starting to see through the white-hot pain. Lyon was back in his human form, standing in the doorway of the cell, sans clothes. He met his friend's amber gaze. "You hurt her, Roar, and I'll kill you."

"We won't hurt her."

Skye slipped out of his hold as Kara stepped into his slowly widening field of sight. Kara came to him, her blond hair in its usual ponytail, her eyes worried as she curled her slender fingers around his wrist.

"Ready, Paenther?" she asked softly.

"Do it."

Kara closed her eyes. Within seconds, her hand began to warm on his wrist. With a flash, her skin erupted in an iridescent radiant glow. But instead of the warm surge of energy he usually felt, a bolt of power shot into his wrist, ramming through his body, knocking him back against the stone wall.

The last words he heard as he lost consciousness were Kara's.

"Lyon, look at his eye! *His Feral mark is fading.*"

Chapter
Sixteen

Paenther hit the wall. He felt Tighe grab him as the radiance burst within him, sending warm energy shooting through his body and into his limbs, raking over the pain that lived within his flesh. With a surge of renewed strength he pushed himself upright again, swallowing a grimace.

"You okay?" Tighe asked worriedly.

He shook his head fast and hard, clearing it. "That was a mean kick of power."

His gaze sought and found Skye watching him with wide, worried eyes from the other side of the cell. He held out his hand to her, and she flew into his arms. Pulling her tight helped ease the turmoil inside him, if only a little. It was enough.

He met Lyon's gaze. "The shackles are off. I'm ready to find that cavern."

Skye made a sound of dismay.

Lyon acted as if he hadn't heard him. "Shift."

Paenther growled. "You think I can't shift?"

"Your feral mark is fading, B.P. I don't know what in the hell that means, but unless you can shift, you can't go near the Mage."

"Fine." He thought about stripping so he didn't ruin his clothes, but a quick glance down told him that ship had already sailed. Even his leather pants were half-shredded from the teeth and claws of his brothers. "I'm not shifting in this cell."

With a gentle squeeze, he released Skye. Lyon stepped back as he brushed by him to stand on the stone floor in the middle of the cell block. Stealing himself for the rush of pain that always accompanied his shift, he pulled on the power of his animal, the power that had been as natural a part of him as breathing for nearly three hundred years. And nothing happened.

Dammit.

"B.P.?"

Paenther shot Lyon a glare. "Give me a minute." He had to be able to shift! Raking his hair back with both hands, he pulled, visualizing his beast, straining to reach that rush of pain and strength until his neck and back were damp with sweat.

"Paenther?" Skye's soft voice had him looking at her through the bars of the cell. "Let me touch you."

"Why?" Lyon demanded.

Skye met his chief's hard gaze and answered without hesitation. "His animal responds to me.

I believe Paenther and his animal spirit have always had a disconnect, but the shackles have wrenched them apart to the point they can barely function as one anymore. I might be able to bridge that gap."

Lyon's gaze swung to the Shaman. "Is that possible?"

The Shaman nodded. "I've always sensed a trauma within Paenther's Feral magic, and there's no denying it's gotten worse as evidenced by his fading Feral marks. Whether or not the witch can help him, I don't know."

Paenther held his hand out to her. "Then we'll find out."

The others stood back to let Skye go to him. She met his gaze, uncertainty in her blue-and-copper eyes.

"Try, Beauty."

She dipped her head and took his hand. "I need to touch you. Let me touch your chest."

Paenther ripped the shredded silk shirt off with a single tug, popping the last remaining buttons. Skye lifted her hands and pressed her warm palms against his chest. Almost at once, he felt a calming.

He covered her hands with his. "If this works . . . when you see the lights, jump back, or you'll wind up under me."

Her mouth kicked up at one corner, a small, intriguing gleam entering her eyes. "I rather like being under you," she said softly.

Unfortunately, Feral hearing was all too sharp.

Out of the corner of his eye, he saw a knowing smirk flicker across Tighe's face.

Paenther held Skye's gaze. "All right, let's give this a try." Once more he pulled on the power of his beast, but like before, nothing happened. The fury he kept carefully contained rose, boiling beneath his skin until he feared he would lose control. He was about to push Skye to safety when he felt it. The power rising from deep inside him. A trickle at first, then stronger, building until the shift came on him in a familiar rush of pain and savage, primal pleasure.

Lights sparkled around him as Skye jumped back, and he shifted at last. Being in his animal had always hurt, but it was worse this time. Shifting had never been right for him.

In his panther's body, he stretched and shook, then lifted his head with a roar, feeling an odd pleasure tug on him through the aching pain.

He swung his panther's head to the source. Skye stood beside him like a beacon of light and warmth, a light radiating outward from deep inside her chest, and he understood on a primal level why the creatures of the Earth flocked to her. A nature spirit, the Shaman had called her.

And he knew it was true.

His muscles twitched, his body begging for a good run through the woods, but not only was there was too much at stake to steal that kind of time for himself right now, he could never leave his Mage witch with his brothers.

She wasn't safe at Feral House.

"Can you shift back?" Lyon asked.

Paenther growled. That was the question of the hour. Closing his eyes, he willed himself into his human body. Again, nothing happened. *Dammit to hell.*

I need your help, Beauty.

Without hesitation, Skye knelt in front of him, her hands sliding over his panther's neck, easing the pain and filling him with an odd, intense pleasure. There was nothing sexual about his reaction to her, not in this form, yet her touch flowed through his body, into his soul, washing away the darkness, sending light into those deepest recesses, warming, cleansing. A purifying in its most fundamental form.

He understood now why the creatures sought her touch.

"Try again," she said softly.

And he did. This time, with Skye's hands on him, the power came when he called, and he managed to shift back into a man.

He faced his chief. "I can shift as long as Skye's with me. We'll leave immediately."

Lyon's expression turned to granite. "No way in hell."

"Roar . . ."

"Look, B.P., I understand all too well your need to reach Vhyper and to stop Birik. And I fully support it. But I'm not sending you out there like this. If you come upon the Mage and get separated from your witch, you'll be right back under their spell. Unless you can shift into your animal, they'll just enchant you again. And that's unacceptable."

The fury escaped his careful control. He leaped at his chief, hard in his face. "And what's the alternative, Roar? I'm the only one who can possibly find that mountain. We leave *now*."

"No."

"Roar . . . *Lyon* . . . I'm losing my connection with my animal. Right now I'm still of some use. Let me do my job while I still can, dammit."

Lyon's expression turned hard, but in his eyes, Paenther saw a fierce caring. "No, B.P. Sending you out there like this is sending you to your death. I won't do it."

"Then you're giving up any chance of saving Vhyper. I'm not going to heal. My connection with my animal is not going to get any better."

"Maybe it will." The Shaman's tone, behind him, was thoughtful.

Paenther swung around to glare at the smaller man in his white ruffled shirt.

"You think he'll heal?" Lyon asked, surprised.

"Not on his own, no. But after watching the enchantress, I think she may be able to help him. With the right training."

Paenther scowled. "*Training?*"

"Hear me out, warrior," the Shaman said. "I know someone who might be able to help, if he's willing. A single night may be all it takes. He's an old Mage. Ezekiel. I've known him for a long, long time."

"You have a Mage friend?" Tighe asked incredulously.

"He's no friend, but I trust him. There's never been any darkness in his heart. He never had much power, and what little he had is mostly gone. His mate was an enchantress. If anyone can teach your witch to call the good energies instead of the dark, it's Ezekiel. If he will. After his mate's death, he turned his back on his own race as well as all others. He sees no one anymore."

Paenther scowled. "Then why do you think he'll see us?"

"Because your Skye is an enchantress. They're exceedingly rare, warrior. She'll remind him of his lost mate." He turned those old eyes to Skye. "Call the animals, witch. Not the gulls. Anyone with a slice of old bread can call the gulls, foolish birds. But if you call anything else, he'll respond."

"Where is he?" Paenther asked.

"He has a house in Corolla on the Outer Banks, but only a Mage can see through the warding. You won't find it without your witch."

"I can fly them down there," Tighe said. "It's a good five-hour drive."

Lyon shook his head. "I don't want you near her that long. If you start shifting when you're in the air . . ."

Tighe grunted but didn't argue. The thought of a fifteen-foot Bengal tiger in the cockpit was enough to put them all off flying.

The Shaman tossed Paenther a key. "I own a

safe house a short drive south of there, right on the beach. Stay there tonight while I see if I can make any headway clearing your witch's magic from these Ferals."

Paenther palmed the key, flexing his hand until the metal bit into his flesh. He needed to get out to that mountain, dammit. He needed to find Vhyper.

"Roar . . ."

"*Fuck!*" Jag disappeared in a flash of light, shifting into his jaguar.

"That's an order, B.P." Lyon's gaze shot daggers at Skye. "Get her out of here and get yourself healed."

Paenther pushed Skye behind him as his gaze went from his chief to the spotted jaguar hissing at Skye, his ears flat to his head.

"We're going."

A short while later, they were on the road. Skye ran nervous fingers over the jeans now covering her legs, a fabric she hadn't worn since she was a child. Before they left Feral House, Delaney had insisted on finding her some clothes. The jeans were a little big for her, but a belt and soft sweater hid that fact. Her feet, it turned out, were the same size as Kara's, and the woman had loaned her a pair of running shoes. She wasn't used to wearing shoes and socks, but these were surprisingly comfortable.

She plucked at the jeans, her pulse far from calm. What if this whole trip was for nothing? What if Ezekiel wouldn't see her?

Paenther's hand reached over and covered hers, giving her a reassuring squeeze. "He'll see you. Maybe he'll even help us."

She turned, studying his strong profile. "Are you reading my mind now?"

Something resembling a smile softened his face for one brief moment. "You haven't stopped playing with your jeans since you got in the car."

"What if Inir's already gotten to him? What if he's lost his soul?"

"He hasn't. The Shaman may not call this Mage a friend, but he wouldn't send us down there if he weren't sure of him." He squeezed her hand again.

Skye covered his hand with her other. "I'm sorry I hurt you when I said the spell to release your shackles."

"It wasn't your fault. I'm sure the blame goes back to Ancreta and what she did to me all those years ago."

"What's going to happen if you completely lose your connection with the animal spirit, Paenther?" The thought of it scared her.

"I don't know. Maybe he'll be free to mark someone else."

"Could he mark you again?"

"I don't think so."

"So you'll go back to being Therian?" She rubbed her hand over the back of his, sliding her fingers between his.

She waited for him to answer. And waited.

Finally, she looked at him, at the hard line of his jaw. "Paenther?"

"Being marked by an animal spirit changes you." His voice was clipped. Controlled. Too controlled. "Being unmarked doesn't change you back." He turned his hand and grasped hers, palm to palm, intertwining their fingers. But he didn't say anything more.

He didn't have to. She understood. If he lost the connection with his animal, he was going to die.

Skye thrashed against her bindings, turning her face against the crushing blows of the sharp rocks being flung at her magically by a dozen Mage. The rocks pummeled her, cutting her cheek, cracking her ribs, tearing gashes into the flesh of her naked body until she was struggling to breathe against the brutal pain of the assault.

Even as the stones continued to fly at her, Birik's face swam in front of her eyes, his own sharp with fury.

"Return to me, Skye, or you'll suffer worse. Every time you sleep, you'll live the tortures I have planned for you, until you're afraid to close your eyes. Until you cease being able to tell the real world from the night-mares. Until your mind collapses beneath the weight of the terror.

"Return to me, now. You'll never escape me, foolish girl. Never!"

"Skye."

She came awake with a start, jerking away from the car window, her body aching, her breaths pained and short, hurting as if she'd suffered the attack for real.

Paenther's warm hand curved over her shoulder. "Your heart's thundering. Was that a nightmare, or something more?"

"More, I think. It was Birik threatening me if I didn't come back."

"He can reach you over this distance?"

"I don't know." She pressed her shaking hand to her damp forehead, trying to clear her mind of the nightmare. "He was wearing a green tunic I haven't seen him in for years. And he was taller. Much taller."

"Or you were smaller. Could he have inserted that nightmare into your cantric when you were a girl?"

"Yes. I think that's what he did."

"Will you tell me about it?"

She glanced at him, at the worried look in his eyes as he met her gaze. "I was being stoned. He said the nightmares will get worse if I don't come back, until I can't tell dream from reality."

Paenther growled low in his throat. "That Mage is going to die." His fingers caressed her shoulder. "No one's going to hurt you again. I won't allow it."

His touch was firm and warm, but not even Paenther could protect her from the living hell Birik would make her life if she didn't return to him. Yet she couldn't go back there, not when she knew the use he would make of her power.

Like a wraith, she floated between one world and the other, unable to live in either without misery. If she stayed away from Birik, her misery would be of the mind and flesh. If she went back and helped him free more of those Daemons, the anguish would be to her soul.

And neither choice gave her the only thing she wanted in life. The only one.

Paenther.

Chapter
Seventeen

Hours later, they reached the small town of Corolla on the Outer Banks of North Carolina. The
sun was setting, the sky a brilliant pink and
orange silhouetting the row of beach houses on
their high stilts. The tourists had yet to begin their
annual migration to the beaches and the houses
stood dark and empty amid the sand and wild
grasses of this narrow, windswept barrier island.

Lyon had called a short while ago to tell him
Hawke and Kougar had found no sign of the Mage
who'd called him through his shackles. It was
possible Birik's control over him extended much
farther than they'd believed. Lyon had urged him
to be careful.

Paenther glanced at Skye, who watched out her
window, her fingers laced with his. He still held

her hand. For reasons he wasn't entirely sure of, touching her calmed him. Grounded him. And seemed to do the same for her.

"We're here, Beauty."

Finally releasing her hand, he handed her the map printout he'd pulled from the computer before he left. An aerial map upon which the Shaman had drawn a star in what appeared to be an empty lot a block from the beach. "This one's up to you. If the Shaman's right, I won't be able to see it."

He drove down the road, per the Shaman's directions.

Skye pointed. "There."

All he saw was a plot of sand between two large, dark beach houses set high on stilts. "I'll take your word for it." He parked the car at the edge of the road and climbed out.

As he helped Skye out, she looked up, meeting his gaze, a worried look in her eyes. "The Shaman told me to call the animals, but the last time I did that, I forced the Ferals to shift, and they couldn't shift back right away. What if it does something bad to you, too?"

Paenther shrugged and ran his fingers through her hair. "Don't call so hard this time."

A small smile lifted her mouth. "Okay."

As she closed her eyes, it was all he could do not to lean forward and kiss her. But her magic was already unpredictable enough. Better to let her do this on her own.

Within a few minutes, three feral cats and two

red foxes ran up to her. As she knelt and greeted each one with a stroke of her hand and a soft word, doves and crows and a dozen seagulls gathered around her, several landing on her shoulders and head. She only smiled and reached up to stroke them, too.

A bemused smile on her face, she stood and looked at him. "Ready?" She turned and opened a gate in a fence he couldn't see.

As Paenther followed her through the sea oats, a man suddenly appeared a dozen yards in front of them, fury on his face. Old, the Shaman had said, but like all immortals, he appeared to be no more than thirty. Except for his clothing. He was dressed much as humans must have been in the early days of civilization, in a simple brown belted robe that fell to his ankles. Worn sandals covered the soles of his feet. His brown hair was long and stringy, a short beard covering his jaw and upper lip.

Paenther snagged Skye around the waist and pulled her behind him, birds and all.

"Who do you think you are?" the Mage demanded.

Paenther growled low in his throat. "The Shaman told us where to find you, Ezekiel."

"Little Therian bastard." With a dismissive wave of his hand, the Mage turned away.

"Skye's an enchantress and needs some guidance."

Ezekiel paused, then turned back slowly, eyeing the creatures on her shoulders and at her feet.

Then his gaze rose and widened, looking beyond them. "Well, I'll be."

At the sound of a low whinny, Paenther turned and stared at the two horses. Skye's face lit. As she went to them, Paenther turned a wary gaze back to Ezekiel. "Mustangs?"

"Aye. Only a powerful enchantress could call them like that."

He looked back to where Skye stood stroking their sleek brown necks. Mustangs ran wild on the island, the descendants of horses brought ashore by Spanish explorers around the time he himself was born.

Skye sent the horses away and came back to join him. "We need your help, Ezekiel." Her voice was firm and strong even as her hand slid into his. "Since I was a child, the archsorcerer, Birik, has used my gift to raise dark power. Now he's trying to open the Daemon blade. We have to stop him."

The Mage grunted. "There's nothing I can do." But he didn't turn away this time.

Skye's cool fingers squeezed his hand. "The Ferals will stop him. But thanks to a couple of Mage attacks, this warrior is in danger of losing his animal. The Shaman thinks I might be able to help him if I learn to pull the good energies. I need you to teach me."

"And what is it to me?"

She released Paenther's hand and started to step forward, but he barred her way with his arm. She glanced at him, but didn't fight him.

"Do you know what Inir's doing?" she asked the Mage instead.

He grunted. "Stealing souls."

"Yes."

"He hasn't stolen mine, and he's not going to because no one knows I'm here! Or they didn't," he added with a grumble.

"The Shaman said there's no darkness in your heart," Skye said softly. "I can see that in your eyes. It's been a long time since I've seen Mage eyes with a soul."

Ezekiel frowned, peering at her. "Why are you with a Feral?"

"He rescued me from Birik. I was the only one in that stronghold who hadn't been turned."

"Birik will be after you, then."

"He's after both of us. He used us to free three wraith Daemons from the blade. I've seen what they do."

The Mage muttered something unintelligible under his breath as he turned away. Suddenly, the run-down lot disappeared. In its place stood a small frame structure, far older than its neighbors. Unlike the other homes, it sat only a few feet off the ground as if only grudgingly acknowledging the nearby ocean. Quaint, with two dormer windows attesting to a small second story, it appeared freshly painted and surprisingly well maintained.

"Come in, then," he said with a motion of his hand, and turned to start up the front steps.

Paenther met Skye's gaze. "You did it."

She gave him a smile that was part triumph and part wary uncertainty. She'd gotten them a pass into the Mage's house. What came next, neither could know.

Paenther kept a tight grip on Skye's hand as they followed the Mage up the steps and into the house, but his knife hand remained free and ready.

The old hermit led them through a spare, dated living room and into a kitchen that looked like it hadn't been updated in half a century. "Sit," he said as he picked up the teakettle and carried it to the sink. "Tea?"

"Yes, please," Skye said, sitting at the rough-hewn dining table.

"No." Paenther's reply was brusque, but he didn't care. He was taking nothing in this place. The Shaman might trust him, but Paenther trusted no Mage.

As Ezekiel pulled down two large coffee mugs and placed a tea bag in each, Paenther studied the man, noting the way his hair hung in stringy hanks around his shoulders. Though he carried no scent of body odor, his grooming habits were far from impeccable. One of the hazards of living alone, Paenther supposed.

Ezekiel glanced at him, his eyes sharp and curious. "How did Birik come by the Daemon blade, Feral?"

"Feral House was infiltrated by a Mage witch several months ago. A witch capable of hiding her eyes from us. One of our own was cut by the blade and turned."

The Mage filled the mugs with boiling water, then carried them to the table and set one before Skye, along with a small saucer and spoon for the teabag.

"Thank you," Skye said softly.

"He's lost his soul," the Mage said, meeting Paenther's gaze.

"No, Vhyper's soul is still there. I talked to him in Birik's cavern after Skye captured me."

Ezekiel looked between them with interest. "She captured you? I thought you rescued her."

Paenther scowled at him. "We rescued one another. As I was saying, there's humanity in Vhyper. It's hidden, forced down, but it's still there. I know what I saw."

"That may be." Ezekiel pushed a large platter of cookies toward Skye, then took one for himself. "Terrible sweet tooth," he admitted, before biting into the treat.

As Skye reached quickly for a cookie, he remembered with a pang that she still hadn't eaten. He'd make it up to her. As soon as they left here, he'd buy her a feast.

"I've been studying this soulless plague on and off for centuries."

"Centuries?" Paenther asks.

Ezekiel nodded. "Whenever a Mage gets infected with dark spirit, the cycle begins all over again."

"What do you mean?" Skye asked.

"When Satanan was captured and incarcerated in the Daemon blade, he left behind wisps of dark spirit around the Earth, hidden in cracks and crevices, in caves and within the ground. Over the many millennia since Satanan's capture, most of these wisps have found their way into beings of one kind or another, generally subjugating the soul that inhabited the body and turning it pure evil. Most of these creatures have been human. They cause tremendous suffering while they live, but humans don't live long, and when they die, the dark spirit dies with them. Lamentable, but not a huge problem. The far greater problem comes when the dark spirit infects one of the immortal races.

"It's largely believed that the demise of the Ilina race over a thousand years ago resulted from dark spirit's infecting their queen, a woman of prodigious power who may have understood what was happening and made the ultimate sacrifice in order to keep the darkness from spreading.

"Unfortunately, the Mage have always had a weakness for the dark power. There have been numerous instances of dark spirit infecting Mage over the millennia, with unfortunate results. The worst, though, is Inir, the current Elemental. He was a dark and dangerous soul before he was infected. And I, for one, believe the spirit that infected him possessed more than a trace of Satanan's consciousness. The dark spirit alone merely turns the individual to evil. But Inir has come into possession of vast stores of knowledge that should have been lost eons ago. I believe Satanan is working through Inir to free himself and his horde from the blade."

When Skye grabbed yet another cookie, Ezekiel frowned at her. "Does no one feed you?"

Paenther grunted. "I tried this morning and failed. Birik served her only the flesh of the animals she calls."

Ezekiel stared at her, then scowled. "Birik's a stupid, soulless bastard." He rose from the table and removed the cookies. "Spaghetti with tomato sauce, a large salad, and garlic bread." He peered at her. "Will that do?"

The smile that spread across her face was so pure, so beautiful, Paenther felt his heart seize.

"That sounds wonderful. Thank you."

A small smile breached the Mage's face for a split second before he nodded and grabbed a pot from one of the cabinets.

Paenther forced himself to focus on the man's words. "How is Inir infecting others if dark spirit can't be shared in that way?"

"He's not. Not exactly." Ezekiel turned on the tap and filled the pan with water. "At least not in the same way. I'm still trying to figure it out myself. It's my belief that the stronger souls he's turned will survive the attack of darkness. That in those individuals the darkness is reversible. The question is, how to free them."

Ezekiel set the pot of water on the stove, then pulled a head of lettuce out of the refrigerator and began making a salad. "So Birik's had you raising dark power for him, Skye?"

"He has."

"Moon rituals with sacrifices?"

"Yes. Every night."

"For how long?"

"Decades."

"Have you ever performed the ritual without the sacrifices? The way it was meant to be done?"

"No. I didn't know there was another way until the Shaman suggested you might know."

Ezekiel nodded. "I do. And you may well be able to heal your Feral friend here."

Skye's gaze flew to his, the relief and excitement in her soft eyes palpable. But he found it hard to believe anything inside him would really change.

"You'll stay here through midnight. After we eat, I'll teach you what I know, though I'm no enchanter. My Barbara was the enchantress, you know."

The ache of love and loss in the Mage's voice twisted something inside him.

Skye leaned forward. "Do you think this could stop the Ferals from accidentally shifting?"

Ezekiel lifted an interested eyebrow, a chuckle escaping his throat. "*Accidentally* shifting? This sounds like a story I need to hear."

Paenther stood in the doorway between the kitchen and living room watching Skye as Ezekiel taught her the chants and dance to raise the power she was born to raise. They'd been working on it for hours, but he found, surprisingly, he didn't mind. He felt her joy and her mounting excitement as midnight neared and he felt his own mounting with hers.

If this worked, she wouldn't suffer Birik's punishment. Instead, she would come into her true purpose for the first time. And possibly help him in the process.

A dozen times he'd prayed to the goddess that this would work, that Skye would be free of Birik's punishment.

"Dancing sky-clad, without clothes, is traditional," the old Mage told her, "though ritual gowns work as well if you have one. Beneath the moon is best, but my Barbara drew just as much joy dancing in tents and caves and . . ." He cleared his throat. "The bedroom."

Skye met Paenther's gaze, a small, secret smile lifting her lips, filling him with a sharp stab of pleasure.

"Keep practicing that dance, lass, while I get us some water." Ezekiel's manner had thawed and warmed hour by hour until Paenther suspected his hermit lifestyle was not by choice but just an attempt to stay beneath Inir's radar. The man clearly enjoyed having the company.

Or he just enjoyed having Skye around. A low growl escaped his throat as the man drew near.

His jealousy must have shown because Ezekiel stopped and met his gaze, his eyes clear and honest. "I would never hurt her, Feral. She's as pure a nature spirit as I've ever met. An exceedingly rare creature." He shook his head. "Birik pulled dark power through her night after night for all those years, and yet it never tainted her. There's not the faintest shadow on her soul. She's a miracle."

"You can't have her."

To his amazement, the Mage smiled. "Does she know you're in love with her?"

"I'm not in love with her."

"No?" An annoying glint of disbelief entered his eyes. "My mistake, then." With a nod, he moved past him into the kitchen to get the water.

Paenther growled low. He wasn't in love with her. Of course he wasn't. And it wouldn't matter if he were. She was Mage, for goddess sake. He could never take her as his mate. A Mage would never be welcome in Feral House.

So, where would she go when this was over? She'd already said she had no way to find her family.

Dammit, *this* is where she should go. Here, with Ezekiel. Hidden from the Mage, who would only use her powers against her again.

He should be encouraging the old Mage, not warning him off.

He wasn't in love with her.

But, goddess help him, he'd rather carve out his own heart than see her in the arms of another.

*Chapter
Eighteen*

"It's time." Skye grabbed his hand.

Paenther looked down at her, at the nervous excitement sparkling in her eyes, the sadness all but gone. She'd never looked more beautiful.

Skye looked over her shoulder at Ezekiel. "Are you coming?"

"No, lass, I'll wait here."

Her face fell just a fraction. "I'd like you to come."

He shook his head. "It would bring back memories that are too painful, if you understand my meaning. The last enchantress I watched dance beneath the moon, was my Barbara. Besides, your Feral is a bit on the jealous side. I'll be waiting for you right here."

Skye released Paenther's hand and went to

Ezekiel, giving him a quick peck on the cheek. "Thank you."

Paenther bit down on his jealousy as the Mage smiled.

"You're welcome, Skye."

Eyes dancing with excitement, she turned back to him and grabbed his hand. It was all Paenther could do not to pull her into his arms and claim her right then and there, but he let her tug him toward the back door. He followed her down the steps to the sand, the sea breeze wrapping around him like a cool, damp mist.

She looked up at him, a smile hovering at her mouth. "This is going to work. I can feel it." She pulled off her shoes, then shed the rest of her clothes as the moon broke through the clouds and illuminated the perfection of her skin.

Paenther tried to resist her for three full seconds and lost. He pulled her into his arms and kissed her again, sliding his hand down her bare back to her finely rounded rear as he slid his tongue inside her mouth to taste hints of dinner mixed with the clean, fresh taste of her.

She pulled away. "I can feel it coming."

Watching her begin to turn, her excitement a palpable force around her, he felt his chest tighten until it pained him. She chanted the words Ezekiel had taught her, dancing as he'd watched her practice for hours.

But little by little, her excitement died, her moves losing their grace and turning frantic.

"Skye, what's wrong?"

"It's not working."

"I'm going to kill him," Paenther vowed between clenched teeth.

"No, it's not him." She looked at him, her eyes turning bleak. "The Shaman bound my magic," she whispered, and arched with pain as the first of the cuts tore across her bare chest.

Paenther lunged forward and slammed his thumb beneath her ear, knocking her unconscious, then swung her into his arms, fighting not to roar his fury to the heavens.

"Bring her in," Ezekiel said, sticking his head out the back door.

Paenther struggled for control and forced himself to look down at her, not sure he could watch her suffer again. To his bone-deep relief, only three harsh cuts marred her skin. Knocking her unconscious had disabled the curse. This time.

Goddess, but he wanted her safe. He turned toward the Mage, jealousy fighting with his deep need to protect her. It wasn't like he could ever keep her himself. Even if he wanted to. She'd be better off here where Birik and Inir would never find her.

"What happened?" Ezekiel asked, holding the door as Paenther swung inside with Skye in his arms.

"The Shaman bound her magic so she couldn't enchant anyone in Feral House. Birik planted punishments in her cantric so she'd bleed if she didn't perform the ritual."

Ezekiel growled. "Damn them both, especially

that distrustful Therian. All he had to do was look at her to see she was pure."

"Can you unbind her magic?"

The old Mage stared at her, then shook his head. "I might have been able to at one time, but I . . . no. I don't have that kind of power anymore."

Standing in the middle of the kitchen, Paenther turned to the old Mage. "Can she stay here with you? Will you keep her safe?"

"For how long?"

Paenther felt the words like gravel in his mouth. "For as long as you'll allow. Forever."

Ezekiel looked at him curiously. "She's your only real chance, warrior. Once that damned Shaman unbinds her magic, she should be able to help you reconnect with your animal. Without her, I fear your days are numbered."

"I'll be okay. There's nothing for her back there. I'm not sure I can keep her safe."

"You protect her at your own expense, yet you don't love her?"

"I just . . . don't want her to get hurt. She's too damned fragile."

The Mage laughed. "She may look as delicate as a dandelion puff, but she's strong, warrior. You know it as well as I. I don't think you'd care for her the way you do if you didn't recognize a strength in her that was a match for your own."

Ezekiel met his gaze with a piercing intensity, the wisdom of the ages in his eyes. "Know this, Feral. You are stronger together than either of you will ever be apart."

* * *

It was well past midnight when they arrived at the beach house in south Nags Head owned by the Shaman. The house was dark but not uninviting, with a colorful windsock blowing cheerily from the upper deck in the moonlight. The house was two stories atop the requisite stilts, weathered gray wood siding, each story with its own wraparound deck.

Skye looked up at the house, exhausted and bitterly disappointed the ritual had failed. She'd thought she'd finally found a purpose for her gift, but nothing in her life seemed destined to go right.

Paenther parked the car in the space beneath the house. Part of her wanted to curl up and go to sleep, but she was afraid Birik would only send her another nightmare.

What she needed more than sleep was freedom. She needed to feel the wind.

As Paenther opened her door, she looked up into his rugged face. "I'm going to stay outside for a while if that's okay."

He held out his hand for her and helped her out of the car. "If you can get me back into my animal, I need a run. We can go down to the beach."

She smiled. "I'll get you into your animal, then we'll both take a run."

"You are a nature spirit, aren't you?"

"I spend almost all day every day in the woods. I'm happier outside."

They went into the house, a casual, comfortable

mix of rustic woods and bright upholstery. Three bedrooms took up the first floor. A high ceiling soared over the living areas on the floor above.

Once they'd taken a look around, they deposited their overnight bags in the largest of the bedrooms. Skye eyed the bed with a mix of anticipation and trepidation. Anticipation because she'd be sharing it with Paenther. But beds ultimately meant sleep. And the risk of nightmares.

Paenther stripped out of his clothes, tossing them on the bed. He turned to her, his large, hard body unmistakably aroused.

A small smile tugged at her mouth. "I thought we were going for a run."

"We are." But he padded toward her like the dark, dangerous predator he was.

She glanced down meaningfully. "Now or later?"

A wicked glint shone in his eyes. "Now." But his hands gripped her shoulders and he hauled her into his arms, pulling her against his hard, ready body, and kissed her until her head spun and her legs felt too weak to stand.

His hand covered her breast. His lips left her mouth to trail across her cheek and down to her neck, where he nuzzled and kissed and nipped until her body was hot and heavy with need.

"We can run later," she murmured.

"No." But his fingers went to the belt at her waist and unhooked it. He slid his hand into the too-large waistband, beneath the elastic of the panties. Reaching behind her, he pressed her hips forward with one hand while the fingers of the other burrowed between her legs and slid deep inside her.

Skye clung to his arms, one hand catching at his armband as her knees threatened to give way beneath her.

"*Paenther.*"

His mouth nibbled at the base of her throat. "I want a run."

"You're sending me seriously mixed messages here."

"You make me lose all thought." His mouth turned frantic as the kisses and the nips traveled up her throat to her jaw. "I want you, but I want to take my time."

Her pulse was racing, her body on fire. "Just come inside me, just come . . . inside. Take our time . . . later."

With fast, frantic movements, he unzipped her jeans and shoved them and her panties down to her thighs, then he turned her around.

"Bend over, Beauty." His voice was husky with need as he pushed her down, one hand in her hair as the other gripped her hip. Pulling her close, he took her from behind. His thickness spread her, filling her, as he rocked against her, slamming his groin to her rear. She gasped with the raw pleasure of this basic act, crying out as she came, loving the sound of his pleasure as he followed her over that sensual precipice. When he was through, he pulled out of her, pulled her around, and kissed gently, thoroughly.

Finally, he pulled back and looked down into her face, his dark eyes warm with an emotion that tugged at things deep inside her chest. His hand brushed back her hair, then he pulled up her clothes and fastened her belt. Taking her hands, he pressed them to his chest. "Help me shift, little witch, then let's go for that run."

As she touched him, the animal within him rose and leaped at her in greeting. Paenther pulled on the power and at the same time she called on the animal inside him to help.

In a flash of sparkling light, the man became a jungle cat, a sleek black panther. Like before, she reveled in his beauty, his emerald eyes, his black pelt.

She knelt and stroked his head and neck. "You're magnificent."

As are you. He licked her face, startling a laugh out of her.

I like the sound of that.

"Of what?"

Your laughter. You don't laugh often enough.

She peered into those emerald eyes, seeing the man she loved. "I haven't had a lot of things to laugh about. But being with you makes me happy."

I'm glad. Let's run.

She took off her shoes and socks, then rose and let them out of the house. Together, they ran down to the beach, the cool breeze in her face, the big jungle cat at her side. His presence thrilled her.

When they reached the dune, the panther took off. *I'll be right back. I need to run.*

Skye waded through the soft sand, but when she reached the hard-packed beach, she began to run, too, feeling her spirit briefly soar. The moon shone on the water, making it sparkle and dance with moonlight. A dolphin breached the surf a distance out, calling to her.

She sent love and well-being out to the beautiful creature. A moment later he soared into the air, spinning, before diving back under the surface of the ocean. Two more dolphins leaped, and she stopped at the water's edge and watched them dance for her.

They were so free. So at one with their world, as she would never be with hers. The panther raced back down the beach toward her and came to stand at her hip. Her hand went to his neck, pressing him close.

Did you call them?

"Not intentionally."

Show-offs. He bumped her hip with his head. *I feel your melancholy.*

"I'm fine." She backed up to where the sand was no longer wet, and sat. The panther sat beside her, then lay at her side, resting his sleek black head in her lap. There was something about him, a tenseness, that didn't feel right.

She stroked his head. "You're in pain."

It's nothing. Just another gift from Ancreta.

"Tell me about it. Please?"

The panther made a sound in her head that was almost a sigh. *When my brothers shift, they experience an incredible rush. A joy. I've heard them talk about it a hundred times. Even when they're not in their animals, they're able to communicate with their beasts. They feel their emotions and hear their growls and roars in their heads. They're one with their animals in a way I've never been, thanks to Ancreta. All shifting has ever brought me is pain.*

"Do the others know?"

Only Vhyper. If Lyon knew, he might take me off draden-hunting duty, and I'd hate that. Because even though I feel constant pain when I'm in my animal, it eases something inside me. I need to be able to shift and to run. It's part of me now.

She stroked his neck, over and over. "I have to try to help you, Paenther. We have to convince Lyon to unbind my magic."

We'll get your magic unbound. I refuse to watch you go through another cutting like that. Once you've done what you can to heal me, I'm leaving for the mountains. I'm not leaving Vhyper there any longer than I have to. He never deserted me, and I won't desert him.

"What do you mean? When didn't he desert you?"

The cat shifted its head, resting his chin on her thigh. As his emerald eyes looked up at her, he told her about Vhyper and Frederick. About how badly Vhyper took Frederick's death at Ancreta's hand.

That night, Vhyper shifted into his snake. He shouldn't have been able to without the radiance and Feral magic, but the vipers have always been different.

"They have poison, don't they?"

They do. In the old days, before the rise of the Dae-mons and the subsequent war that ended most Therian and Mage magic, the vipers were the bad boys of the Therian world. They were the outcasts. The villains. Now there is only ever one with the ability to shift, and he's a Feral Warrior. Vhyper is one of the finest I've ever known. The real Vhyper, anyway.

When he shifted that night in Ancreta's dungeon, he shrank his size until he was barely bigger than a worm and escaped unseen. After months of captivity and torture, he was out of there. Free. But instead of taking off to find Feral House as he should have done, he mounted a one-man rescue. Of me. He should have gone to find the Ferals and come back with the might of the shape-shifters behind him, but he didn't know where Feral House was and didn't know how long it would take. Travel was slow in those days, especially in winter, which it was. He was afraid they'd move me, and he'd lose me.

Vhyper risked his freedom, his life, *to get me out of there. And succeeded. Now he's the one trapped. I can't leave him in there. I have to save him as he saved me.*

Skye stroked his fur. "I'm going to help you, Paenther. I'm going to heal you, I swear it. Then I'll do whatever I can to help you free him."

The panther rose onto his haunches and leaned forward to lick her cheek. *Thank you, Beauty, but I'm not letting you get anywhere near that cavern again. My men and I will get him out.*

"I don't think you'll make it through the warding of that mountain without me to guide you."

We'll see. I've promised to keep you safe, little witch. That's a promise I mean to keep.

"I know." She buried her face in his fur and loved him.

Help me shift.

"You'll be naked."

He chuckled in her head. *A naked man on the beach will draw a lot less attention than a black pan-ther. There's no one out here to see, either way. I need to kiss you, Beauty. It won't wait.*

His words brought tears to her eyes. She did as he asked, and a moment later, the man was beside her, pulling her onto his lap and into his arms.

Paenther pulled Skye tight against him as he sat naked in the sand. The night was clear, the moon dancing over the waves as the soft roar of surf melded with the hard beating of his heart. Need poured through him as he slanted his mouth over that of the woman in his lap, kissing her thor-oughly, tasting her, inhaling her sweet scent of violets. The need to touch her, to be close to her, was becoming a craving he couldn't fight. God-dess, what was she doing to him? The more time he spent with her, the more he needed her. And not just sexually. Touching her was becoming as important to him as breathing.

As she wrapped her arms around his neck, he reached beneath her sweater and covered her breast, neatly tucked into a lacy bra. He growled, low, not liking the feel of anything between them.

With a light tug, he pulled off her sweater and tossed it aside, then followed with her bra. Her skin glowed in the moonlight like mother-of-pearl, drawing his gaze . . . and his mouth. He bent his head and closed his lips over her shoulder. She tasted of forests and raindrops and sweetness, and she stirred emotions inside him he'd never felt for anyone.

Her fingers went through his hair. "Aren't you worried about draden?" she asked softly.

"I'll shift if I have to," he murmured, then slid his tongue along the line of her shoulder and slowly up her neck, drawing a gasp and a hard shiver from her. Skye was in no danger from the little fiends—they rarely attacked Mage. And he had a fiery need to make love to this woman beneath the stars.

His hand closed over one perfect breast, her nipple tight and hard as it grazed his palm, sending need coiling low inside him. Curving one hand beneath her knees and the other at her back, he turned her until he was cradling her in his arms.

Skye laughed and slid one arm behind his neck. "What are you doing?"

He met her gaze with his hunger, he was certain, written all over his face. "This." Lifting her, he brought her breast straight to his mouth. He groaned from the sheer sweetness of her flesh as he closed his lips around her and suckled. He flicked his tongue across her nipple, over and over again until her fingers dug into his neck where she held on, and into his scalp, where she held him tight against her until she was moaning with pleasure.

With a last tug on her breast, he lowered her back to his lap, gazing at the damp, swollen flesh with satisfaction. He looked down at her, at her small, sexy smile.

"You're even more beautiful in the moonlight," he said softly. "I didn't think it was possible."

Her smile widened and turned shy. "So are you, my warrior. I want you inside me."

"There's nowhere I'd rather be." He kissed her, sliding his tongue into her mouth as he laid her on the soft sand and stroked her body, his hand sliding down her torso, to bump up against her jeans. "These have got to go."

But as he rose to his knees to unfasten her belt, she sat up, her hand sliding over his arm.

"Paenther . . ."

His movements stilled at the uncertain tone in her voice. She was watching him with raw need, but something more.

"What, Beauty?"

Slowly, she reached for him, cupping his erection in her cool palm. He sucked in a breath at the exquisite pleasure of her touch.

"In the cavern . . . you wouldn't let me kiss you here. Yet you brought me so much pleasure when you kissed me down there. Is it different for a man?"

So innocent. He stroked her head and met her gaze. "It's no different. It can be an incredibly erotic feeling . . . when it's done by the right person, in the right way. Ancreta used to force my arousal like that. Bad memories, I'm afraid."

Yet even as he said the words, the truth, the thought of Skye's mouth, replacing the perfect touch of her hand, nearly brought him to release.

He stared into her eyes, cupping her cheek. "You are the right person, Beauty. If you want to . . ."

Her eyes searched his. "I don't know how to do it in the right way. I've never done it at all."

"There's no wrong way. Whatever pleases you. But first, I want you naked, little witch." He kissed her, then set about unfastening her belt. "You're wearing far too many clothes."

Paenther moved between her legs and pulled off her jeans and panties, tossing them onto the pile, his gaze fixing hungrily on the sweet flesh between her legs. But she closed her knees and rose, pressing her hands to his shoulders.

"My turn."

He could have overpowered her in an instant, but he rather liked the touch of bossiness in her tone.

"Lie down for me, Paenther. Please?"

He did, lying back on the cool, damp sand, watching her as she knelt beside him and studied his cock as if unsure where to begin. His body thrummed with anticipation, throbbing with desire. His chest tightened until he thought it might explode from the pressure of his feelings for her.

Her hand closed around him. Then slowly, so

slowly, she lowered her face. Her tongue flicked out, marking him with a fast, damp lick across the tip of his head, tearing a groan from his throat.

She watched him, their gazes locked as she held him upright, opened her mouth. . .

He froze, suddenly struggling not to grab himself out of her hand and push her away.

She saw and released him. "I'm sorry."

Paenther sat up and grabbed her shoulders as she started to lean away. "No. Don't stop. But I think I'll sit up while you do it."

She nodded, understanding in her eyes. Being on his back brought it all back too clearly.

Once again, she slowly lowered her face to his lap, but this time she didn't stop. As he slid his fingers into her hair, he felt her damp mouth close around his cock. His eyes nearly rolled back into his head at the unbelievable pleasure.

"Ah, Skye, that's good."

She tongued him, sucked on him, driving a desperate need to touch her in return. His hand slid down her silken back until his palm cupped her rear, kneading and flexing into the soft flesh. Then his fingers slid into the crack between her cheeks and down until he found her heat.

As she twirled her tongue around his head, he shoved two fingers deep inside her, eliciting a deep sensual moan from her throat.

His other hand slid into her hair, holding her, caressing her. Loving her.

Her damp mouth began to suck on him, riding his length until he thought he was going to lose it.

Goddess, but he had to be inside her.

He pulled his fingers out of her and lifted her face.

"Enough, Beauty. I need to be in you."

With a soft smile, she lay back on the sand, opening her arms and her body to him. The moonlight lit her face, setting her eyes to sparkling, tightening a band around his chest.

Skye reached for him. "Love me, Paenther."

He stared down at her. "I do." And he knew it was true. Against all odds, against everything he'd ever thought possible, he'd fallen in love with a Mage witch.

He fell into her arms and cradled her face. "I love you, Skye."

She stared at him, tears and joy flooding her eyes. "I love you, too. So very much."

Her words stroked his heart, filling him with warmth and rightness. Holding her with his gaze, he entered her body, sliding his length into her tight, wet sheath, fitting together two halves of a whole.

She was his. And yet there were a dozen reasons she could never be.

He pushed the dark thoughts aside as she wrapped herself around him. Over and over, he slid inside her, then most of the way out, then deep inside her again. Faster and faster, he drove them both as Skye met him, thrust for thrust, groaning, her body straining right along with his.

She came on a cry of joy, and he followed her

over, spilling his seed in a moment of such perfection, he wasn't certain it would ever be matched.

But as he kissed her and pulled out of her, reality pressed in, threatening to steal this one brief moment of happiness.

They returned to the beach house without any sign of draden, showered, and fell into bed, exhausted. A short while later, Paenther woke to the sound of Skye's distress.

He held her close in the bed, her body curled around his, her head tucked beneath his chin. As he stroked her back, her trembling slowly eased.

"Birik again?" he asked softly.

"Yes."

He felt so damned helpless. He'd promised to keep her safe, but in those dreams, Birik hurt her, and there was nothing he could do about it. All he wanted to do was keep her safe—lock her within the walls of Feral House, where no one would ever hurt her again.

But Feral House was the one place she could never stay. No Mage witch would ever be welcome there, he knew that.

He kissed the top of her head, her soft hair brushing his chin. She pulled back and looked up at him with love in her eyes. Within that love, he saw a raw, desperate hope for the future. A future he was all too afraid would never be theirs.

Chapter
Nineteen

Skye clung to Paenther's hand as she accompanied him up the front walk of Feral House, her heart warm and full with a fragile joy.

Paenther loved her.

The entire trip home, he'd held her hand, refusing to let go, filling her with happiness and hope beyond anything she'd ever thought possible. There was so much at stake still, and the other Feral Warriors still distrusted her, but Paenther would bring them around. She had to believe.

Because he loved her. And she loved him so much in return, she ached from it.

They were nearly to the front steps when the door burst open. Paenther grabbed her around the waist and hauled her back as Tighe ran out the door, Delaney close behind him.

"Jag and Foxx found a pair of Mage." Tighe paused at the base of the steps. "They called for backup."

"Where?"

"Jefferson Street."

Paenther released Skye and swung her to face him. "You need to stay here."

"Paenther, no." The last thing she wanted to do was face Lyon alone. "You may need to shift."

He thought about it for three seconds, then grabbed her hand. "All right. I'll drive, Stripes. The Escalade's warm."

Tighe eyed her with a look that was neither friendly, nor truly antagonistic, but he nodded.

The sunshine disappeared, the day turning gray in an instant. The wind started to kick up. Tighe looked up and frowned.

"I'll ride in back," Skye suggested, as they reached Paenther's black SUV.

"No." Tighe's response was quick and sharp, leaving her no choice but to get in front with Paenther. It was clear he didn't trust her with his mate. As soon as they were in, Paenther took off. The trees bent to the fury of the wind, a small branch tumbling across the drive in front of them. The wind was definitely kicking up.

They drove the short distance in silence. "There's Foxx's Mustang," Paenther said, when they turned onto the residential road only a few streets from the one where Feral House sat.

A red car sat on the side of the road appearing empty and abandoned.

"Do you see them?" Paenther asked.

"No. They're probably in the woods." But a moment later, Tighe's tone matched the sudden tension in the car. "I called them telepathically, but there's no answer. If they're chasing Mage, they should be in their animals."

Paenther pulled out his cell phone and punched some numbers. "No answer."

"We're going to have to track them."

Paenther pulled over to the side of the road. As the car slowed to a stop, Tighe threw open the door and leaped out, shifting midleap into a house cat.

"He can change his shape," Skye murmured, surprised.

Delaney leaned forward. "A lot of the Ferals can. It helps them blend into the human landscape. Zoo animals tend to draw unwanted attention."

Skye glanced at Paenther, tempted to ask him if he could change size, too, but his concentration was elsewhere. She suspected Tighe was talking to him.

As if in answer, he shoved open his door. "Let's go."

"Did they answer him?" Delaney asked.

Skye opened her door, having to hang on tight to keep it from getting away from her as the wind tore past.

"No." His expression was grim. "He smells blood."

Paenther grabbed Skye's hand, and the three ran into the sharp wind to where Tighe, now a man, stood at the edge of the woods. Skye smelled the carnage before they reached it and prayed Tighe hadn't found the bodies of the Ferals. But when he looked up, a hint of grim satisfaction weighed in his eyes, and she knew he hadn't.

"Mage," he said as they joined him. "Now I understand the sudden turn of bad weather. Mother Nature is pissed."

Skye covered her nose as she looked down at the two badly mutilated bodies. The men's chests had been torn open. Their hearts were almost certainly gone. But enough of their faces remained for her to recognize them.

"I know them."

"Friends of yours?" Tighe asked carefully.

She met his gaze without rancor. "I have no friends among Birik's Mage."

Tighe nodded, seemingly satisfied, but his expression quickly turned to one of confusion. "These two were killed by animals. Feral animals. So where are Jag and Foxx, now?"

Paenther released her hand and stepped back, stripping off his shirt. "Let's find them." When he was fully undressed, she stepped forward and pressed her palms to his chest. He covered her hands briefly, then released her as he began to shift.

Skye jumped back as the panther emerged where the man had stood. He took off into the woods but the tiger didn't immediately follow. The great striped cat was staring at her with deadly green eyes.

Tighe's voice cut through her head with hard warning. *If you harm Delaney, witch, you die.*

She answered him in kind. *She's a good person, Tighe. I would never hurt her.*

With a warning growl, he turned and bounded off after Paenther.

"Was he threatening you?" Delaney asked beside her. The wind whipped at her loose hair, sending it flying about her face like a dark mist.

Skye threw her a wry look, then went back to watching the cats. "You know him well."

"Oh, yeah. They're prickly as hell about who they let in their inner circle, but once you're in, watch out. The cavemen had nothing on these guys for sheer stubborn protectiveness."

"That's nice for you. To be protected like that."

"Do the Mage do that?"

"Protect their females? Some do. When I was a little girl, I lived among Mage would have risked everything to keep me safe from the outside world. Unfortunately, it was another Mage who wanted me, and there was nothing they could do to stop him." She sighed. "The only one who ever tried to protect me in the caverns was Paenther. And he was chained at the time."

She felt Delaney's probing gaze. "He's more than protective of you. I've seen the way he looks at you, Skye. It's a lot like Tighe looks at me. Some of the Ferals think you've enchanted him, but I don't think it's that simple."

Skye met Delaney's gaze. "I love him. And he told me he feels the same."

Delaney grinned. "Well, there you have it. Sounds like we're going to be sisters-in-law . . . or whatever it would be. Feral Warrior wives-in-law?"

Skye smiled, the rush of longing making her chest ache. "I'd like that." She'd more than like it. Having friends, a home, a family again was a dream she'd barely dared to imagine.

Look left!

Tighe's voice rang in Skye's head, tearing her thoughts from the fragile hope. At her side, Delaney's head jerked left and she knew he was speaking to them both. *Two men. Do you recognize either of them, Skye?*

She saw the two he was talking about a distance away, walking casually, like humans out for a stroll. They were dressed in casual jeans and barn jackets rather than the blue tunics of Birik's sentinels. But as one of them turned, she caught his profile. *They're Birik's men, Tighe.*

The two cats gave chase. Immediately, the Mage took off, running in two different directions.

Get in the car and lock the doors, Tighe barked. *Both of you.*

Delaney made a sound of disgust. "I hate getting relegated to the role of helpless . . ." She whirled, pulling her gun. "Freeze!"

Skye spun around to find a third man running directly for them. A man she recognized all too well. Devrell, one of Birik's cruelest sentinels.

"He's Mage." In her head she screamed, *Tighe! Paenther!*

The sound of gunfire exploded in her ears as Delaney shot at the man, but he was immortal and the bullets did nothing to slow him down.

"Skye, run!"

Skye hesitated, wanting to help her new friend, but there was nothing she could do. Besides, she knew it was her the Mage wanted. She turned and fled in the direction she'd watched Paenther go.

Beauty! What's happening?

There's a third Mage. Delaney shot at him, but. . .

She glanced behind her and gave a mental shriek. *She's down! He's coming for me.*

Run, Beauty! I'm coming.

Her feet felt awkwardly heavy in the borrowed running shoes as she ran through the woods, leaping over the uneven ground, the forest-scented wind whipping at her face. The heavy thud of her heartbeat pounded in her ears as terror crawled up her spine.

She wouldn't go back there!

All around her, birds landed on nearby branches. Squirrels chattered angrily in the trees as if preparing to come to her aid, but she didn't call them. They'd only get hurt.

Behind her she heard the low chant of a Mage spell and her heart sank. Seconds later, a rock the size of her fist rose from the ground and flew at her. She turned her head and raised her arm, but the rock slammed into her shoulder, knocking her off stride. More rocks flew at her, as if Birik's nightmare had come to life, hitting her legs and sweeping her feet out from under her. With a thud, she landed on her back on the forest floor, the wind knocked out of her.

Before she could leap to her feet, Devrell was over her, staring down at her with cold eyes ringed in a copper as bright as her own. He grabbed her and hauled her to her feet. Skye fought him, struggling against his hold as he dragged her back toward the road. Even though his strength was nothing compared to Paenther's, it was still far greater than her own.

Paenther!

I'm coming, Beauty.

Moments later, a flash of black caught her eye.

Devrell released her, pulling a knife from his belt. As the panther leaped at him, going for the throat, the Mage slid the knife between the animal's ribs. The sleek animal knocked the man to the ground with his powerful body, taking two more stabs to the chest and throat before he bit clean through Devrell's wrist, tearing off his hand.

Blood sprayed from the Mage's arm as the great cat lay across him, lengthwise, his deadly teeth mere inches from Devrell's face. Tail twitching, blood matting his fur, the cat stared down at his captive like a hunter about to take a juicy bite out of his prey.

Paenther snarled, his eyes glowing green. But as Skye stepped closer, he swung his head toward her. *Are you okay?*

"Yes. What about you?" she asked worriedly.

Fine, Beauty. The panther growled and turned back to the Mage. *Who sent you?*

"B-Birik," the man stuttered, his voice thready with shock.

"Where are my friends?"

"Took them. The others . . . took them."

"Why?"

"The Feast of the Moon Spirit. Three Ferals . . . to open the blade."

Skye's heart seized. "He's going to *sacrifice* them?"

"Yes. Birik wants you, too, if we can get you. Otherwise, he'll use the viper shifter and pull his own power."

You'll not get her. Ever. The panther turned to look at her. *Is there any reason I should spare his life?*

"Other than the Earth getting even angrier than she already is?"

Paenther tilted his face to the wind as if just realizing the weather had changed. *Other than that?*

"None. He deserves whatever you do to him."

Paenther watched her through his cat eyes, his body ablaze with pain as it always was when he was in his animal, trebled by the knife wounds. Wounds he could feel healing slower than they should be. He shoved away the deep worry clouding his mind and concentrated on Skye, on the echoes of old pain and deep hatred swimming in her summer-sky eyes. A pain that cut him deeper than the knives had.

He hurt you. It wasn't a question. The truth was written all over her face.

"He enjoys bringing pain to others."

To you?

She looked away, then met his gaze, her mouth tight. "When Birik chained me to that rock where you were kept, he invited his sorcerers and sentinels to use me, too, figuring the worse it got, the quicker I'd cave. His men still had souls at the time and few took him up on the offer. This one joined me on that rock every night, usually with two blades. One of flesh, the other of steel."

Paenther snarled deep in his cat's throat, his gut twisting with rage for the child subjected to such brutality.

He stared down at his captive. *You die. For her, you die.* He made sure Skye heard the words as clearly as did the Mage beneath him.

The man yelled in fear as Paenther struck, ripping out his throat before tearing at his chest until he had the heart in his mouth. He looked up at Skye. If he'd seen horror in her eyes, he'd have tossed the heart aside and ended it there. But those blue eyes blazed with gratitude and vindication, so, his gaze fixed on hers, he ate it.

For you. Thunder rumbled angrily in the sky.

"I'd kiss you, but you're a little messy."

Paenther gave her a feline smile, then called to Tighe.

Is Delaney okay?

Yes. You?

We'll be right there. He looked at Skye. *Help me shift back, Beauty.*

Small pellets of hail began to fall. The Earth was angry, all right. She was going to get a hell of a lot angrier once he got his hands on Birik.

Skye slid her hands in his fur and helped him shift back with a burst of pain that nearly sent him to his knees. When he was standing on two feet again, he pulled her against him, shielding her from the hail, and led her back toward the road.

"Where did the blood go? You're clean."

"That's the upside of not being able to keep my clothes on when I shift. I don't retain much of anything."

"You don't even have to take showers?"

"It doesn't work *that* well. Besides, I've found I'm rather fond of showers."

He could almost feel her blush. Holding her against him like that, he felt that overwhelming protectiveness well up inside and spill over. Never again would anyone hurt her. Not as long as he drew breath.

The hail grew in size until he could feel it tearing at his bare back. Hell, his Escalade was going to be dented for sure. But he didn't care. Goddess, he didn't care. He'd slain one of Skye's dragons, and for that he felt on top of the world.

Skye's hand touched his arm. "Are you sure you're okay? Those stab wounds healed?"

"They healed." For the most part. Things weren't right in his body, and it was seriously starting to worry him. He remembered all too well the way Frederick's body had turned mortal just before he died.

The rage burned through his mind stronger than before, requiring a control greater than he'd ever had to exert. And the pain when he shifted was getting worse. A pain that was as much of the soul as the body. A pain that whispered of loss and isolation. And a rending inside him he wouldn't survive.

If he lost the panther spirit, he would die.

Only now, within the arms of an enchantress, had he finally begun to live.

Chapter Twenty

Skye shielded her face from the blowing snow as Paenther ushered her into the foyer of Feral House. The hail had ended, but Mother Nature had yet to forgive the Ferals for the death of three Mage. Souls or not, the Mage were a part of nature as no other creatures could ever be.

Behind them, Tighe carried his mate, who was protesting loudly.

"Tighe, I'm fine!"

But the tiger Feral ignored her as the four ducked into the house and shut the door against the blizzard.

"Let me down, Tighe. Now."

"What happened?" Lyon demanded as he strode into the foyer, Kara close behind him.

Paenther's big hand brushed at Skye's hair, dislodging a small shower of wet droplets around her shoulders as he met the gaze of his chief. "Foxx and Jag are missing, Delaney was attacked and knocked unconscious—"

"But I'm fine. Tighe, put me down!"

"—but she's fine. We found two dead Mage when we got there and killed a third after learning Birik means to sacrifice Foxx, Jag, and Vhyper at midnight tonight. Did I miss anything?"

Tighe grunted. "Nothing but the fact that you still can't shift without the help of your witch."

Lyon's expression turned hard, his gaze flying from Paenther to Tighe and back again. "*Hell.* In the war room. *Now.*"

"I'll ask Pink to bring coffee." Kara turned toward the kitchen. "You all look like you could use something warm."

Paenther stroked Skye's head, then slid his arm around her and ushered her down the hall, following Lyon.

As they entered the room, Skye looked toward the big window, surprised to see that the snow had stopped as abruptly as it had begun, leaving several inches on the ground. Mother Nature seemed to be over her fury.

Paenther pulled out a chair for her, and she sat at the big table. Instead of sitting beside her, he stood at her back, a strong, protective force behind her.

He loved her.

Tighe and Delaney took seats across from them. Wulfe and Hawke sat at the end.

Lyon paced. "How did Jag and Foxx get captured?"

"We don't know. We found three live Mage and two dead when we got there. And no Jag or Foxx. There's no telling how many Mage they ultimately had to take on."

"They still shouldn't have been captured. They're Ferals, for goddess sake!"

Kougar joined them, remaining by the door as Lyon's hard, worried gaze raked his warriors.

"The Mage are no longer the enemy we once knew, Roar," Tighe said quietly. "Dark power is damned strong."

Lyon growled, the sound of a lion rumbling from his throat. "Tell me about the sacrifice."

Paenther's hands cupped her shoulders. "If the Mage I killed is to be believed, they've taken Jag and Foxx to the caverns. Birik intends to sacrifice them at midnight tonight during a moon feast, along with Vhyper."

Lyon's gaze dipped, and he met her gaze with an amber intensity that felt as if he tried to see deep inside her. "Can he raise power this way? Dangerous power?"

She braided her fingers together in her lap. "I believe so, yes. Birik's a snake enchanter. Vhyper's death will help him tap into his gift. The deaths of the other Ferals, along with many snakes, could be dangerously potent."

"Enough to free more Daemons, or even Satanan himself?"

She desperately wanted to give him the answers he needed, but she just didn't have them. "I don't know. I'm sorry."

Lyon frowned and looked over her head at Paenther. "We have to get into the cavern and we have to do it now. Are you healed?"

"No. The Shaman's not-a-friend, Ezekiel, taught her to pull good power instead of dark, but it didn't work with her magic bound." Paenther's hands left her, and she glanced over her shoulder to see he'd crossed his arms over his chest. "But it doesn't matter. I'm ready."

"No." The word came out of her mouth like a shot.

Paenther's gaze dropped to her, a hint of displeasure in his eyes. But Lyon had to understand even if Paenther was too stubborn to admit it.

She turned to meet Paenther's gaze. "You won't survive it."

"Beauty . . . I'll be fine."

"That mountain is warded with magic, Paenther. There's no telling how much more damage it might do to your connection with your animal. And if you get captured, they'll put you in shackles again. Your animal can't take it, Paenther. You're going to lose him."

"There's no choice. I'm the only chance Vhyper and the others have. No one else has been able to find that mountain."

"What about Skye?" Tighe asked.

Skye whirled to face him, but she shook her head. "I don't know where it is. Until this past week, I'd had no contact with the human world; nor had I been off the mountain since I was taken there as a child. If someone can get me *to* the mountain,

I can find the cavern with ease. But I don't know where the mountain is."

"Was there a town nearby? Anything you might remember?"

"Nothing I could see from the forest. Just farmland. And the one small country store where I met Paenther. If there was a human town nearby, I never heard it discussed."

Tighe's gaze swung to Lyon. "So, Paenther can lead a team to the mountain, then wait behind."

"Like hell."

Hawke tapped his fingers on the table. "If the magic around that area was so strong we were getting disoriented just trying to find the Market, there's no reason to believe we'll be any more successful getting up the mountain and into the cavern. We're almost certainly going to need a guide." His gaze swung to Skye.

Paenther's hands squeezed her shoulders. "She's not going near that place again."

Hawke didn't back down. "It might be the only way for us to get in."

"I can lead you." Skye said the words before she lost her courage.

"Not without me," Paenther said behind her. "And as soon as we're at the cave's entrance, you'll run right back to the Market."

A lion's growl rumbled in Lyon's throat. "And what about you, B.P.? What if she's right? What if the warding damages you further?"

Paenther met his chief's gaze with stubborn determination. "There's no alternative. I'm the only one who's been inside that cavern or knows what Birik looks like. Besides, Skye's not going without me."

Stubborn Feral. He wouldn't survive it. Skye shoved to her feet, forcing Paenther to back up. "There is an alternative. I may be able to heal him. Now. Before we go."

Lyon's eyebrows rose. "I thought your power only came at midnight."

"My power is at its height at midnight. But I raise my power through the animals. Maybe if I call the forest creatures, I can raise enough to help him."

"Could radiance help?" Kara asked, walking through the door with a tray of coffee mugs.

"A power raising." Hawke tapped the table in front of him. "We need to call the power of the beasts. The power of the panther."

Lyon scowled. For long minutes, he paced silently, his face hard, his amber eyes alive with a thousand thoughts.

Skye stood there, waiting for his acceptance of her gift. She could help Paenther, she knew she could. But he had to give her a chance.

Lyon finally stopped and turned to face Paenther. "She's a Mage witch, B.P. A witch who's already demonstrated a disturbing power over our animals. If she's not what she pretends to be and seizes control, or uses the power she draws to incapacitate us, she could destroy us. If the Ferals go down, Satanan wins. Are you positive . . . *positive* . . . you can trust her? Without a shadow of a doubt?"

Skye clasped her hands in front of her, waiting for Paenther to tell them what he'd told her. That he loved her. Of course he trusted her.

But the room rang with an ominous silence. He made no such declaration. He said nothing at all. A chill stole over her skin.

Slowly, she turned and saw him watching her with a myriad of emotions in his eyes. But the only one she felt, the one that drove a stake through her heart, was the doubt.

He'd said he loved her. How could he love her when he didn't even trust her not to betray him and all he cared about?

Pain ripped through her chest, tears burning her eyes.

He didn't love her. He didn't even know her if he thought she could ever willingly betray him.

She shoved past him and ran for the door.

"Skye . . ." Regret laced Paenther's voice. But he didn't try to stop her.

With a sudden, desperate need to get outside, she ran through the house and out the door, into the yard. She stood in the snow, holding herself tight, tears slipping down her cheeks as she shredded the foolish dreams she'd woven in her head since the moment Paenther told her he loved her. She'd let herself believe, *hope,* that his loving her would change everything. That he was finally able to look past what she was, if not quite forget.

He'd said he loved her. If he loved her, he should trust her, shouldn't he? But he didn't. He couldn't.

Because of what she was.

The cold wind froze the tears on her cheeks, the chill seeping deep inside, spreading a spiderweb of cracks across her heart.

I love you, Paenther. I can help you. But I can never be other than what I am.

Paenther stared out the window to where Skye stood, creatures flocking around her. Dogs and deer, squirrels and cardinals, they went to her, pressing against her, seeking her attention. Offering her comfort.

But for once she didn't touch them, didn't acknowledge them. Her arms wrapped around her middle as if she didn't even know they were there. Never had he seen anyone look so alone. And his heart broke. He'd done this to her. He'd caused her this pain.

"I hurt her. I doubted her."

Lyon had demanded his promise that there was no chance she could betray them. But before he could give it, memories had flooded his mind, tearing out his guts. Ancreta running toward him that day just before she captured him, her gown torn, her cries tearing at his heart. And the way Foxx looked at Zaphene, poor lovesick Foxx with his starry eyes, head over heels in love with a Mage witch who'd spun her web over him so thoroughly he'd killed Beatrice, his Radiant, without ever knowing he'd done it.

For one horrible moment he'd wondered if he was Foxx all over again, snared by a witch's web of magic. How could he risk the lives of his men, of his brothers, on a Mage witch? Any Mage witch?

But how could he doubt Skye?

Lyon came to stand beside him. "Knowing what I do of your background, I'm amazed you've been able to trust her at all."

"I do trust her, Roar. I can't always get past *what* she is. But I know *who* she is. She's one of the purest souls I've ever met."

As they stood together, watching the creatures gather around her, Lyon murmured, "They say animals and children see the heart of a person. There's a lot at stake here, B.P., but we don't have many options. If I've learned anything from Kara, it's that sometimes you just have to trust your heart."

"I trust her with my life, Roar. If my life were the only one at stake, I wouldn't hesitate."

Lyon clasped his shoulder, drawing his gaze. "You're my second for a reason, B.P. If you trust her with your life, that's enough for me. I'll call the Shaman and get him back here to unbind her magic. Then we'll head out to the goddess stone."

Paenther felt the weight of the world on his shoulders. And at the same time, an incredible lightness of spirit. Goddess, he loved her. What was more, *he knew her.*

He clasped Lyon's shoulder in return, then turned and hurried out of the room.

Sometimes all you can do is trust your heart.

And his heart belonged to Skye.

* * *

Skye stood staring into the woods, unseeing, as the animals gathered around her, seeking a comfort she didn't have to give. Tears continued to skate down her cold cheeks, but she couldn't stop them any more than she could stop the cracks from forming over and over in her heart.

She felt rather than heard Paenther approach. He walked too silently for her ever truly to hear him.

"Skye." He said her name softly before sliding his hands on her shoulders from behind. "I'm sorry."

"It's okay." The thing was, she couldn't blame him for being cautious when so much was at stake. It was her own fault, and the fault of her foolish heart, for reading too much into his declaration of love.

He turned her to face him, but she wouldn't meet his gaze, not when the tears refused to stop. But he pulled her into his arms anyway, one hand at her back, the other sliding into her hair as he lifted her face to his. With eyes swimming in regret, he brushed away her tears.

"Don't cry, Beauty." His face dipped, and he kissed her without hesitation, without doubt, with a fierce tenderness that claimed her, body and soul. A kiss of possession. Of declaration. Of promise.

Finally, he pulled back. Shaken, confused, she kept her eyes closed and clung to his waist, not even remembering reaching for him.

"Look at me, Skye." As she looked up, his hands rose to frame her face. "I trust you, little witch. With my life."

She sighed. "Paenther . . . it's okay. I understand. You have a lot of reasons not to trust a Mage."

"I do. You're right." He stroked her jaw. "But you've never given me any reason not to trust *you*."

Her mouth pursed ruefully. "Other than the fact that I enthralled you and captured you?"

To her amazement, a small smile flickered across his face. "Other than that. I love you. I trust you because I *know* you. I've seen the goodness in you from the beginning even if I had a hard time believing such beauty of spirit could possibly have been born a Mage. I trust you with my life, Skye. I only hesitated because . . ." He sighed and pressed his forehead to hers. "Trust comes hard for me. And these men are my family. My brothers. Until you, they were the whole of my life."

She clung to the love in his voice and in his words. "I'd never do anything to hurt them. Or you."

He pulled back to look down at her. "I know that."

With her fingertips, she traced his mouth. "You've become *my* life, Paenther. I can't let you suffer if I can help you. I can't let you die if I can do something to save you." *I can't live without you.* But the last she kept to herself. Because, despite his declarations of love, she realized now that not once had he talked about the future, most importantly, a future that included her.

He stroked her damp cheek. "Lyon has called the Shaman to unbind your magic. We'll do the power raising as soon as you're ready."

"Lyon agrees?"

"He does."

"That's good." But a host of butterflies took flight in her stomach. She'd wanted them to give her a chance, but now that she was getting it, she was suddenly overcome with doubts of her own. What if she couldn't pull it off?

Paenther looked at her quizzically. "What's the matter?"

"What if I forget the words?"

He kissed her forehead. "I remember them. We're going to make this work. Together."

A head pushed between them, that of a big black Lab looking for attention.

"Jealous thing," Skye scolded fondly, laughter in her voice.

Ignoring the dog, Paenther kissed her one more time, sweeping his tongue into her mouth, as she savored the heady taste of him. But the dog refused to be ignored, and she started to laugh.

With a chuckle, Paenther released her and stepped back. "Go ahead. They deserve a little of your time, and the Shaman won't be here for at least an hour. Not with the sudden turn of bad weather."

She saw the glimmer of humor in his eyes and laughed. How was it possible to love another person so much that she honestly wondered if her heart would simply stop if his did? As she turned to her animals, her joy flickered and died beneath the weight of her fears.

What if she couldn't help Paenther at all?

Chapter
Twenty-one

Two hours later, the Ferals and their mates trudged through the snow-blanketed woods. As they climbed down to a broad, flat stone, *the goddess stone*, Skye stared down at the glory of the raging Potomac River far below.

Though the snow had ended a while ago, the wind still whipped, cold and biting.

Paenther pulled her against him. "We'll call a Feral Circle to enclose the magic and keep out prying eyes."

Lyon joined them. "Kara's going to pull the radiance to melt the snow so Skye's feet don't freeze." His hand went to Paenther's shoulder. "Wish you could join us, B.P. Maybe if this works . . ."

Skye shivered, and Paenther pulled the leather coat he'd loaned her tighter around her. All she wore beneath was a thin, flimsy sleeveless silk gown. A ritual gown, Kara had called it. Kara and Delaney had taken her aside to dress her, choosing a beautiful gown of a vibrant blue they said brought out the color in her eyes.

"Once we're ready, we'll call down the power of the panther." Lyon looked at her. "I want you to wait outside the circle with Kara and Delaney until I call you. Then you can do . . . whatever it is you do."

Skye nodded, leaning back against Paenther as she watched the other Ferals gather around Kara, the five huge males dwarfing the woman. Lyon took Kara's hands while the others touched her neck or arms or ankles.

Skye had seen this once before, in her prison cell, and looked for a repeat with anticipation.

"Ready?" Kara asked.

"Do it, little Radiant," Lyon replied quietly.

Just like that, Kara lit up as if she'd swallowed two dozen lightwicks. The effect was even more amazing outside beneath the clouds. She looked like an angel come to Earth. Or the sun in human form.

"Amazing, isn't it?" Delaney breathed, standing beside her, the collar of her own coat turned up against the wind. "I'll never get used to this stuff."

Skye met the other woman's gaze, seeing warmth and intelligence, a strong soul and friendship in those dark eyes. She smiled warmly in return. "It is amazing."

Around Kara's and the men's feet, the snow melted as if someone were warming the stone from within. When Kara's light went out, the men stepped back, stripping to the waist. Golden armbands wrapped around thick arms glowed dimly beneath the heavy clouds. To a man, the Ferals were beautifully built, powerful and strong. But the only one who set her heart to racing was the one at her back.

Paenther gave her a squeeze, then released her to turn her in his arms. The warmth of his hands seeped into her bare flesh beneath the coat's leather. "Are you ready?"

The warm scents of leather and male cut through the cold air, heating her blood. As she stared into his dark eyes, she told him the truth. "I'm scared that I might not help you. Otherwise, I'm ready."

He squeezed her shoulders. "You're going to do the best you can, Beauty. That's all any of us can ask."

"Ready, B.P.?" Lyon called.

Paenther kissed her, a quick peck that sent his soft black hair sliding against her cheek. Then he released her and pulled off his shirt, and went to join the circle.

Kougar led the chant as the Ferals cut their chests with a sharp knife, one after the other, slapping their palms to the bloody wounds. Finally, Paenther cut his own chest, bloodied his hand and shoved his fist into the air. One by one, the other Ferals slapped their hands on top of his in a savage ritual of blood and power.

"Skye, join us," Lyon called.

She shrugged off the long leather coat and handed it to Delaney, then stepped out of the borrowed boots. Taking a deep breath for courage, she walked barefoot across the wet rock to enter the circle and stand before Paenther.

He stared down at her, his gaze falling to her knees and rising again, slowly, male appreciation warm in his eyes. Then he tilted his head back and yelled to the clouds, his deep, strong voice ringing out over the rocks and wind, "Spirits rise and join. Empower the beast beneath this sky." The others joined in, the words drifting and sliding around her. Thunder rumbled. The rock beneath her feet began to shake.

"Dance, Skye." Paenther threw back his head, and roared, "Empower the spirit of the panther!"

As the energy flowed around her, Skye closed her eyes and spun, her feet moving as she chanted the words Ezekiel had taught her.

"Stop!" Paenther's voice barked in her ear as his rough hands clamped onto her shoulders, stopping her abruptly. Her eyes flew open and she stared with horror at the Ferals around her bent double with pain.

She jerked free of Paenther's hold and spun to face him. "What happened?"

"Those are not the words Ezekiel taught you," he growled, his own face a mask of pain.

"They were." Her trembling hand went to her forehead. "I thought they were." She whispered some of the syllables.

"No. Those are the words I heard in the cavern."

Violent quakes tore through her body and she covered her face with her hands. This was the very thing she'd feared! That she'd hurt them. That Birik and his darkness had stained her soul.

"Shh . . ." Paenther's strong arms went around her and he pulled her against him, holding her too tight, his body strung taut with pain. Soft in her ear he said the words he'd heard as many times as she had last night.

Skye began to whisper the words with him, over and over, louder as she pulled out of his hold and turned. The Ferals straightened, their faces slowly clearing of the terrible discomfort.

Deep within her she felt the power begin to rise. *Praise the Mother.* But as she spun, the pain attacked her instead, a sudden searing wound through her chest as if someone had stabbed her with a dagger. She clutched her chest, forcing her feet to keep moving, but the pain intensified until it was a searing mass of fire and she couldn't breathe. She stumbled, gasping, dizzy with pain.

Paenther gripped her shoulders, holding her upright. "What's the matter? I could feel it working."

"My chest." And suddenly she understood. "The cantric. It won't let me . . ." she gasped. "Damn him. Damn him!" She looked up. "Help me. Say it with me."

"No. Not if it's going to hurt you."

"Say it!"

His jaw tightened, but he said the words with her, helping her dance when she could barely stand upright, when her vision threatened to fail. When she could hardly speak.

She felt his panther fighting to get back to him. But the harder she struggled to keep going, the worse her own pain became.

Paenther stopped her. "That's enough, Beauty."

"No! It's not." His panther growled, demanding her help. And she would help him!

"That's enough, Skye. I feel better. Stronger. It's enough."

The panther inside him howled with frustration.

"It's not enough! He's trying to reach you. I can help him reach you."

His face went hard and he hauled her against him, pinning her to his body. "No. This is killing you. I'm okay."

"Paenther . . ." Slowly, the pain in her chest ebbed to a throbbing ache. "I need to heal you."

"Look at his eye," Tighe said.

"Your Feral marks are back, B.P. See if you can shift on your own again."

Skye pulled back and looked up into Paenther's face. The scars across his eyes were indeed back. She released him and stepped back as he shed his pants then, with a flash of sparkling lights, shifted into the panther. A moment later, he returned to human form and donned his pants.

Lyon's voice rang with quiet satisfaction. "Thank you, Skye."

She nodded, but deep inside Paenther, his animal continued to charge at her frantically, begging her to continue.

She'd helped him.

But not enough. Not nearly enough.

"It's not working!" Paenther growled, hours later. The rage inside him twisted and turned like a living thing.

He and Skye were back in the Blue Ridge, standing behind the Market with Tighe, Delaney, Hawke, and Wulfe. It was nearly dusk, the gray sky growing dark. Vhyper, Jag, and Foxx only had a handful of hours left. But try as they might, they couldn't get through the warding.

He'd found the Market as he'd known he could, but getting up the mountain was proving impossible. Three times Skye had tried to lead them and each time, just past the place where he'd made love to her that day, things had started to fall apart. They started becoming disoriented. Confused. Hawke had shifted and tried flying over the warding, only to wind up spiraling to the ground, breaking his wing.

The last time, he and Skye had gone alone, but it was no use. Unless she could carry him, and she sure as hell couldn't, she wasn't going to get them into that cavern. Unlike some of the other Ferals, he had no ability to change the size of his animal. When he shifted, he was a large, full-sized panther. Period.

Tighe, Delaney, and Hawke sat on the remains

of a discarded sofa. Kougar leaned against the brick wall of the Market while Skye sat beneath the trees on the hill, surrounded by the creatures of the forest.

Paenther paced. "Ideas?" he threw out to the group.

"There's one," Skye called softly, then rose and came down to join them. "I remember the counterspell. I can go in alone and try to free Jag and Foxx."

"No."

"If they escape, Birik probably won't bother to sacrifice Vhyper. The death of one Feral won't be enough for what he wants."

"You're not going in there alone."

She looked at him helplessly. "I can't get you in."

A chill slid down his spine. "You can take me in the same way you did before. Enthrall me."

Tighe growled. "Don't even think about it, B.P. You'll just wind up sacrifice number four."

He met his friend's gaze. "It's a chance."

"A hundred things could go wrong."

Skye stared at him, her eyes alight with worry and misery. "Tighe's right."

"It may be our only chance. Can you unenthrall me once we get inside?"

"Not easily or quickly." She clasped her hands together in front of her. "I had to open your mind to unenthrall you when I helped you escape from the cavern. Sex with an enchanted man isn't quick, and Birik will know I'm back as soon as I walk through the warding on the doors. I doubt I'll be able to get you up and off before someone finds us. And I'll have lost any way to pretend I've returned on my own. We'll both wind up in chains and be of no use to anyone."

"So the only way is for me to go in as your prisoner."

Shackled. Again. Fury threatened to rage through his body at the thought of it, but he had to get in there, dammit. He had to save his men.

Yet his only chance at success was if Skye went with him to get him out of the shackles. He stared at her, memorizing every line of her face. If he failed, she'd go back to being a captive and slave to that monster.

Skye slid her hand into his. "I don't like this plan, Paenther. But it may be the only one."

He pulled her around and cupped her shoulders. "I can't give you back to him."

"He won't kill me." She reached for him, pulling his head down where she could kiss him. He let her, feeling the soft, tender brush of her lips before she pulled back. In her eyes he saw his future and his past.

"I know what will happen if you hold back and do nothing," she said softly. "If you let Vhyper die when you might have been able to save him, you'll die inside, little by little, until there's nothing left." She stroked his cheek. "I can't be the cause of that. We can do this, Paenther. Trust me to do my part. I'll give you the chance you need to do yours."

"Tighe's right. A hundred things could go wrong."

"I know. But we don't have a choice. Birik really might succeed in freeing Satanan tonight. Against that possibility, the risk to our lives means nothing."

He gathered her close to his heart and held her, burying his nose in the scent of violets. All he wanted to do was keep her safe. He didn't care about the risk to his own life.

Her hands slid over his back. "I'm stronger than I look, Paenther. No matter what happens, I'll be okay."

He couldn't deny her strength. It was he who was hesitating. Because he couldn't bear for anything to happen to her.

It dawned on him that he'd barely blinked at the prospect of intentionally letting a Mage witch enthrall and capture him. He trusted her. Completely. Implicitly.

Her safety was his only concern, and while it was huge, his little witch was right. There was no choice but to try.

And pray that fate was on their side tonight.

They were going to need all the help they could get.

Chapter
Twenty-two

"This is as far as we go." Paenther stopped beside the very tree against which he'd first made love to Skye and pulled her into his arms. Night was falling fast, and the draden would be out soon. It was time to get into that cavern.

The thought of letting himself be enthralled again, of walking into the enemy's lair blind, deaf, *witless*, turned his blood to ice. But his men were depending on him. He was their only hope.

Skye locked her arms around his waist and pressed her cheek to his chest. He knew she was scared. Hell, he was terrified. *A hundred things could go wrong.* He was a man who survived on rigid control, yet he was relinquishing every ounce of it into another's hands. He was a man who trusted few and had hated the Mage for centuries.

Yet he willingly placed his life and the fate of the Feral Warriors, if not the entire world, into the hands of the Mage witch in his arms. Amazingly, he did so without a qualm. She would do everything she could to help him pull this off.

What terrified him was that it wouldn't be enough. That she wouldn't be able to free him, and he'd never get a chance to fight. Every warrior expected to die in the midst of a blazing battle. It was the only way to go. The thought of dying like a fly trapped on flypaper, unable to save his friends, let alone himself, made his muscles tense with fury. The thought of being unable to save the woman he loved from the monster who had hurt her so many times nearly claimed his soul.

But he was out of options.

He buried his face in Skye's fragrant hair and drew strength. "This is going to work," he murmured against her temple. "Whatever you have to do, Beauty, get me free."

She pulled back and looked up into his face. "I won't fail you. I promise."

Looking down into those blue-and-copper eyes, he saw his future. His world. And he knew that somehow, despite everything, he would find a way for them to stay together.

"I love you," he said softly, falling head over tail all over again.

"And I love you." Tears formed in her eyes. Doubts swam with the tears, but she didn't voice them out loud. Instead, she pulled one of his hands from her cheek and placed a kiss in his palm, the tears running free.

He knew what he had to do. There was only one way for her to enchant him and even if there wasn't, he needed to make love to her at that moment more than he needed to breathe. One hand cupping the back of her head, he kissed her, the taste of her tears on his tongue.

Skye kissed him back with a fervor and a tenderness that filled him with love and raked at his heart. *He couldn't lose her. He wouldn't.* He loved her. How could that single emotion make him feel so powerless, yet at the same time fill him with the strength of the gods?

The passion that erupted every time they touched one another rushed over them, turning the kiss hot and needy. Paenther slanted his mouth over hers, needing to reach farther into her mouth with his tongue, needing to be one with her in every way possible.

He unfastened her jeans and helped her out of them and her panties, then slid his hand beneath her thighs as she opened for him. Her flesh was warm and soft, the core of her damp and ready. As much as he wanted to make proper love to her, they were out of time. He freed his erection then pulled her against him, pressing his cheek to hers.

"Hold on to me, Beauty," he whispered against her ear, then lifted her. As she wrapped her bare legs around his waist, he pushed home, burying himself in her warmth, her love, in the only place he wanted to spend eternity. His gaze locked with hers. Love blazed between them.

"I love you, warrior," she said as he came. The veil of enchantment once more fell over his mind.

Skye straightened both their clothes, then led Paenther through the woods to the main entrance of the cavern. She could see no reason for subterfuge. Birik would know she was here soon enough. Her heart thudded until she thought she might be sick.

The smell of damp limestone and lightwick smoke greeted her, filling her with bitter memories as she led Paenther down the steep cavern stairs. If this failed, if after knowing freedom, she wound up trapped here again, her soul would shrivel and die. Then again, her heart would already be dead. Because the only way she'd be trapped here was if Paenther were no longer alive.

If he lived, he'd find a way to save her. She knew that.

A sentinel's shout echoed off the stone, relaying the news of her return with a prisoner. The sound would surely call Birik to her in a heartbeat. The knowledge made her hands damp with sweat.

If only she had the powers of a television witch. She'd blink Paenther and the other Ferals out of there, then send one of Birik's snakes to eat out his heart.

Her gaze caught a flash of white hair on the stairs below, and she knew he was coming for her. Her legs began to shake. She squeezed Paenther's hand tightly, gaining strength from the feel of his warm flesh against hers and his strong, masculine presence, even if there was nothing he could do to protect her.

As Birik neared, Vhyper close behind, part of her, the part of her that had fought him so stubbornly all those years ago, wanted to stare him down and refuse to quake in his presence. But her only chance of freeing these men depended on his believing nothing had changed. That she hadn't changed.

Fortunately, acting fearful around him was all too easy. Unfortunately, it was no act at all.

The two men reached her, Vhyper towering over the smaller man, his bald head gleaming beneath the floating lightwicks.

Birik stopped three steps below her and stared up at her with curiosity and suspicion. "You're back."

Vhyper smiled, a cruel, smug smile. "Paenther might have been tricked once, but he'd never make the same mistake twice. He let you enchant him this time, didn't he, little witch? He *wanted* back in here."

Skye looked away, her pulse racing. "Yes."

Birik lunged forward two steps and grabbed her jaw, squeezing until pain shot through her skull.

"What is his plan?"

Tears blinded her. "He wanted me to hide him until the enthrallment wore off so that he could find his friends and escape."

She looked up at Vhyper, meeting his gaze.

"All his friends," she added softly, praying Paenther was right and that the Feral's soul still lived behind those eyes.

Vhyper snorted. "Hell of a way to hide him, parading him right through the front door."

Skye looked away before either of them saw the lie in her eyes. "I knew I couldn't hide him. I told him that, but he insisted I try anyway."

Birik scowled. "Fool. Why would he ever think he could beat me?"

Vhyper chuckled. "Ferals are a stubborn lot. I told you he'd be back, didn't I? Out of some misplaced sense of honor and justice, he thinks he owes me his life for my role in saving his years ago."

Without warning, Birik backhanded her across the mouth. "Why did you escape?"

Skye pressed the back of her hand to her throbbing, bleeding lip. "I didn't. He took me against my will." The truth.

"You released him?"

"He came out of the enthrallment before I had him locked down." A lie. He'd come out of the enthrallment buried deep inside her.

"You showed him a way out."

"He forced me. He would have killed me otherwise." Truthfully, it had been Birik, not Paenther, who'd forced her. By unleashing those Daemons on innocent people, he'd forced her to make some hard choices. Choices she would never regret.

Birik stroked her cheek. "Meek little mouse. And he forced you to come back here."

"No. I offered to help him. I had to come back." She allowed her fear to break in her voice. "I just want the punishments to stop. Please, Birik. Please. I never meant to thwart you. He forced me to leave, but I came back. And I brought him to you."

"Who removed his shackles?"

"The Shaman." It wasn't entirely true, but it was close enough. And Vhyper was likely to believe it.

"I don't really care why he's here. Now that I have you both again, that blade will almost certainly open tonight. And nothing will be as it was before."

Birik grabbed Paenther from her and motioned to two sentinels nearby. "Get rope and escort the enchantress into the forest," he told them. "I want four deer, fully grown, tied and delivered to the Hall of Feasts at midnight. Do not let her out of your reach. Where there's one Feral, there are likely to be more. Once she has the deer, lock them all in her cell until midnight with a guard at the door."

He grabbed her jaw one more time until she was seeing stars. "You'll not escape me again, Skye. If you try to thwart me in any way, I'll have you begging me to give you to the Daemons just to end your torment."

A moment later, she stared at Birik's retreating back. His orders rang in her ears. She was to be locked in her cell until midnight. With no chance of finding Paenther. No chance of freeing the Ferals from their shackles until the very last moment.

A moment that might well be too late.

* * *

"Welcome to the party. Great rescue, Geronimo."

Paenther fought his way out of the fog of enchantment, following the sound of Jag's caustic voice. Slowly the mist parted, and he found himself in a small alcove in the cavern rock. He was standing upright, at least, but chained with his hands above his head. Beside him, chained in the same manner was Jag. And beside Jag, Foxx.

Foxx frowned at him. "Did you really come back here on purpose?"

Paenther met his gaze. "What do you think?"

"Superman to the rescue," Jag drawled. "Couldn't get the rest of the war party to join you, Cochise?"

Paenther growled low in his throat. "There's only one way in, and that's enthralled. And the only way Skye can enthrall is by opening a man's mind."

Jag grunted. "Couldn't stand the thought of anyone else fucking her, could you?"

"No way in hell." He tested the chains, struggling against them as he'd done a hundred times the last time he was here, but as before, they didn't budge.

Being chained like this, with two others, brought back memories of those days in Ancreta's dungeon. Vhyper, or Vincent, as he'd known him then, and Frederick, had kept up a steady stream of patter—most of it black humor. Paenther had never joined in—his personality had always been more serious—but they'd sometimes made him smile with their antics, which in turn had made them chortle with glee.

Frederick shouldn't have died.

He looked at the two men with him now, Foxx, whom he'd known a couple of years, and Jag, whom he'd known almost the entire time he'd been a Feral. Sometimes he wondered if he knew Jag at all.

Yet they were his brothers.

His only goal was to save their lives and Vhyper's, and to get Skye to safety. To get them all out of this cavern alive. If he were able to reclaim the Daemon blade while he was at it, all the better. But the men were his reason for being here. Especially Vhyper.

"How'd the Mage get you?" he asked his companions.

Jag scowled. "The cub turned on me!"

"I did not!" Foxx shot back.

Paenther's brows lowered as he looked from one to the other. "What happened?"

Jag frowned. "We were running to the grocery for Pink when Mr. Intuition here got a feeling there were Mage in the neighborhood. Of course, he didn't tell me why we were driving down Jefferson until we were on them. Two Mage. I called it in, we shifted and took them on. As we were taking care of them, two more showed up. Then suddenly fox-face forgot who he was supposed to be fighting, upped his size until he was bigger than my jaguar, and went for my neck. The Mage slapped shackles on both of us while Foxx had me pinned, and the next thing I knew, I was here."

"I didn't attack you," Foxx said sullenly.

Jag's jaw dropped. "Are you trying to say your fangs *accidentally* went through my neck? Do you think I'm a fucking moron?"

Paenther's gaze went from one to the other, not liking what he was hearing. Not liking it at all. "What do you remember, Cub?"

The kid met his gaze, a mix of anger and confusion in his eyes. "I wouldn't have attacked him!"

"But you don't remember."

Foxx looked away. "No."

Paenther looked at Jag and saw the same disquiet in his eyes as he felt himself. "They enthralled you, Foxx. That's the only explanation for it."

The cub's head swung around. "In my *animal* form? Without ever touching me?" He scoffed. "That's impossible."

"Do you have a better explanation for what happened?"

Foxx struggled against his bonds, the chains rattling on the stone. "No! But how? The Mage can't enthrall us through our animals. Everyone knows that."

"The Mage can do fucking anything they want these days," Jag grumbled.

"Maybe not." Paenther looked at Jag. "They didn't enthrall *you*."

Foxx scowled. "What are you saying?"

"I'm saying Zaphene's control over you may have extended beyond what we realized."

"I'm their puppet, now?"

"I don't know, Cub." Paenther and Jag exchanged a look of foreboding. If they could no longer trust Foxx, they were in deep shit.

Chapter Twenty-three

Paenther wasn't sure how much time had passed when Vhyper walked into the small cell, grinning the old Vhyper grin, his bald head gleaming. But no warmth lurked in his eyes.

No humanity.

"Looks like old home week. Nice of you to join us, B.P. I told Birik to set a place at the ritual table for you, so to speak. I knew all he had to do was let you know we'd all be losing our heads tonight, and you'd come riding to the rescue. Do I know my friend, or what?"

"You fucking turncoat," Jag snarled.

"He's not Vhyper," Paenther said evenly. "Vhyper is as trapped by the evil as we are."

Vhyper snorted. "You wish. I'm who I always was, but changed." He lifted one ironic brow. "In a *good* way, of course."

"You're wrong. The man I would give my life for is still inside you. And he isn't going to let us die."

"Right." The word was dry, Vhyper's eyes hard. "Even if you were correct, and I could be *saved*, it wouldn't be enough to get you out of here. I'm not the only Feral weapon in the Mage arsenal."

Paenther glanced at the cub. "We're aware Birik can control Foxx."

"Oh, he's doing a lot more than controlling him, B.P."

Foxx made a sound of disbelief. "What do you mean by that?"

"That's the beauty of it, Cub." Vhyper tugged on his earring. "Even you don't know what you've become. Which is what made you such a powerful weapon."

Paenther's blood turned cold.

"What have I become?"

"Zaphene's pawn that Birik claimed once she was dead. Zaphene carved out your soul but left your conscience and personality in place so none of us knew. Not even you. Your youth combined with your intuitive talent made you especially malleable. You killed Beatrice, then switched the Daemon blade for the ritual blade that night on the goddess stone when we called the power of the lion. I lost my own soul that night thanks to that blade.

"When I found the Mage and turned over the blade to Birik, I told him about you. I knew Paenther would come looking for me. I suspected, correctly, that he'd bring you and your intuition. Of course, it wasn't really your intuition that led you here. All the time, you were acting on Birik's commands. He ordered you to come to the Blue Ridge and to stop at the Market, where Skye was waiting to choose a Feral."

Paenther's head was beginning to pound. Meeting Skye was no coincidence. It had never been an accident. Foxx had delivered him into her hands.

"Why are you telling us all this?" Jag grunted. "You're starting to sound like some movie villain, spilling your guts like this."

"Jag . . ." Paenther groaned. If he ever got out of here, he'd string that cat up by his tail.

Vhyper glanced at Jag with a smirk. "Just thought you'd like to know." But when his gaze swung to Paenther, something moved deep in his eyes. *His friend.* The real Vhyper was the one spilling the plan. Hoping Paenther could use the information?

"So I didn't escape capture when Skye caught B.P.?" Foxx's voice rose with his mounting disbelief.

"Of course not. They called you into the caverns, fucked with your mind to make sure you were firmly under Birik's control, then stole your memories of the mountain and sent you away so the Ferals wouldn't find us." Vhyper grunted. "Birik misjudged the grit of his little enchantress and B.P.'s determination to escape. Once they left, he sent minions to call Paenther back through the shackles, but when that didn't happen, he called you."

"To Jefferson Street," Jag muttered.

Vhyper shrugged. "The rest fell into place as I predicted, with B.P. riding to the rescue and Skye his only way back in here." His look turned smug. "Now everything's in place, ladies and gents. Tonight, we just might free Satanan."

"Zaphene didn't steal my soul," Foxx wailed. "She didn't!"

" 'Fraid she did, Cub. Look on the bright side. Birik's sacrificing you tonight just saves the Ferals from having to destroy one of their own."

Foxx had turned pale, his freckles stark against his skin. "I'm ruined," he whispered.

Vhyper chuckled. "Birik plans to strip away your conscience before the ritual tonight just in case anything unforeseen happens. You'll be firmly in his camp soon enough. And after midnight? You'll be dead." He shrugged. "We all will."

"Vhype." Paenther nailed Vhyper with his gaze. *"We'll get out of this, Vhyper. Together. Don't ever doubt it."*

He saw it again. That flicker of awareness, of humanity behind those cold eyes, and the memory of those words that Vhyper had said over and over again as they'd lain trapped in Ancreta's dungeon all those years ago. His friend had heard him.

Vhyper frowned, then turned toward the door. "Enjoy your fantasy, B.P. I have a feast to indulge in before our big night."

With Vhyper's departure, the small cell turned quiet as a tomb.

Paenther eyed the youngest Feral, a deep regret encasing his heart. "Don't despair, Cub. The evil controlling Vhyper is a liar. We can't trust anything he says." But, if he was right, if the real Vhyper had been behind the gut spill, he'd been telling the truth.

Foxx looked up, his eyes at once furious and terrified. "She didn't take my soul, B.P. I know it. *I know it.*"

Jag grunted. "Doesn't really matter whether or not you have a soul. They're controlling you." He eyed Paenther ruefully. "I hope to hell you still have a plan."

Paenther sighed. "So do I."

Skye's stomach was in knots, her eyes burning with unshed tears, her skin crawling with fear as she led Faithful and the other three deer down to the Hall of Feasts as Birik had ordered. Behind her, the two sentinels followed. All four deer pressed against her, feeling her fear, but it was Faithful she clutched the tightest.

The moment she'd stepped outside, with the two sentinels at her back, she'd realized what would happen. Faithful would be the first to answer her call. She'd tried to send her away, but her friend had refused to leave her side. And one of Birik's sentinels had slipped a rope around her neck.

Skye struggled to take a deep breath, to find some semblance of calm. If all went as planned, the deer wouldn't die. None of them would, creature or Feral.

But *nothing* was going as planned. And it was nearly midnight.

A hundred things could go wrong, Tighe had said. And it seemed they already had.

As she neared the Hall of Feasts, she heard the sounds of the tables being cleared and removed. The hall was huge, with a soaring, irregular ceiling covered in stalactites, and a floor cut this way and that by columns and curtains formed over millions of years from the stone. Not only was the hall the largest of the rooms in the caverns, it was also one the most sumptuously furnished after Birik's apartments.

Thousands of lightwicks floated through the air, gleaming off the gilt, crystal-laden tables and red brocade dining chairs. Thick rugs covered the floors, for though the stalactites remained, like icicles frozen in time, none dared drip in this place.

When she'd first come to the caverns, musicians had played, accompanying every meal with a symphony of sound. But that was before. No music sang in hearts robbed of souls.

As she led Faithful and the other deer down the wide entrance passage she saw that the cavern had been decorated for the Moon Feast—the most powerful night of the Mage calendar, when the energies of the moon and Earth were at their zenith. The lightwicks floating above the hall had been shot through with rainbows, the colors snapping and glittering over the rock.

As she'd suspected, the hall was being cleared, the tables carried out and the rugs rolled and removed. She'd never done the ritual in this hall, and she wondered why Birik needed such a large space. The question did nothing to ease the ever-tightening knots in her stomach.

Already, in the cleared area on the near side of the natural columns that divided the hall, fires had been lit in great caldrons, forming a large ritual circle. Set within the circle were four cages. Leading her companions into the hall, she saw that the cages were filled nearly to overflowing with snakes.

How many creatures does Birik intend to kill tonight?

It was a moment before she realized that beyond the columns were other fires. A second ring.

Two circles?

Of course. Birik would raise power through the sacrifice of Vhyper and his snakes, while he expected her to do the same with the other Ferals and her deer. If the two energies melded and joined the way he obviously hoped they would, the combination might well be explosive.

She skirted the first circle, heading toward the second. As she cleared the columns, her pulse began to skate, fast and erratic.

Within the fire ring sat three wood platforms, tilted at a slight angle. Jag and Foxx lay chained and unconscious on two of them, their heads at the lower ends. On the floor beneath each platform sat a large vat ready to catch the blood.

Paenther lay on the floor in the middle of the circle, naked and staked as he'd been the night they'd freed the Daemons. But like his friends, unconscious. Or enthralled.

Her stomach rolled. She'd been practicing the chant to remove the shackles since she entered the caverns, but it wasn't going to do an ounce of good if they stayed like this.

Unconscious Ferals weren't going to be able to fight, shackles or no shackles.

Dear Mother, what am I supposed to do, now? Please don't let these men or these creatures in my care die.

She led her small menagerie between the fire pits and into the circle, trying not to stare at Paenther, but fear and love welled up inside her until she couldn't look away. His black hair hung back from his face, revealing the tattoo on his chest and throat, and the claw marks across his eye. Even enthralled, there was a latent power about him that drew her, that excited her on a hundred levels. A hard strength and a silent bone-deep promise of retribution to anyone who dared cross him.

How was she ever going to live if he died?

She forced herself to turn away. *He wasn't going to die.* She refused to allow it.

With a touch of her hands, she ushered the deer to the empty platform she knew Birik intended for her pets' slaughter. Struggling against tears, she tied them loosely around the necks with the ropes attached to an eyebolt screwed into the rock. Then she knelt and calmed them as best she could, meeting Faithful's dark-eyed gaze, praying she could save them all. At the sound of quiet steps behind her, she turned to find Vhyper approaching.

Part of her, the part beaten and abused too many times within the walls of these caverns, wanted to ignore him, or to run and cower against the wall. But something had happened to her in Feral House. Within Paenther's strong, gentle arms, she'd recovered a lot of the strength she'd once had. And it was a strength she refused to lose again.

Taking a deep breath, she rose and faced him, her fists clutching the skirt of the dress she'd donned after she returned.

"Big night," Vhyper said with a grin that didn't reach his eyes.

She tried to reconcile this cold, dangerous man with the friend who had once risked everything to keep Paenther alive.

Lacing her fingers together at her waist, she cocked her head at him. "You do know Birik means to kill you, right?"

"Of course."

"Why would you sacrifice your life for him, Vhyper?"

He tugged at his earring. "Not for him, little witch. For Satanan."

"You'd give up your life to free the very evil you're sworn to fight? An evil that will destroy everyone and everything you've ever cared about? That will decimate this world?"

Something flickered in his eyes. A knowledge. *A pain.*

Paenther was right. The real Vhyper, the one with the soul, was still in there. But it was the other one who struck with the speed of a snake, backhanding her and knocking her to the ground. Face throbbing, she watched the large Feral walk away.

Pushing herself to her feet, she turned to find Birik coming toward her, a black snake wrapped around his arm, a second curved around his neck. As he neared, she looked away as she always had.

"It's time to begin. When I tell you to, start your dance, then mount your Feral. You'll have to ready yourself this time, unless you'd like one of my men to do it."

She jerked her head, going cold at the thought. So many times her body had been used, in so many ways. But after knowing Paenther's touch, the thought of anyone else touching her made her ill. "I can do it."

Birik nodded. "The sorcerers will drench you in the blood of the deer. But not until you climax will we sacrifice the three Ferals, and we'll do it all at once. The surge of power should be . . . astounding. Prepare yourself."

He turned away and lifted his voice, sending a high call echoing over the stone, signaling the Mage to gather. Sorcerers, sentinels, and witches alike appeared through the doorways and rushed toward the circles.

Skye's heart clutched. The Ferals were still unconscious.

"Birik . . ." As he turned back, she looked away

before he saw the worry in her eyes and started to suspect its cause. "I need . . . I need them awake."

"They're safer this way. Order the panther to get hard for you and you should be able to mount him. If not, use your hand."

If they remained unconscious all was lost. And if Birik suspected anything, he'd never release them from their enthrallment.

Her heart pounded as she hazarded a glance at her tormentor and risked saying too much. "I can't feel their animals. I'm . . . I'm afraid I won't be able to call the power through them." It wasn't entirely true. She could still feel the animals, but their energy was low beneath the magic. It was possible she really wouldn't be able to pull the same level of power through them.

She felt Birik's eyes on her, his cold gaze chilling her. "You're right. Their power is greatly dampened." But he didn't move. He continued to stand there, spearing her with his frigid gaze until she was certain he knew every thought in her head, could read every plan. She didn't move. Didn't react. Her gaze held steady in the center of his tunic-clad chest.

Finally, he turned and went to the Ferals. One after the other, he touched them, freeing them from the enchantment that would have eventually worn off on its own if there had been time.

Skye watched them, her breath held as she waited, but nothing happened. They didn't move. Birik's enchantment was like a drug in the system, a drug that took minutes to wear off. And they didn't have minutes. Midnight was upon them.

Their animals woke, rising, greeting her sluggishly. But the men remained enthralled.

They were out of time!

As the sorcerers in their bloodred hooded robes assembled outside the twin circles of flames, Birik laid a knife on top of the half column between them. Skye looked at it and knew it must be the famed Daemon blade, the prison of Satanan and his horde for five thousand years.

A chill slithered down her spine.

Birik nodded at her, a silent admonition to prepare herself, then stripped off his tunic, leaving his skin bare. Like her, he would perform the ritual sky-clad, wearing nothing but the blood of the sacrifices.

She watched Paenther, trying not to stare, not to make it too obvious she was desperate for him to wake up. She felt as if her heart would stop from the pounding fear.

She gripped the hem of her dress and pulled it off in a single move, tossing it below one of the platforms.

As she watched, Paenther's eyes opened and blinked, but didn't stray from the ceiling. *Wake up completely, Paenther. Please wake up.*

Glancing at Jag and Foxx, she found them both watching her with eyes that were still glazed.

The cool, damp air of the cavern caressed her skin as she went to Paenther. Birik had told her to prepare herself, but the thought of touching herself with the two Ferals watching was too much, even for her. But there were other ways. She knelt beside Paenther.

"Can you hear me?"

"I can, Beauty, though my head feels clogged with cat hair."

She bent low over him. "Maybe I can help you clear it." She kissed him, pressing her lips to his. His mouth opened beneath hers, his tongue sweeping in to claim hers. Moment by moment the kiss changed in intensity, from soft and lazy to hard and demanding. When she pulled back, sharp clarity cut through his eyes

"Where are the others?"

"They're here. It's midnight."

"Beware of Foxx, Skye. He's been turned."

She wanted to ask him why he thought so, and how it had happened, but there wasn't time. Instead, she stood to find the sorcerers circling the fire pits, Mage sentinels standing in a larger circle around them. If Paenther was right, and Foxx was no longer on their side, it was two against so many. It would take a miracle for them to win.

But if she didn't free them, they would absolutely die.

As the sorcerers took up the midnight chant, Skye turned into her dance. In her head, she repeated the spell to free their shackles. Her gaze went to Foxx, then skirted to Jag. He watched her, waiting. Ready. When she looked down at Paenther, she found him staring up at her with hatred in his expression and love in his eyes.

"Witch," he snarled loudly. "Beauty," he whispered, his voice low nearly to the point of silence. That single word, said with reverence, sang in her heart.

It was time.

Skye flung back her head, closed her eyes, and said the words to release their shackles. She felt the moment the animals within them roared in approval. She opened her eyes to a flash of sparkling lights as the Ferals shifted into their animal forms.

"Stop them!" Birik roared from across the hall.

Within a heartbeat, the Mage were on the animals with knives and magic.

On two of the animals. Foxx walked toward her, still a man, unmolested by the Mage. In his eyes was a coldness she'd never seen before. A coldness she knew all too well.

Paenther was right.

They'd stolen Foxx's soul.

She turned and ran, but Mage blocked her way, and Foxx caught her before she'd gotten out of the hall.

Skye! Get out of the cavern. Paenther's voice rang in her head.

But it was too late. For all of them.

Foxx jammed his thumb beneath her ear. Darkness descended over her mind.

Too late.

No sooner had he shifted into his animal form and leaped onto his feet, than Paenther found himself surrounded by Mage wielding knives. They couldn't enthrall him in this form, but if he didn't move fast and lethally, they'd rip out his heart before he ever got a chance to attack.

The only way to beat a Mage in battle was to remove his hands so he couldn't enthrall, and that was exactly what he did. He leaped at the nearest opponent, clamped his jaw around the Mage's wrist and ripped his hand off his arm. The bastard would grow another within the hour, but for now, that was one hand that wouldn't enchant or wield a knife against him. He only had to dispose of about fifty-nine more.

Jag! Paenther called telepathically. *Find Skye and the Daemon blade and get out of here!*

No way.

Beauty?

Searing pain tore through his abdomen as a blade slid between his ribs. Out of the corner of his eye, he saw the jaguar in the middle of a battle as fierce as his own.

Beauty?

Where was Foxx? If he'd already gotten to Skye. . .

That's an order, Jag!

Jag's snort sounded in his head. *Tough shit, Geronimo. You're not expendable. We're leaving this place together, or not at all. How many Mage do we have in here?*

Thirty something. And two turned Ferals.

Oh yeah, forgot about that. We're fucked.

Paenther grunted. *Get free if you can and find Birik. He's the only one who has to die.*

Roger.

Paenther tore off another hand, and another, as a blade sliced through his right hindquarter. He stumbled beneath the pain and muscle damage. He'd heal, if he got the chance. The Mage were bearing down hard.

His gaze searched frantically for Skye. *Beauty?*

No answer. And there was no sign of Foxx.

In his heart, he knew the young Feral who'd fought by his side now fought for his enemy.

And he had Skye.

Skye? The beloved voice rang in her head.

Paenther.

Beauty! Where are you?

I don't know. Murmured voices sounded all around her, but she was still struggling back to consciousness and had yet to open her eyes. How long ago had Foxx grabbed her, knocking her out? Now she lay on her back on a thick rug, still naked, as she'd been when the ritual had begun.

Paenther, are you okay? Is Jag? So many Mage.

We have our hands full—or our mouths full, as the case may be—but we're holding our own. I'm fine now that I know you're all right. I'll find you, Skye. When you figure out where you are, tell me. I'll find you!

Skye opened her eyes slowly, a little at a time, taking in her situation, her surroundings. Her heart sank as a familiar gleaming, sumptuous decor filled her sight.

I'm in Birik's apartments, Paenther.

The chambers gave away nothing of their cave roots. The walls had been painted and hung with bright red and yellow silk; though thick stalactites clung to the ceiling, they'd been sealed against the moisture that pervaded most of the rest of the cavern. Gilt furniture filled the chamber, ornately carved tables laden with decorative crystal and power orbs.

On the walls hung the heads of animals, beasts whose lives Birik had sacrificed in the hunt for more power. The heads included several black bears who'd come to her in the woods over the years, a couple of wildcats, and four stags, with their huge racks of antlers. Each one had been drawn to her gift. Each had died at Birik's hands as she'd danced in their blood.

She hated him. Hated him!

"What are we doing in here?" Foxx asked. "Why aren't we out there fighting?"

"Seal the doors!"

As Birik's voice broke through the others, she froze, then slowly turned her head.

Birik sat on a large throne at the far end of the room, his three most powerful sorcerers on one side, Vhyper and Foxx on his other. In an arc around them, stood twelve sentinels, each armed with half a dozen blades. Birik's private guard.

Paenther . . . She quickly told him what she saw.

Birik looked at the young Feral with the disdain he held for all Therians. "You're in here instead of out there because I won't have you destroying them. Or helping them."

His cold gaze flicked over her and stilled. "You're awake."

Skye struggled to her feet and forced herself to face him.

Birik stepped down off his throne and crossed to her, clamping his hand around her neck the moment he reached her. "You freed them. How did you learn to remove the shackles?"

She couldn't speak through the hand cutting off her air.

"Mind-skinning," Foxx replied for her, his voice bored.

Birik squeezed. "You helped them."

Foxx snorted. "She's B.P.'s girlfriend. If she weren't Mage, he'd probably make her his mate."

If she weren't Mage. The words cut, yet she knew they were the truth. Even if they managed to make it out of here alive, there was no future for them. Paenther could never take her as his mate.

Birik's grip tightened until she could barely stand, could barely see through the pain. A fraction more and he'd crush her windpipe or snap her neck. "You willingly spread your thighs for that piece of animal trash?"

Fury erupted through the desperation. He wasn't trash! The Mage had always considered themselves superior to the Therians, yet it was the Therians, the Ferals, who acted with honor and courage. Who fought to save the world instead of destroy it.

She speared him with her gaze, something she had not had the courage to do in too many years. The flicker of surprise in his eyes pleased her.

Skye! Paenther's voice cut through the pain. *I need a distraction. Pull the power, for me, little witch. The good power.*

Can't . . . remember.

I'll say it with you.

As Birik's hand threatened to snap her neck, Paenther's voice began chanting in her head. The words Ezekiel had taught them.

Skye closed her eyes, mouthing the words, saying them in her head as she pulled her power, the true power, through the only warm-blooded animal in the room, the one inside Foxx.

Pain sliced through her chest as her cantric objected, but with the pain came a warm rush of energy. Gathering the power close, she let it grow and grow, then opened her eyes, trapped Birik in her gaze, and threw it at him.

Disbelief flashed in Birik's eyes a split second before he released her and flew backward, crashing into the table behind him. Crystal and power orbs shattered as the table collapsed beneath his slender weight.

Behind her, the door splintered, deep growls filling the room as the two jungle cats leaped inside. A jaguar and a black panther, the beautiful black panther she'd fallen in love with.

Skye, behind you!

She whirled too late. Birik hadn't stayed down and now his arm went around her neck, yanking her against his chest as his knife slid deep into her chest on a river of fire.

"You blast your power again, and your heart goes with me," he said loudly enough for all to hear. "And if your Feral makes another move, the result will be the same. If you move, cat, she dies."

Paenther froze, poised to spring at the Mage whose blade was sunk hilt deep in Skye's chest.

Beauty!

Paenther, no. Don't stop. Kill him!

He'll kill you without hesitation, I can see it in his eyes.

My life doesn't matter.

It matters. You matter.

The trouble was, how in the hell was he going to save her without getting himself enthralled in the process? A knife between Birik's eyes, another in that wrist. Tricky, since he had to be in human form to throw.

Jag, can you free a knife or two from these bastards?

Nothing I'd enjoy more, Hiawatha. But unless you've learned to throw with your tail, you're seriously risking enthrallment.

Just get me the knives, Jag. I'll do the rest.

Without hesitation, Jag went on the attack, tearing the blade hands off the closest two sentinels and tossing the metal. In a flash Paenther shifted and grabbed the knives.

But as he prepared to throw them, he froze, caught in some kind of magical net. Too late, he saw them, the three sorcerers on Birik's right staring at him with eyes of evil, murmuring beneath their breaths. Pain sliced through his head and down through his body.

Jag, get out! They've caught me. Get out before they trap us both.

Shit, the jaguar muttered, but the shout of the guard told him Jag had done as he'd commanded for once.

"Let the jaguar go," Birik said. "The others will catch him. And if they don't, I don't really care. This is the one I want."

Pain leaped inside him, scorching him from the inside out, but he watched with tearing relief as Birik slid his knife from Skye and pushed her away from him.

Skye fell to the floor, struggling for breath, but her heart was still in her chest, still beating. To an immortal, that was all that mattered. Her head turned, and she met his gaze, those blue eyes pained. For him.

"What are you going to do to him?" Foxx asked with a bored drawl. Paenther turned to study the young Feral he'd known for three years, still trying to figure out if he were merely being controlled by evil or if he had in fact been turned. At the moment, though, it didn't seem to matter. Not unless Foxx was one hell of an actor. Because he seemed utterly in league with Birik. "Are you going to kill him?"

"Kill him? No. I'm merely taking his soul. I have three Ferals at my disposal now. When they catch the jaguar, I'll have four. I'd never believed catching all the Ferals was a possibility, but I'm beginning to realize, your foolish loyalty to one another might make it ridiculously easy. As long as I have you, the others will come to me. And when I have you all, and have taken all your souls, you'll open the Daemon blade the way it was meant to be opened and free Satanan once and for all."

Like hell. But he was right. The Ferals were loyal to a fault. The others would mount rescue attempt after rescue attempt until they succeeded or were all caught. Just as *the seventeen* had all those years ago, and died, their animals never to return. It wasn't in the nature of a Feral to abandon his friends and brothers. And it was that very loyalty that would be their undoing.

The pain began to swirl in his head, a strange-colored fog encasing his mind and body. Sharp, invisible hooks dug into him, pulling. He found Skye, locked his gaze with hers, holding on against the magical forces trying to remove his soul.

Pain and fear for him bled from her eyes.

With a swift and terrible understanding he knew the moment he lost his soul his love for her, for anything, would die. He'd hurt her as he became a tool of evil, a weapon against the men he'd sacrifice his life to protect.

His body would continue to live and to kill, but the man he was, the man capable of love and sacrifice, would die.

As the pain overtook him, he yelled to the heavens, pouring out his rage and despair.

Skye stumbled to her feet, her wounds nearly healed, her heart crumbling beneath the weight of the terrible crime Birik was perpetrating on the man she loved. On the Ferals. On the world.

Vhyper stood well behind Birik, now, a man with a cold, emotionless face, his hands clasped behind his back.

Skye went to him.

"He loves you," she said quietly. Desperately. "He risked everything to come back here to save you."

"He's a fool," Vhyper said coldly. But something

flickered in his eyes. "There's nothing I can do." His voice was different, warmer, filled with pain. The good man.

Risking everything, she gripped his arm. "You're the only one who can save him, Vhyper. Ancreta made you what you are. She caused the injury inside you that let the Mage get their claws into you. Now they're going to destroy Paenther."

Vhyper's gaze looked elsewhere, but the fact he hadn't shaken her off or hit her gave her hope he was listening. But listening wasn't enough.

"Vincent!"

His gaze snapped to hers, a look of terrible struggle in his eyes.

"Don't let Ancreta win, Vincent!"

Skye saw the moment the cold rushed back into Vhyper's eyes, dousing the humanity. With a casual flick of his wrist, he backhanded her, sending her slamming against the wall. She slid to the floor, her head pounding, her body aching. But she felt the creature inside Vhyper rear up, hissing and spitting. Not at her. At something within him. An invisible foe. A battle between good and evil in its purest form raged inside the viper shapeshifter, each seeking possession of his body. His mind. His soul.

She tried to rise, but her head spun dizzily, and she sank back to the floor and crawled close to him, trying to murmur the words to give him power, but they wouldn't come!

Paenther! But Paenther was no longer in his animal form and couldn't hear her telepathically.

If she called to him out loud, she'd only attract Birik's attention to herself and possibly to the battle going on inside Vhyper.

Her head and body aching, she struggled to her feet, where Paenther could see her. Where she might be able to catch his eye and beg his help.

But when his gaze turned toward her, his eyes held no warmth, no love. Only pain.

And the cold emptiness of the soulless.

The cold that rushed through Paenther as the evil spread over his heart was sharp and biting, but wondrous. A frigid cleansing that rid him of doubts and worry, of guilt and sorrow and conscience.

His body bled with pain at the transformation, but it was the pain of rebirth, and he exulted in it.

Behind Birik, Skye rose, her gaze clinging to him, boring into him. In a voice so soft, only a Feral would hear, she whispered to him.

"Paenther, I need the words. Help me save Vhyper! Help me save you!"

Why would he want to be saved?

"Paenther, give me the words!"

She needed the chant. But the chant gave her power.

"I love you, Paenther."

What difference did it make how she felt about him? The old Paenther was gone. The reborn Paenther had no need for love.

But deep inside his slowly hardening heart, a fire flared. A desperate love. A fierce need to help her. The fire battled back the cold that tried to encase his heart. And suddenly he was saying the words, his voice ringing through the cavern.

Birik shouted. "Cease! Stop him."

Skye grabbed Vhyper's arm, her mouth moving to the words as she whispered them along with him. Her face contorted with pain, her pain fueling the battle inside him, strengthening his resolve to hold on, to fight for her. For Vhyper. For his own soul. Discord rippled through the evil, as he felt the battle raging inside Vhyper even as he was consumed by a battle of his own with Skye's power struggling to save them both.

"Stop him!" Birik yelled a second time.

"He'll stop on his own," one of the sorcerers said. "Once we have his soul."

Birik whirled on Skye instead. He grabbed her from behind, slamming her jaw closed as he pulled her away from Vhyper.

Paenther felt the cold surge inside him, the evil pulling at him, tearing him apart at the most fundamental level. Darkness swirled around his head, but he continued to chant, clinging tenaciously to Skye. She was all that kept him tethered. All that gave him the might he needed to hold on.

But he was losing. The chanting went silent as the words would no longer come.

Through the dark fog, he saw lights flash and sparkle. Where Vhyper had stood, now sat a great snake, growing by the second until it was the width of a man and five times as long.

The snake slithered across the floor, coiling and rising beside the sorcerers. As the darkness closed in on him, the snake rose, his eyes pinning Paenther. And in those eyes, he saw pain and joy, grief and love. He saw his friend.

The snake struck lightning fast, tearing off the heads of two of the sorcerers before they could move. The third ran.

For one searing moment, Panther thought it was too late, then warmth rushed in, dispelling the cold as the invisible bonds disappeared. In a rush of dizziness, he fell to one knee. And felt his soul tumble back into place.

Vhyper's voice, warm and rich with the deep bond of brotherhood, whispered in his mind. *The head or the heart, B.P.? Birik is going down.*

Paenther looked up with a fierce grin. *The heart. Welcome back, Vhype.*

He called on the power within him and shifted into his cat's form in a burst of pain and furious joy, then leaped to Vhyper's side.

The snake let out a hissing sound Paenther knew well. A viper's battle cry. *We're getting out of this together, B.P. Now, let's do it!*

"Capture them!" Birik yelled.

As the sentinels drew their swords, Skye's voice

rang in his head, ringing with excitement and love. *Paenther, help me say the chant again!*

Paenther's gaze swung to Skye, loving her with his panther's eyes. He said the words as he leaped at Birik, Vhyper at his side. Skye chanted loudly, her voice ringing over the stone as she raised her unique power and sent a blast at the sentinels, knocking them back. He felt her pain, heard it in her voice, but his witch was at heart a stubborn little fighter, and she kept the guards at bay.

Birik tried to run for the door, but Paenther leaped on him, taking him down. As he sank his teeth into the bastard's chest, the great snake bit off his head. Paenther pulled out Birik's heart and ate it.

Beneath him the ground began to shake. Chaos erupted in the room as the Mage fled, sprinting for the door. Paenther shifted back into his human form and ran for Skye.

She flew at him, her arms wrapping around his neck as he gathered her tight against him.

"You're okay," she whispered.

The sound of battle erupted behind them. Animal battle. Paenther set Skye on her feet and pushed her behind him as he whirled to find Jag and Foxx fighting as no Ferals should, going for one another's throats. Mortal combat. Jag's fur was soaked with blood where the huge fox had taken a chunk out of his neck. Part of Foxx's face had already been torn away. Each was fighting for his life.

"Foxx!"

But the fox ignored him.

I tried to stop him from leaving, Jag said. *He attacked me again. His eyes are empty, B.P. There's nobody home.*

"Wait here," Paenther told Skye, but as he prepared to shift, Vhyper struck the fox, six-inch-long fangs burying deep in the animal's hindquarters.

Almost at once, the fox fell back, shifting to a man as he hit the floor. A chunk of rock fell from the ceiling not far away, crashing and splintering as the ground shook even harder.

Paenther grabbed Skye, shielding her in case anything else fell. "We've got to get out of here."

Vhyper and Jag both shifted back into men as Paenther and Skye joined them. At their feet, Foxx lay groaning, twisting in pain.

He looked up at them, his gaze locking on Paenther's. A gaze as cold as any he'd ever seen. *Soulless.*

"Vhyper . . . was right." Foxx's face twisted with pain. "All this time . . . didn't know. The Mage's weapon and . . . I didn't know."

Paenther looked at Vhyper. "How bad?"

"The poison? A lethal dose."

Paenther stared at his friend, then nodded and looked down at Foxx. "I'm sorry, Cub." And, goddess, he was. The kid had shown some real promise. He could have been a damn fine Feral once he matured. Once more the Mage had cut off a promising life before it had a chance to bloom. "It shouldn't have ended this way."

Foxx opened his mouth as if to speak, then said

nothing as his body relaxed, his head lolling to the side.

"He's gone," Skye said quietly.

A massive stalactite dropped from the roof and shattered, spraying them with stinging bits of limestone.

"Out," Paenther said. *"Now."*

Vhyper lifted Foxx in his arms as Paenther shielded Skye.

"Where's that Daemon blade?" Jag asked.

Vhyper shook his head. "The last time I saw it, it was sitting between the two circles."

As they reached the door, Paenther turned right, but Skye pulled against him, fighting him.

"This isn't the way out?" he asked her.

"It is. But I have to get Faithful. Go with Vhyper. I'll meet you outside."

"Like hell. Who's Faithful?"

"One of my deer. I have to save my deer."

"Skye . . ."

"I'm not leaving them in here to die!"

Jag grabbed her arm, but his gaze met Paenther's. "I'm going after the blade. I'll bring the deer."

"I'll go with you . . ." Paenther began, and cut off as a chunk of ceiling nearly crashed on top of them. He hauled Skye out of the way barely in time.

"Go, B.P.! Get her out of here."

"You've got three minutes, Jag, then I'm coming after you."

"Deal."

* * *

Vhyper led the way out of the caverns and into near-hurricane-force winds and driving rain. Mother Nature was furious, but Skye could hardly care. Paenther was alive, Birik dead, Vhyper saved. Now if only Jag, Faithful, and the other deer made it out alive.

Paenther held her tight against his chest as cold rain lashed her body. She glanced at Vhyper as he held Foxx, his gaze searching the forest. No longer was he the cold, casually cruel Feral she'd known in the caverns. But the dark, swirling intensity she felt in him made him seem every bit as dangerous. Inside him, she could feel the snake, coiled and agitated, but she didn't think it had anything to do with her this time.

"Do you see any sign of them?" Paenther asked.

"None. The Mage may be soulless, but they're not stupid. There's nothing more for them here."

"Three minutes," Paenther said softly, as if to himself. "Then I want you to take Skye and get out of here, Vhype. She can lead you to the others."

"No," Skye said. "I have to see Faithful."

Paenther stroked her, the cold rain sliding between their naked bodies. "We're not going to have room in the car for a deer, Beauty."

"I wouldn't take her from her family. I just need to know she made it. I need to say good-bye."

Vhyper laid Foxx on the ground and stripped him, tossing Paenther the clothes. "You need these more than he does."

Paenther slipped Foxx's shirt over Skye's head, a soft cotton dress shirt that fell nearly to her knees, then pulled on the pants and boots for himself.

Beneath them, the ground rumbled and shook. "Get her off this mountain, Vhyper, before it implodes."

But Skye shook her head. Deep inside she could feel the pull of the animals. "Jag's coming." As the Feral cleared the entrance to the cave with four deer, elation flared inside her. It was done, and they'd all made it. Except Foxx.

Skye pulled away from Paenther and ran to Jag as he led the deer by the ends of their tethers. He might be holding them by the ends of ropes, but she noted with interest that Faithful was pressing as tightly against him as she usually did her. Which was extraordinary, really, considering the man was part predatory cat.

She also noticed that Jag's hand stroked the side of her friend's neck, long, gentle strokes. Skye pushed between the deer gathered around him and gave the Feral a kiss on the cheek.

He scowled as she knelt to pull the tethers from around the deer's heads, his face screwed up against the driving wind and rain. "Can the gratitude, Glinda. I told you I'd get 'em, and I got 'em. You saved us, I saved your friends. We're even."

"The blade?" Paenther called.

"No sign of it. And that hall is gone, now. It pancaked about two seconds after I got Bambi and her friends out of there."

One by one, Skye looked into the beautiful creatures' eyes, sharing her joy in their survival, feeling their warming love in return, then sent them far away.

Finally, she kissed Faithful. "Go, dear one. Be safe." Faithful hesitated, then pressed her cheek against Skye one last time and took off.

Skye rose and turned back to Jaguar, tears in her eyes. "You're a better man than you want the world to think, Jag," she said softly.

He scowled at her again. "You're wrong, Sabrina. My heart is as black as they come, and it always has been."

She could see the utter truth of his words in his eyes. Or at least, a truth he fully believed. He was wrong.

But she had a feeling telling him that wouldn't do a bit of good.

The ground rumbled again, violently. Paenther's hand landed on her soaked head. "We have to go. Now! Just how many Mage did you kill in there, Jag?"

"Eight. Maybe nine."

Vhyper laughed. "Serves the fuckers right."

"Yeah, well let's hope we can get out of here before Nature's fury rips this mountain out from under us."

Skye grabbed Paenther's hand and ran as the earth began to cave in behind them. Birik and the caverns were gone. There was no going back.

But she feared the only future she wanted, one with Paenther at her side, was nothing more than a dream.

* * *

"How did Foxx die?" Tighe asked grimly as he drove them back to Feral House.

"I killed him." Vhyper's raw confession rang through the closed car.

Paenther looked at him sharply, hating the pain he heard in his friend's voice. They were in Tighe's Land Rover, Delaney riding in front with her mate, Vhyper in back with Skye and him. Foxx's body lay in the cargo area behind them. Hawke was driving Jag and Wulfe back in Paenther's Escalade.

"You didn't kill him, Vhype," Paenther said, willing his friend to believe the words he knew were true. "The Mage killed him when they stole his soul."

The car went silent except for the swish of the windshield wipers and the gusts of wind buffeting the Land Rover. Any rejoicing at Vhyper's and Jag's return was dampened by the hard truth of Foxx's death and Vhyper's earlier announcement that the three wraith Daemons had been set free just that morning. Goddess knew where the Daemons had gone, but Paenther felt certain they'd know soon enough. Just as soon as the first bodies of their victims were found.

His own satisfaction at finally freeing Vhyper was tempered by the pain lancing his body in harsh, regular waves. He didn't know what the sorcerers had done to him when they tried to steal his soul, but he felt strange in a way he never had before. Like there was still something inside him.

Skye lifted her head off his shoulder. "Something's wrong with your animal spirit, Paenther. He's acting like he's sick. I'm worried about him."

He looked down into the copper-and-blue eyes he'd come to love. "Me, too, Beauty. Me, too." Pressing her head against his shoulder again, he held her, needing the feel of her against him.

"If this is too insensitive, tell me and I'll shut up," Delaney said from the front seat. "But what happens now? With Foxx? Or the fox spirit?"

Tighe answered her without hesitation clearly relieved to end the silence. "Within the next few weeks a new Feral will be marked. Sometime in the next year or two, he'll find his way to us. If he doesn't, he'll die, clearing the way for one who will."

Vhyper met Paenther's gaze over Skye's head. "I can't decide if I should thank you for freeing me or kill you for it." His eyes swam with a guilt thick enough to choke. "I'm not sure I can live with the things I've done, B.P."

"You will, Vhype. Because you didn't do them. The darkness that held you captive did. And because I'm not ever giving up on you. Just as you've never given up on me."

He saw Skye's hand reach out and take Vhyper's. To his surprise and relief, his friend didn't pull away but curved his hand around her smaller one and held on as if her touch alone kept him from flying apart into a million pieces. A tiny curl of jealousy slid around Paenther's heart, then dissipated. He was about to take as his mate a woman, an enchantress, to whom all the Ferals would be drawn on some level. And while she'd told him she had no particular affinity for snakes, she had a heart big enough to care for all creatures, two-legged and four-. And those without any legs at all, for that matter.

It was a moment before his mind backpedaled to the words he'd thought without hesitation. *He was about to take as his mate. . .*

He stared out the window, stunned, and yet . . . certain. He was taking her as his mate. If she agreed, if she wanted him, he would willingly bind himself to her for all eternity.

They wouldn't be able to live at Feral House, of course. Not with her being Mage, but it didn't matter. He'd find a safe house nearby and split his time between them. This woman wasn't getting away from him. Ever. He just hoped whatever was going on inside him gave him the time to make good on that promise.

Chapter Twenty-six

Once more, Skye stood on the goddess stone, dressed in nothing but a filmy ritual gown, Kara and Delaney on either side of her as they waited for the Ferals to raise the Feral Circle. The winds weren't as bad this far from the mountains, and the rains had ended, but the sky was still dark despite sunrise being nearly upon them.

Paenther stood with the others, his strong form tense with a pain she prayed she could ease. Inside him, the panther no longer leaped to greet her. He barely lifted his head at all. But she felt his will, felt him demanding help that only she could give.

Tighe had called Lyon as they'd driven in from the mountains and told him Paenther was in bad shape.

When they'd arrived at Feral House, the Shaman had been waiting, ready to clear Birik's spells from her cantric now that the Mage was dead. Kara had helped her change into the ritual gown once he was done. The moment she was ready, Lyon had ushered them all down to the goddess stone.

All but Vhyper. Vhyper alone remained at Feral House, at Lyon's command. He was glad to have the warrior back, but he didn't entirely trust him yet. None of the Ferals did, except Paenther. Sadly, they seemed to trust her not to hijack the ritual more than they trusted one of their own.

Paenther came to her and took her hands. "Are you ready?"

"I need to know something. I've been thinking about how to make this work, and I need to know what Ancreta did to you to cause this rift in the first place. It might be important to repairing it." She touched his face, loving him with her eyes. "Tell me what you remember."

"As little as possible." He gazed down at her, his eyes pained, yet filled with love. Once more, the feral mark across his eye was nearly gone. "She opened my mind, then chanted some words I can't begin to remember."

"I don't need the words. My power's enough. But I think we need to open your mind as I pull the power."

He released one hand to stroke her jaw, his eyes gentle on her face. "Do you want to do this somewhere more private?"

She gave him a rueful smile. "I got over any shyness about my body a long, long time ago. No, I think we need to do it here. We're going to need to raise the power of the panther again. He's the one who has to do most of the work, and he's weak, Paenther. He has to breach the gap Ancreta formed between you, and he's going to need all the strength you can give him to do it."

She pressed her palms to his bare chest. He was wearing his leather pants again, but all the Ferals had doffed their shirts to prepare for the ritual. Through the link of flesh, she stroked the animal spirit inside him, telling him with her heart that she would do what he wanted and try to get him the power he needed to find his way back to Paenther.

"Does he know what we're doing?"

The panther brushed her mind, a growl of gratitude and approval. She nodded. "He knows. He's ready."

"It amazes me you understand him."

"If this works, you will too, soon enough."

"Then let's do it." He led her down to the circle, told his friends what they were going to do, then swept her into his arms, kissing her with a hot, deep-throated kiss. When he pulled back, he growled to his men, "Close your eyes. This is about to get private."

Grunts and groans rose around them, but Skye closed her eyes, shutting them out. The only thing that mattered was healing Paenther. The only one who mattered was the one she loved.

"Look at me, Skye."

She did, gazing into Paenther's strong, beloved face, and tumbling into the dark depths of his eyes.

Holding her gaze, he reached for her breast, kneading, teasing, then grabbed the back of her head and tilted her face to meet his hard, passionate kiss. She knew his intent was to drive her up, hard and fast, and he knew just how to do it. The hand on her head slid down her back and grabbed her rear. Then he yanked on her gown until he was able to reach beneath. His warm hand slid between her thighs. His fingers stroked that sensitive flesh, nearly melting her, before they dove deep inside.

His scent, his taste, the feel of his muscled shoulders beneath her hands combined with the blissful feel of his fingers inside her, had her quickly weeping with need.

He pulled away, unfastened his pants to free his erection, then grabbed her hips.

"Wrap your arms around my neck and hold on, Beauty."

Paenther lifted Skye's dress to her waist, then gripped the backs of her thighs, spreading her wide for him as he lifted her. He probed between her legs with his shaft, seeking her entrance. Finding it, he pulled her hips toward him and thrust inside her tight, wet sheath on a stab of ecstasy.

Skye threw her head back with a moan of pure pleasure.

"Oh, *Paenther.*"

His name on her lips destroyed his control. He pulled nearly all the way out of her before pressing home a second time and a third, over and over, each thrust more desperate than the last.

So intense was the pleasure he nearly forgot the reason for it. "Say the words, Beauty. I'll help you say the right ones." Together they called her power.

His voice broke off, midchant. "I'm getting close. Goddess, you send me up faster than . . ." He kissed her hard and pulled back on a groan. "The power of the beasts!" he called. "Now!"

Skye gripped his head from behind, and he knew she fought to reverse the damage Ancreta had done to him all those years ago.

The men circled tight around them even as Paenther continued to thrust inside her.

The scent of fresh blood mixed with the heady scent of sex teased his nostrils. He didn't have to look to know they were cutting themselves.

"Lean back, Skye," Lyon's voice said. "I need to cut his chest."

She curved her back, giving Lyon minimal room to get a knife between them. Paenther shifted her, holding her rear with one arm as he slid his hand against his bloody chest, then shoved his fist in the air.

"Empower the spirit of the panther!"

Like before, thunder rumbled. Power roared up through the Earth. The rush of pleasure and pain sent them both over the edge in the next thrust of his body inside her, sending them tumbling in a single spiral of ecstasy. As the orgasm tore through his body, he felt the power erupt within him ten times stronger than before. Paenther shouted, half pleasure, half pain. Skye screamed.

Around them, the other Ferals shouted, but he heard no pain in the sound. Pleasure, yes. And triumph.

"Holy shit!"

"Did you feel that?"

The Ferals' excited voices bombarded his ears.

Skye continued to whisper the words Ezekiel had taught her, alone this time. Now that her cantric had been disabled, she no longer needed his help. As she murmured the words, the pressure mounted in his head until he thought it would explode.

"Paenther, reach for him!" Skye cried. "He's trying to get to you. Reach for him!"

Paenther closed his eyes, desperate to help, yet uncertain where to reach, where to turn. And suddenly he felt it, the second presence struggling toward him through a thick, bright barrier. With his Feral's strength and determination, he pushed against that invisible wall with every ounce of mental power he possessed.

It shattered. In a burst of light that rained down over him like broken glass, the barrier burst. And standing within a rainbow mist was a sleek and beautiful black panther. A creature, a spirit, he'd never seen, yet knew in the deepest reaches of his being.

The panther roared, a jubilant sound of triumph

and rapture. Then he leaped, and suddenly they were one, their minds brushing, intertwining, snapping together like two pieces of a puzzle. And as one, they swung their gazes to Skye, who was still in his arms, still cradling him deep within her body. The woman they both loved.

For one sharp moment Paenther felt a pinch of jealousy that the beast inside him loved her as thoroughly as he did. Then he laughed at himself. Laughed out loud. And felt the beast's pleasure caress his mind.

Within him, a sudden pressure built, a desperate need to shift. He pulled out of Skye and set her down. With a swift kiss, he stepped back.

For the first time, he didn't have to pull on the power. All he had to do was think of himself as an animal, and in a sparkling flash of light, he became one. The shift was amazingly, incredibly, without pain. Instead, he felt a rush of such pleasure he could barely credit it. The pleasure raced through his body, extinguishing the pain, flushing the rage he'd lived with for three hundred years.

He stood on the rock, the cold damp wind blowing in his cat's face. His vision was clearer, his senses keener, his body stronger, more vibrant, more alive as he drank in the feel of the spirit bounding through his mind. One. After all these years, one, at last.

His gaze swung to Skye. One with his beast, perhaps, but not whole. Not completely. Not yet.

Thinking of his man form, he shifted, smooth as glass.

Belatedly, he realized the wind had stopped, the sky had cleared, and in the east, the sun was starting to rise. He reached for the beauty who owned his heart . . . and stopped midreach as he stared at the sleeve on his arm.

"How is this possible? I lose my clothes when I shift. I always have."

"Your gifts come through the power of your animal. You've been lacking a lot of that power." Skye's smile was the sweetest in the world. "Now that he's with you, you'll both be stronger."

He gathered her hard against him, then swung her around, laughing. Finally he set her down and turned to his men, who were all watching him, bemused.

"I don't think I've ever heard you laugh," Tighe said, a quiet grin on his face and wonder in his eyes.

"I feel . . . reborn," Paenther said.

His brothers gathered around him, slapping him on the back, and pulling him into hard, male hugs. His only disappointment was that Vhyper wasn't there to share it with him. But he was up at the house, free of the evil. Trust might take a while, but it would come. He had to believe that.

Lyon grasped his forearm, then pulled him into a hard hug. When he pulled back, a rare smile lit his friend's face. "You look like a new man, B.P."

"I am. Thanks to Skye." Paenther reached for her where she'd stepped aside and pulled her against his side.

Lyon held out his hand to her, his amber eyes

turning serious as he offered her this purposeful act of trust.

Her expression uncertain, Skye placed her hand in Lyon's. He sandwiched it between the two of his. "The Feral Warriors are in your debt, Skye. If you ever need us, all you have to do is call. And you're welcome at Feral House for as long as you wish to stay."

Paenther watched her eyes tear as a warm, sweet smile creased her face. "Thank you, Lyon."

His heart burned with love.

Skye looked at Paenther in surprise as he gave a tug on her hand, pulling her to a stop as the Ferals and their women made their way back through the rugged, rocky woods after the ritual. She'd heard Paenther say he felt reborn, but she didn't think he had anything on her. For the first time in her life, she'd pulled good power instead of dark, without pain, and the rush had been breathtaking. Wonderful warmth had flowed through her body, full and strong and right.

She'd healed Paenther. And pleased Lyon. The Chief of the Ferals had accepted her and told her she could stay.

A bittersweet smile twisted her lips. While his offer had brought tears to her eyes, the decision wasn't hers. She could only stay if Paenther wanted her to.

"Problem, B.P.?" Tighe asked, his arm looped around Delaney's shoulders.

Paenther smiled, tumbling her heart all over

again. "I just want to talk to Skye without an audience, Stripes. We'll be right behind you."

As the others passed, he took her into his arms and held her against him. Just held her, his arms telegraphing a tension that had her starting to worry. Was this when he would tell her that a part of him would always love her, but of course she couldn't stay? That he appreciated her help and wished her the best of luck in her life?

She buried her face against his warm chest and steeled herself for whatever he needed to say, refusing to let her grief show. She wouldn't do that to him. To either of them.

Paenther stroked her hair. "Look at me, Beauty."

Taking a deep breath, struggling to hide the heart that was breaking, she pulled back and looked up into his beloved face.

His expression melted, turning infinitely tender. "I love you, Skye. Since the moment I saw you in the Market, I've been obsessed with you. Even while I still thought I hated you, I was falling in love with you. And I know now that even though my panther and I are finally one, we're not whole. And we never will be without you."

Tears sprang to her eyes. "What are you saying?" she breathed.

He lifted his hand and cupped her cheek. "I want you to be my mate, Skye. To be by my side. Forever. I can't live without you."

She stared at him, hearing the words that had lived in her deepest dreams for days now. Hearing them, but not quite believing.

"Paenther . . . I'm Mage."

He grinned at her. *Grinned.* "You don't say."

But it wasn't funny. Tears burned her eyes, tears that were part joy and part heartbreak. "Don't joke, Paenther. They'll never accept me."

He was immediately serious again, but his expression never lost that wonderful tenderness.

"Don't cry, little one. They'll accept you. Sooner or later, they'll accept you. But until then, we won't live at Feral House. I'll find a place nearby and have it warded against draden attack. It'll work, Beauty. I promise. I'll make it work."

His expression became intense, almost desperate. "You're a fighter, Skye. Don't let them scare you. Please don't. Fight. For me. For us. All three of us."

"Three of us?"

A tiny smile formed on his mouth. "You, me, and the panther. He's a stubborn cuss. He's growling at me to make you say yes." He cupped her face in his hands. "You're my world, Skye. My heart. My soul."

Leaning forward, he kissed her forehead, then pulled back to look into her eyes again, love shining from his own. "Be my mate."

The tears slipped down her cheeks. "Yes. A hundred times yes, Paenther. A hundred times yes."

Paenther pulled her into his arms and kissed her thoroughly, the kiss tender and fierce. Everything she'd ever dared dream of.

The others were waiting by the cars when they finally caught up with them.

"Skye's agreed to become my mate," Paenther announced. "We'll find a place to live not far from here."

"You don't want to live at Feral House?" Kara asked. Her gaze turned to Skye. "It's a little crazy, but I think you'd like it."

Lyon looked at his second. "I'd rather you be at Feral House, B.P." He turned to her. "If you don't want to live with us, Skye, I'll accept your wishes, but I'd like you to reconsider. I meant what I said. You're welcome in Feral House. Period. We'd be glad to have you join us as a permanent addition."

Skye looked up at Paenther, but he didn't return her gaze.

Inexplicably, his jaw had hardened. "Does that go for everyone? I won't subject her to prejudice day in and day out."

"Prejudice?" Tighe asked. "Were you paying any attention to the rest of us out there on the goddess rock? We were grinning like loons. That woman of yours has a magic touch, B.P. And I mean that in the best possible way."

Jag growled. "What if her people come looking for her again? She's ours, now. She stays here where we can protect her."

"Does that go for everyone?" Paenther asked.

To a man, they nodded. Skye felt the tears threatening to spill over again.

Paenther turned to her. "What do you think?"

She lost her battle with the tears. As they slid unheeded down her cheeks, she told them all,

"I lost my family when I was eight. I've waited a long time to find another one." Her voice broke on the last.

Kara bounded over to her and wrapped her in a joyous hug. A moment later, Delaney joined them, grinning at Skye.

"What did I tell you? Wives-in-law."

Kara shook her head, looking from one to the other. "No. Sisters."

Delaney nodded. "Sisters it is."

As the women pulled apart, Skye turned to Paenther, crying openly now.

Paenther swept her into his arms, cradling her like a child as she wept.

"I hope those are happy tears."

Skye laughed and wrapped her arms around his neck, pressing wet, teary kisses to every part of his face. "What do you think?"

Paenther grinned. "I think I'm the luckiest man alive."

Skye pressed her hand to his cheek and pulled back where she could see his eyes. "I intend to make it my life's goal that you always feel that way."

The wicked gleam that entered his eyes had them both laughing. Then he kissed her, and the outside world disappeared.

Epilogue

One week later

Paenther stood at the foot of his bed, his arms crossed over his chest, one shoulder leaning against the high post, a smile pulling at his mouth as he watched Skye. She sat in the middle of his bed, her legs crossed in her brand-new fitted jeans, her slender form and small breasts displayed to fine advantage in the soft purple shirt she'd donned that morning.

On her shoulder, her cockatiel leaned forward to rub its cheek against hers. In her lap, the black schnauzer puppy played with the tabby kitten. Sweet laughter burst from Skye's throat, and he grinned outright. He'd never tire of hearing her laugh.

They'd been officially mated exactly twenty-four hours, and the Ferals were still showering her with gifts. Tighe, under Delaney's direction, had bought her two new outfits, including the one she wore now. Hawke had given her the cockatiel. Jag had dropped the kitten in her lap during the mating feast yesterday afternoon while Wulfe had left the puppy tied to their bedroom door during an intimate moment that had been quickly aborted at the sound of the animal's high-pitched cry. As she'd held the puppy with tears in her eyes, he'd quickly forgiven Wulfe the interruption.

Hell, every Feral had brought her something. Except Vhyper. Vhype spent all night every night fighting draden, usually alone. During the day he rarely left his room. Paenther had tried to talk to him, but each time Vhype had calmly, but firmly, turned him away.

Skye looked up at him, her happiness dimming. "What's the matter?"

"Nothing." Nothing a bit of Feral persistence wouldn't solve. Vhyper would come around. Paenther would see to it. Meanwhile, he wanted the happiness back at full brightness in his mate's eyes.

He grinned and shook his head at her.

"What?" she asked, laughter in her voice.

"I'm thinking we may need to buy a second house just for the animals. Maybe a farm."

She gave him an impish smile, but the touch of worry was genuine. "Do you mind?"

"Never." He sat on the bed beside her, leaned forward and kissed her. "All I want is to see you happy, and animals will always be a part of that."

She reached for him, touching his face. "All I need to be happy is you."

He kissed her again, a long lingering kiss that promised to evolve into something far deeper. Until he heard a rap at the door.

"Come in."

Lyon poked his head in the door. "You ready?"

"We'll be right there."

Skye looked up with confusion. "Are we both going?"

He stood and held his hand out for her. "Lyon's gift to you is a little complicated. We'll be gone all day. Kara's offered to watch the menagerie."

"Where are we going?"

"You'll see."

Several hours later, the car Lyon had rented at the airport pulled up in front of Ezekiel's house.

Skye looked at Paenther with confusion and no small amount of trepidation. Because they hadn't come alone this time. Lyon, Tighe, and Wulfe were with them, Tighe having flown them to the Outer Banks in his small, private airplane. And all four Ferals were heavily armed with knives.

Paenther squeezed her thigh as Lyon turned off the engine. "Trust us?"

She pressed her head to his shoulder. "I do. But he's Mage."

She felt Paenther's lips press against her hair. "Not all Mage are the enemy." When she looked up at him, love shone from his eyes, and something else. Something sharp and expectant.

"What's going on, Paenther?"

"I'll show you."

The four big men piled out of the car. Paenther held her hand, helping her out, and together they walked up the walk. Belatedly, it dawned on her that the Ferals hadn't asked her to lead them.

"You can see it?"

"He's expecting us," Paenther told her.

At that moment, Ezekiel opened the front door and stepped out onto the stoop wearing fresh, modern clothes, his hair clean and pulled back at his nape. As if he'd spruced up for company. Behind him stood the Shaman. A frisson of nervous excitement frayed the edges of Skye's calm. But as she accompanied the Ferals up the stairs, she felt their tension mount, and her own followed.

Ezekiel smiled at her and she went to him and kissed his cheek. "What you taught me saved the day."

"I'm glad, Skye. I'm glad. Now go on in. There's someone here who's anxious to see you."

She glanced at Paenther, who took her hand. Lyon and Tighe went through the door first. Not until Lyon nodded did Paenther lead her into the house.

Three people stood in the middle of the living room, a lovely woman with long dark hair, fine features, and tears filling her copper-ringed eyes flanked by two heavily armed Mage sentinels with looks of soft joy on their faces.

Skye stared at them, one after the other, shivers of sweet recognition fizzing beneath her skin. Her own eyes filled with tears as they found the woman and clung.

"Momma?" Her voice broke beneath the weight of her joy.

"Baby. My Skye." Her mother's voice fell on a sob. "It's really you." Skye rushed into her arms and was quickly enveloped in a group hug as the two sentinels, her beloved uncles, joined them. One by one, she looked into their eyes, seeing tears and love and warm, caring souls.

Her hands went to them, touching their faces, one after the other, unable to believe this was real. "Inir didn't get to you."

"No," her mother whispered. "I've dreamed of this day for forty-one years, baby. I never thought I'd see it."

"Me either." Skye laughed and turned to look at Paenther. "Did you do this?"

He smiled at her, a suspicious moisture in his eyes. "I'd love to take the credit, but this was Lyon's doing with the help of the Shaman and Ezekiel."

She hugged her mother, then pulled away to go to Lyon and place a kiss on his cheek. "Thank you."

The big Chief of the Ferals nodded, warmth lighting his amber eyes. "You're welcome, Skye. But I have to admit, this was more than a little self-serving. Ezekiel?"

As Paenther drew her back into his arms, Ezekiel explained.

"After you were here, I did some checking and discovered your enclave disappeared soon after the soul-stealing began. About half the strongholds did." He winked at her. "I may be a hermit, but I'm a well-connected hermit. I found your mother and contacted the Shaman."

Lyon nodded. "Those Mage who oppose Inir have had to go underground. We've agreed it's time to join forces as we did five millennia ago if we hope to defeat this evil. This wouldn't have happened without you, Skye. We'd forgotten, after hating for so many centuries, that there have always been good, honorable men and women of every race. Your purity of heart and spirit reminded me of that. Reminded us all. Trust won't come easily. It never does. But with you as the bridge between the races, I have every hope that it will come."

"Sometimes you just have to trust your heart," Paenther murmured against her hair. He pulled back and looked down at her, pride and love shining from his dark eyes. "And my heart is yours."